The Class Assignment Is Murder

CAROLYN KLEINMAN

MILFORD HOUSE
an imprint of Sunbury Press, Inc.
Mechanicsburg, PA USA

MILFORD HOUSE

an imprint of Sunbury Press, Inc.
Mechanicsburg, PA USA

FIRST MILFORD HOUSE PRESS EDITION: October 2023

Set in Adobe Garamond Pro | Interior design by Crystal Devine | Cover by Lawrence Knorr | Edited by Lawrence Knorr.

Publisher's Cataloging-in-Publication Data
Names: Kleinmann, Carolyn, author.
Title: The class assignment is murder / Carolyn Kleinman.
Description: First trade paperback edition. | Mechanicsburg, PA : Milford House Press, 2023.
Summary: In *The Class Assignment is Murder*, a Jewish college professor encourages three of her students to examine an old murder case, never dreaming that her students' investigation will not only trigger more deaths but will also resurrect clues related to her mother's unsolved murder. In addition, the novel comes equipped with Reader Discussion Questions.
Identifiers: ISBN : 979-8-88819-122-4 (paperback) | ISBN : 979-8-88819-123-1 (ePub).
Subjects: FICTION / Mystery & Detective / Amateur Sleuth | FICTION / Mystery & Detective / Women Sleuths | FICTION / Mystery & Detective / Jewish.

Product of the United States of America
0 1 1 2 3 5 8 13 21 34 55

For the Love of Books!

For my family – I love you all with all my heart

My son David Kleinman and his wife Erin Nightingale

My daughter Julie Goldemberg and her husband
Daniel Goldemberg

My grandchildren: Max Goldemberg, Lucas Kleinman,
Nina Goldemberg, and Sophie Kleinman

And as always – many thanks to my wonderful husband
Steven Kleinman for his love and support

Chapter 1

Tuesday, June 11

"Why did the boy pick up a knife and repeatedly stab his father? Did he want to kill his mother or just silence her screams? And why, after murdering his parents, did he kill his sister, too?"

With the skill of an expert angler, Hannah Stein, an English professor at Buchanan College, had deftly cast her line and captured her three disgruntled students' attention. She had used a gruesome lure, a tragedy that had haunted her for fourteen years. Hannah felt goosebumps rise along her arms. Remembering this event was chilling. Was it wise to have her students look into this old case? It was, after all, her obsession and not theirs. However, there was no backing out now. This is what she lived for: her students were excited and eager to start their research. They were hooked. There was no time to lose. She quickly reeled them in.

* * *

One day earlier

Professor Hannah Stein sighed. It was the first day of Buchanan College's summer session, and the twelve students in this freshman-support class were a sorry group. They twitched in their seats. One stared at the clock on the wall. Another looked out the window, checking out a pretty girl sitting in the quad. Two students were openly texting on their cell phones.

Hannah was surprised. These local students did not have strong academic credentials, but they all had been identified as having "a special spark." Today, however, they looked burnt out, and she struggled to find a way to ignite them and get them to focus on the class.

Come on, Hannah thought. *Give me a break. You are all lucky to be here. With your poor grades and low test scores, you never would've gotten into an elite college like Buchanan on your own. You should be grateful for this special community scholarship program.*

After Hannah handed out the class syllabus, she heard loud groans. When Hannah asked for an explanation, she got an earful. She heard tales of misery and failure. Her students hated writing research papers in high school and resented that they were required to write one for this class.

"Professor Stein, we talked it over at our orientation session. We all agree that this program is dumb. We have to pass this class, or we won't get our scholarships. You must know that we weren't great students in high school. And just look at these class assignments. They all lead up to completing a research paper. Really? We've been set up to fail. If we lose our scholarships, we're all outta here. None of us can afford this college. This class is just a big fat waste of time." This dismal prediction came from a stocky young man sitting in the back row of the classroom. The others nodded in agreement.

"Come back tomorrow," Hannah said. "Give this class a chance. I know you need your scholarships, and I'll help you hold onto them. I promise."

* * *

The next day, Hannah asked her class a simple question, "What interests you?"

The students were quiet and surprised.

"Just think about this," Hannah said. "It doesn't matter whether your topic is Shakespeare or Dracula. You use the same research and writing skills for all papers. I'll teach you those skills and guide you through the process. You will be able to write a good paper, but first, you have to find a topic you like. Then, you'll enjoy writing your research paper."

Some students laughed, and others grimaced.

"Okay, enjoy may be a bit strong, but you're far more likely to complete a paper if the topic interests you. Come on, tell me what you'd like to research."

Hannah picked up a dry-erase pen and quickly filled a large whiteboard with the topics her students suggested. After permitting them to open the floodgates, ideas gushed out of the class. Hannah could feel it; the room had a fresh, enthusiastic vibe. Students latched onto subjects, woke up their laptops and tablets, and began to hunt for sources. But three students still looked sullen and unhappy when the class ended. They were the ones who remained behind when the rest filed out of the room.

Brad, a tall, slim fellow with multiple tattoos and a buzz haircut, said, "If we can't find a subject we like, do we get to skip the paper?"

A girl named Gina, who wore a strong musky perfume, nervously laughed. She added, "Sounds good to me. After all, Professor Stein, you said we could each choose a topic that interests us. It's not our fault we can't come up with anything."

Hannah replied, "You're free to choose your own topic, but if you can't come up with a topic on your own, you're also free to choose one of mine. You know, there is something I've been meaning to look into for a long time. Perhaps, you might like to help me? A fourteen-year-old boy killed his family and then raped his cousin right here, in Parkerville, Pennsylvania, in 2005. You could each research an aspect of this case and then cite your findings in your papers."

"Did you just say we can investigate a crime?" asked Frank, the stocky fellow who had made it very clear that he did not want to write a research paper.

"Yes," Hannah said, "I did, and it was a terrible crime. Let me tell you a bit about it."

And that's what Hannah did. She told her students just enough about the old murder case to intrigue them. Certainly, there was no harm in that. Then why, after these three left the classroom, did Hannah feel so strange? Her stomach was churning, and her heart was racing.

Chapter 2

Thursday, June 13

Drake Hall was the oldest building on the grounds of Buchanan College. It dominated a corner of the campus and resembled a fortress made of heavy old stones held together by cement. The rooms inside it were drafty in the winter and sweltering hot in the summer, but Hannah Stein was sentimentally attached to her office in the building because the previous occupant had painted a fireplace on the wall. The fake fireplace had been crafted with care. A colorful counterfeit fire blazed in the grate, and there was a real wooden mantle. This was the type of whimsy that charmed Hannah.

Two days had passed since Hannah had recruited three students from her class to look into the murders and rape committed by Matthew Baker in 2005. Now, these same three students were sprawled on the old, saggy couches near the imitation fireplace in Hannah's office. The group had been working there for some time. Crumpled paper coffee cups littered the table, and only crumbs remained in the large family-sized doughnut box. The old-fashioned blackboards on three sides of the room were filled with chalk markings, and they showed that the group had made considerable progress.

Hannah leaned back in her chair and sighed. "We have a lot here. Your initial research has yielded lots of facts and speculations. Now our job is to divide all of this into three meaningful research topics for you to develop more fully. Any thoughts about how we should proceed?"

Today, Gina, a striking brunette with a curvy figure, lacked her usual swagger. She looked pensive, bit her lip, and said, "I'd like to write about the rape. It bothers me. Questions keep bouncing around in my head.

Why did the killer rape his cousin after the murders? Was it part of his plan or a spontaneous act? Did the girl ever suspect that something so terrible would happen to her? Does it still haunt her now? Normally, I don't like to think about rape. It's horrible. But I need answers, and I'd like to find out more."

"I think you may be onto something, Gina," said Brad of the many tattoos, "and I think the rape victim is more likely to talk to you than to Frank or me. Is that a sexist thing for me to say? Am I in trouble here?"

Hannah said, "I think you're right, Brad. We have to be realistic. The teenage girl who was raped is now a young woman. She still lives in the Parkerville area, and it would be helpful for one of you to interview her and hear her side of the story. Rape, however, is a sensitive topic. The victim probably will feel more comfortable talking to another woman than to a man. Let's face it. That does give Gina an advantage. Okay, Gina can research the rape. What about the rest? How do you want to divide up what pertains to the murders?"

"Well," said Brad, "My uncle's a lawyer, and he says he remembers this case. I could talk to him, and he knows lots of people at the courthouse I could talk to as well. I think I'd like to look into the legal stuff, the charges and trial and sentencing. I don't know how I feel about a fourteen-year-old kid being charged as an adult. Sometimes teenagers who commit crimes are punished as minors, but sometimes they are sentenced as adults. This bothers me. Is it okay for me to research this part?"

"Sure," said Hannah, "That will cover the legal end. What about you, Frank?"

Frank was surprisingly agile for a heavy guy, perhaps because he had been a high school wrestler. He sprung off the couch he was lounging on, picked up a colored piece of chalk, and paced back and forth in front of the blackboards. He underlined words here and there. He drew arrows to connect sentences and added several question marks. He looked very pleased when he was done.

"There," Frank said, "I think I've found what I will research."

"Okay," said Gina. "I give up. I like your flashy arrows and the underlining, but what does it all add up to?"

"Don't you see it?" Frank asked.

Brad said, “Nope. You’d better explain.”

“A lot of what we have left on the board is about how the community dealt with the crime, who forgave and who didn’t and why,” Frank said. “I didn’t bring this up before, but I’m a member of the Parkerville Mennonite Church. My family goes way back. We’ve belonged to the church forever, and Matthew Baker, our killer, and his family were congregants, too. Not just members of the church but really active, important members. I’m still living at home, and last night my aunt and uncle came over for dinner, and they brought my grandparents along. I talked about this project while we were eating, and you wouldn’t believe what I stirred up. I never heard my family argue like that before. My mom glared at me all night. She was so upset that I had brought up the name Matthew Baker and got everyone all riled up. I didn’t know my family was so divided. Some were really for and others were really against forgiving this guy. I think this is something I just have to look into, so I can make up my own mind.”

Hannah said, “It sounds like you all have found subjects to explore. Do more research, see where it leads you, and then you’ll each have to form a thesis statement that you can support. We’ve been at this for some time. You’re all doing well. Right now, it’s time to head out.”

“Wait,” said Gina. “Professor Stein, before we go, aren’t you going to tell us why you’re interested in this particular crime and want us to research it?”

“I was wondering when one of you would ask that question,” Hannah said. “The answer is simple. The people who were murdered by their son were neighbors of mine. I never could reconcile what I knew about the Baker family with their violent deaths. I’ve always felt that something is missing, that there is more I need to know. Now, with your help, maybe I’ll find out what that missing something is and be able to put this matter to rest.”

Hannah was tired. She was not ready to elaborate and wasn’t sure she should.

“See you in class tomorrow,” Hannah said.

Hannah unplugged her laptop and slid it and her cell phone into her bag as her students gathered up their gear. Hannah listened to their chatter as they left the room, and, as her office door was open, she could hear their voices bouncing off the walls of the stairwell as they trudged down the stairs. They were still discussing the case. That was a good sign.

A short time later, Hannah was crossing the campus to get to her car. She smiled. She was pleased with her newly formed investigative team; they were off to a good start. She had just reached the entrance to Parking Lot B when she spotted a tall woman walking alongside a small girl dressed in lavender. The child started to skip and hop, and the woman impatiently pulled on the girl's arm.

Hannah froze. Something was wrong. Danger. There was danger here. Her heart started thumping wildly, and her underarms were sticky with sweat. She began to run. She had to reach the child. She had to warn her. Hannah's long, gauzy peasant skirt was in the way. She clutched a handful of her skirt's bright print fabric to hike it up, to free her legs. She had to move faster. Faster. Suddenly, a blue car whizzed by her. She caught a glimpse of two figures. One was small, wearing pale purple clothes. She was too late. The girl was gone. Hannah stopped. She was shaking, and she felt dizzy. A thin layer of sweat covered her face.

"Oh no," Hannah moaned. "Not again. I can't go through this again."

Chapter 3

Twenty minutes later, Hannah parked her car in her driveway. She was glad to be home, happy to be in a safe place. But what exactly had frightened her and set off her panic attack? Hannah unlocked the door to her house and performed her "coming-home rituals." She tossed her keys into the bowl on the entryway table, slid her computer from her bag, placed her computer on her desk, and checked her cell phone for messages. She was only vaguely aware of what she was doing. Her mind was on the little girl she had seen in the parking lot. What was it she felt compelled to tell that child? What was so important?

Hannah was still holding her phone, and its ringtone startled her, but she relaxed when she saw the name "Jodi" on the phone's screen. She quickly answered the call.

"Hello there, friend. How did you know I need you?" Hannah asked.

"What's up?" Jodi Kingston's husky, warm voice was, as always, a soothing balm when Hannah was upset.

"I had an odd thing happen today. Maybe you'll be able to help me make sense of it. But first, tell me how you are. And have you seen Sophie lately?"

"Okay. I'll talk about Sophie first. I know you can't wait to hear about your daughter."

Hannah said, "It's only because you get to see her far more often than I do since she transferred to the University of Pittsburgh. I depend on you to tell me the truth. I fear Sophie only tells me what she thinks I want to hear. How is she doing? How does she look? Is she still heartbroken over her break-up with that political science student she was dating?"

"Whoa, Hannah. Take a breath. I do enjoy taking Sophie out to lunch whenever we can arrange it. Yesterday we met at a coffee shop near campus. She looked good. No, she looked great. She was seated at a table with a group when I arrived, and the guy sitting beside her was hot. After her friends left, Sophie talked about the engineering classes she's taking this summer, but she didn't talk about dating. I have no idea what her relationship is with the hot guy she was sitting next to, but she seems to be busy and happy. That's all I, your personal spy, can report right now."

"Good. That sounds good. And what about you?"

"I'm doing okay. The new job is working out. I often want to kick myself for buying an old townhouse that needs so much work, but the renovations are coming along. I do like my contractor. Speaking of hot guys, he's sizzling, age-appropriate, and interested in yours truly."

"Oh, Jodi, I was worried you'd be lonely when you moved to Pittsburgh, but I should have known it wouldn't take you long to find a handsome man. I love that about you. You never change."

"And why should I when I have everything a man could want in a single woman in her early forties? I have money, wisdom, power, and lots of curves. I'm the perfect middle-aged package."

"And," Hannah teased, "you're so modest and demure, too."

"I'll go for confident over modest and demure any day. Now that we've covered all my fine qualities, it's your turn. What happened today? What can I do to help?"

"I think I need you to be both a therapist and a friend," Hannah said.

Hannah told Jodi about her panic attack in the parking lot, and her voice trembled when she described how she had run after the little girl.

Hannah said, "And for the life of me, I can't figure out why I so desperately needed to reach that child. Yes, the woman I saw was pulling on her arm and hurrying her along, but I don't think I was witnessing child abuse."

Jodi responded with a non-committal, "Hmmm."

"That's not helpful. I need you to bore into this with your laser-sharp mind and tell me what's going on."

"Have you ever felt this way before?" Jodi asked.

"Four years ago. I had a panic attack right after Aaron died. I knew I had to tell my children their father had been killed by a drunk driver, but

I couldn't get the words out. I started to shake and sweat, and my heart raced. Just like it did today. I also had some panic attacks when I was a child, right after my mother died. Those were terrible, but I understood why I had them. I was overwhelmed, unable to cope with those deaths. But my reaction to seeing that little girl today makes no sense at all."

"Relax, Hannah. You're overwrought right now. Give your mind time to figure things out. The subconscious doesn't respond well to pressure. A solution often materializes when you're calm and thinking about something else."

"Jodi, you're a professional therapist. Is that the best you've got?"

"It is for right now. Let's change the subject. It might help. I was surprised when I read your last email. Why are you encouraging some of your students to write research papers based on an old murder case? And why the Baker murders? Why go back there?"

"Why not? You know I still feel guilty about not reporting what Helen Baker told me to the police."

"But it wouldn't have made any difference. Matthew Baker was guilty. He killed his parents and his sister. When he was caught, he was holding the murder weapon, and there was more than enough evidence to convict him. Case closed."

"But, Jodi, maybe it wouldn't have been such a simple open-and-shut case if the police knew what Matthew Baker's mother suspected right before she was murdered."

Chapter 4

Friday, June 14

Early the next morning, Hannah was at her kitchen table sipping coffee and nibbling on an English muffin. She read her son Seth's email as she ate her breakfast. She chuckled, in all the right places, as she read Seth's long, rambling email. Whereas Sophie, his twin sister, was reticent about divulging too much, Seth enjoyed sharing his life with his mother. He was afraid she would be lonely this summer, so he called home or emailed from Paris regularly. Each time he entertained her with wonderful tales about the places he visited and the people he met. He was thoroughly enjoying his study abroad program, focusing on French literature. Hannah sighed. She was happy her son and daughter were doing well but missed the twins. The house was too quiet. She had too much time to wonder what she would do after her offspring graduated college and took off on their own. Now that Jodi, her best friend, had moved away, there was no one to pull her into spontaneous adventures. What would become of her when her children permanently left home, too? She loved her work, but would it be enough to fill her life?

Hannah was surprised when her cell phone rang; she saw that Jodi, who was not a morning person, was calling her.

"Good morning, Jodi. It's just a bit past seven. It's not like you to call so early in the morning. Is anything wrong?"

"Nothing's wrong," Jodi replied. "I had trouble sleeping last night, just randomly dozed. Since I'm awake, I thought I'd check up on you before you left home. How's it going? Anything come to mind yet related to your panic attack?"

"No, and it's maddening. There has to be a reason I felt the need to run after that little girl yesterday, but I don't know what it is. I had trouble sleeping, too. I kept going over this, but I didn't make any progress."

"Your attack may be linked to a buried memory. I have a suggestion. Park in the same parking lot again today, and I'll check in with you tonight. Let me know if you see or hear anything that makes you feel anxious."

"Ah, I knew you'd have a trick or two up your sleeve."

"No tricks, Hannah. This is just a suggestion that may or may not help you. This attack could be tied to something that happened in your past. Is there anything you've repressed?"

"Now that's got to be a trick question. How would I know if I'm a master at deceiving myself?"

"Fair enough. I'll talk to you again tonight. Good luck, my friend," Jodi said.

"Thanks, Jodi," Hannah said and ended the call.

A short time later, following Jodi's instructions, Hannah parked her car in Parking Lot B on campus.

"Okay," Hannah said aloud, "I did it. I'm here."

She looked ahead, to the sides, and behind her car. She saw lines of parked cars and several students wearing backpacks and carrying books. She noted that two professors she knew had stopped to chat near the entrance. She felt nothing. She closed her eyes, waited a bit, opened them, and looked about her again. Everything looked normal, and she felt fine.

Well, I won't have much to report to Jodi tonight. Nothing to fear here, she thought. *All I'll be able to tell Jodi is that the car parked next to mine needs a new muffler. Boy, it's really loud.*

Hannah climbed out of her car. She was locking her car's door when she felt a thump on her shoulder. Hannah swung around. She was shaking. Not again. No, not again. This time she would not freeze. This time she would not run. This time she would fight.

Chapter 5

"Sorry I startled you, Professor Stein. I just tapped you on the shoulder to get your attention. You didn't hear me when I called out to you. That car next to yours is really noisy," Brad said.

Mercifully, the car in the adjacent parking spot had stopped rumbling, and Hannah could hear Brad's apology. Still, it took Hannah a few seconds for everything to fall into place. All was well. Her tall, tattooed student just wanted to talk to her. There was no danger. She slumped against the side of her car in relief. Her hand holding her computer bag fell to her side. She had been ready to use it as a defensive weapon.

"I'm really sorry. I truly didn't mean to scare you, Professor Stein," Brad said.

Hannah could see that Brad looked concerned and contrite.

"No problem," Hannah said to reassure him. "I was just startled. I guess I had too much coffee this morning. I'm a little jumpy."

Brad hesitantly smiled. "I thought I might find you here. I heard that most of the faculty parks in Lot B. I wanted to catch you before our class."

Brad stopped speaking and turned when he heard his name called. A square, compact figure jogged over to them. It was Frank.

"What did she say?" Frank asked when he reached Brad and Hannah.

"I didn't get a chance to ask her yet," Brad replied.

"I think one of you should explain," Hannah said. "And I'm afraid you'll have to be quick. We all have to get to class on time."

"Let's start walking, and I'll start talking," Frank said.

Frank told Hannah that he had learned that Ronald Chambers, a member of his church, believed it was his Christian duty to help Matthew Baker. Chambers and other like-minded congregants visited Baker in prison and raised money so that Matthew could purchase items from the prison canteen. Frank had tracked Chambers down and had a long conversation with him about Matthew Baker.

Chambers had religiously visited Baker twice a month for years, traveling more than seventy miles to a decrepit old prison. Fortunately, when that facility became overcrowded, Matthew was among the prisoners who were moved to the new prison outside of Harrisburg. This prison favored video chats, a more efficient and less expensive way for prisoners to visit with relatives and friends. Chambers had these regularly now with Baker and had arranged for other congregants to join them. To facilitate matters, Chambers had handed over a copy of his church's congregational directory to the prison authorities, with Baker's permission, so that all the congregants could be registered as verified guests. Chambers was stretching the rules, but he managed to pull it off as he never allowed more than five other congregants at a time to join him on a video call.

Frank paused for breath at this point, and when Hannah raised a quizzical eyebrow, he said, "And now I'm getting to the part that involves you, Professor Stein. Ronald Chambers' next video chat with Matthew Baker is scheduled for today, at three in the afternoon, and Chambers said there was room for me, a fellow congregant, to participate. I really want to meet Baker, to see what he looks like, and to hear what he has to say. Brad is curious, too, and wants to be a silent observer. We both will be on campus at that time, and we need to find a quiet spot to set up my computer, a place where no one will interrupt us during this video meeting. We gave it some thought and wondered if we could use your office. What do you say?"

Hannah nodded in assent, pleased that Frank had found a good lead and had arranged this. Yes, by all means, the boys could use her office for this video chat, and she would be there, too. She also wanted to hear what Matthew Baker had to say.

* * *

Hannah, Frank, and Brad were gathered in Hannah's office at a quarter to three that afternoon. Frank was stationed at Hannah's desk, with his laptop open and ready for the video call. Hannah and Brad were sitting on carefully positioned folding chairs, out of the computer's camera's range. They were all ready, and the conference call began promptly at three o'clock.

A gray-haired lady's wrinkled face and neck filled a square on Frank's computer screen. She must have been a regular as she chirped, "I'm back for my monthly visit. Hi, Matthew. It's me, Sarah. I've been praying for you."

Ronald Chambers' face filled another square on the screen. With his rosy cheeks, head of white hair, and long white beard, he could easily pass for Santa Claus. He introduced Matthew to the others on the call, to Frank and a middle-aged couple who were also members of the Parkerville Mennonite Church.

Matthew Baker's face filled the center square. The skinny teenage boy Hannah remembered from newspaper pictures had been in jail for many years and no longer resembled his younger self. Matthew Baker was now a twenty-eight-year-old man with a wide face, receding hairline, and dark circles under his eyes. He was wearing round wire-rimmed eyeglasses; he looked like an older, sleep-deprived, and pudgy version of Harry Potter.

Matthew said, "Hey, everybody, thank you all for being part of this call. I've got something to tell you. Especially you, Mr. Chambers. Finally, I've been able to remember what happened on that awful night, the night when my family was killed. Everything is much clearer now. You've got to help me get out of this place because I don't belong here. I'm not a murderer. I didn't kill them."

Chapter 6

There was a hush, and then everyone on the conference call started talking at once. Chambers put the group on mute.

A few seconds later, he clicked on his microphone and spoke slowly and emphatically. "Matt, I don't understand. I've been visiting you for years. We've prayed together, and you've asked for forgiveness. I believed you were sincere. There's no reason for you to change course now. You've accepted responsibility for your actions. Don't backslide and blame others for your sinful acts."

"But I just accepted what everyone said. Nobody was on my side. Everyone was so sure I was the murderer, even my lawyer. I thought it must be true. I felt I had no choice, and I had to believe it, too," Baker replied. "But now, when I think about that night, I'm not doing anything. I'm watching. I'm watching someone else kill my parents and my sister. So, you see, it wasn't me. It wasn't me."

Matthew leaned forward. "I replayed that horrible night in my head over and over, but it was always blurry. Shapes kept shifting. The only thing that felt real was the knife. I do remember picking up the knife. Then, after the trial, I had to stop. I just couldn't think about my family anymore. I felt so low and dirty. I wanted to curl up and die."

Chambers said, "We've gone over all of this, Matt."

"Yes, I know. For years I've just focused, as you suggested, Mr. Chambers, on getting through one day at a time and on turning myself around. That's what I've been doing. But now, everything has changed. Finally, I can see things clearly. I'm still a sinner, but I know I'm not a killer."

Ronald Chambers cleared his throat. "I'm going to let Sarah and the others talk to you for a while. I won't argue with you, Matt, but I do want you to know that I'm disappointed. I thought all our visits and prayers were helping you to be a better man, to grow and mature. I hate to see you lose the ground you've gained. Please think about what you've said. Think over everything very carefully."

Chambers took the group off mute, and Sarah's high-pitched soprano voice commandeered the meeting. She rattled off inconsequential news, telling Matt what her church committees were doing and relating the latest exploits of her Siamese cat. The middle-aged couple spoke next about their recent trip to Yellowstone Park. Frank was wiggling in his seat. He anxiously awaited the chance to speak to Baker and turn the conversation back to what Frank deemed important. Baker had just said he was in prison for a crime he did not commit. Why were these people wasting time on other matters?

Finally, it was Frank's turn. He introduced himself and explained that he was a concerned church member looking into Matt's crime for a college research paper.

Baker straightened in his seat. "A paper? Hey, that's good. You'll want to write the truth. You do want to help me, right?"

Frank said, "I'll see what I can do. It all depends on what I uncover. I don't know much yet. I'd like to hear your side of the story. What was happening in your life right before the murders?"

Matt explained that he had just started hanging out with a group of high school dropouts before his family was killed. He did this because he was lonely and wanted to belong somewhere. And he admired the guys in the gang. They weren't kids. They had cars and money. It was easy for them to get money; they sold drugs. And he liked experimenting with drugs. He no longer felt small and weak when he was high on drugs. He had some peace. That's all he wanted, a little peace. He wanted his dad to stop yelling at him and his mom to stop looking so disappointed. He wanted people to stop comparing him to his older sister Dara.

Matt said, "Okay. I admit it. Dara was better-looking, smarter, and more popular than I was. I got it. I knew I would never measure up. I just wanted people to leave me alone and let me be. But no. No one would do that. They all said it was a shame I wasn't as good as Dara. Teachers, neighbors, relatives, and so-called friends. Just everybody. They made me so mad. They all thought they were so high and mighty and could judge me. There were times when I just wanted to lash out and cut them all down to size."

"Look, Matt," said Chambers, "I know many years have passed, but could you be experiencing some sort of flashback from the drugs you used? Maybe they're clouding your thinking now. Maybe that's why you've turned things around in your head and now believe you're innocent."

"No, I know the truth now. Everything is much clearer, no longer blurred. You see, I've been working in the prison library for a couple of months. That's where I found Stevenson. Stevenson helped me to understand everything better. Now I know I didn't hurt my family. Someone else did."

Ron Chambers said, "We're running out of time. We have to wrap up this call. I'll try to arrange for another call soon."

"Listen, Mr. Chambers, I really do appreciate all you and the church have done for me. I can't tell you how much your visits have meant, and I'm so grateful for the money you've collected for me, too. I couldn't have made it in here without your help. But now, you've got to believe me. I always knew I could never rape anyone, and I wasn't charged with that. Now, it's equally clear to me that I'm not a killer. You've got to help me get out of here. I shouldn't be punished for something I didn't do."

* * *

"Well," said Brad immediately after the call ended, "what should we make of all that? Is Baker right? After all this time, is he suddenly not guilty of the murders and really innocent?"

"And how do we find out?" Frank answered Brad's questions with another question.

Hannah noticed that Frank's fingers were doing a fast-paced tap dance on the keyboard of his computer.

"What are you typing, Frank?" she asked.

"A list of things to look into," Frank replied. "I think I should find out how PCP works. According to the newspaper articles I read, that was the drug Baker had in his system on the night of the murders. Matthew admits he was high when his family was killed. And I'd like to learn what Baker actually said to the police when they questioned him."

"That's what I'd like to know," Brad said. "I asked my Uncle Bob, the lawyer who has agreed to help me with my research, if I could get a hold of Baker's police interview. He said that would be really tough, but if an interview is used as evidence in a trial, it will show up in the trial transcript. And Uncle Bob found out that parts of Baker's police interview were introduced at his trial."

"Can we get a copy of the transcript?" Frank asked.

"It took some doing, but I found a way to get parts of it," Brad continued. "Uncle Bob once dated Matthew Baker's attorney, who has a copy of the transcript, and, luckily, they parted as friends. He's going to treat this lawyer to dinner at some hot new restaurant she likes, and, in exchange, I'll get copies of some of the pages of the transcript. To repay him, I have to mow Uncle Bob's lawn for a month, so I sure hope the parts of the transcript I get will be worth it."

"That's great, Brad," Frank said. "And there's one more thing that's bothering me. What did this Stevenson say or do? Why is Baker suddenly convinced that he's not a murderer now? I need to talk to Matthew Baker again."

Chapter 7

TGIF, Hannah thought as she collapsed onto the sectional in her family room in her home. *Yes, thank God it's Friday. What a week!*

Hannah kicked off her shoes and stretched out on the comfy cushions. Her cell phone's ringtone yanked her back up to the surface. She had been in the depths of sleep, a dark dream place where she had been falling down a twisted staircase. She reached for the phone, swiped at the screen to answer the call, and groggily said, "Hello."

"Well, hello to you, too, sleepyhead. I obviously woke you up."

"Oh, hi, Jodi. I didn't intend to nap. I came home and thought it would feel good to close my eyes for just a few minutes. I must have fallen asleep, but I don't feel rested. I was having a strange dream. I'm glad you woke me. What time is it, anyway?"

"It's six-thirty. I'm also exhausted, but I'm trying to rally. I have a date with my contractor, and I don't want to fall asleep over dinner. He'll be by to pick me up soon. I wanted to check in with you before I left. How are things going? Any more panic attacks?"

"No. I did what you suggested. I parked in the same lot, and everything was normal. Well, almost normal. I almost hit one of my students with my computer bag."

"What?" Jodi asked.

"My back was turned to him, and he startled me when he tapped me on the shoulder. Not a big problem; no one was hurt. We both were embarrassed. It was just an awkward moment. Nothing more."

"Well, that's good. So, no adverse reactions to the parking lot?"

"Nope. And I didn't feel the need to run after anyone today. I'm just tired because I didn't sleep much last night. Say, this morning, you said you had trouble sleeping, too. What kept you up?"

Jodi said, "Yesterday, we were talking about the Baker murders. I was thinking about them last night. Remember, we both were shocked that those terrible crimes had taken place just a short distance from our homes. It was such a horrible time, but we got through it together. You do remember, don't you?"

"Of course, I remember. How could I ever forget? You saved me. I knew no one here, and you became my first and best friend."

"But, Hannah, I do feel guilty that it took something as big as the Baker murders and the rape for me to reach out to a new neighbor. I was in such a bad place back then. I still don't understand how the guy I was seriously thinking of marrying could be so cruel. He had his secretary call to inform me that he had moved on, and I was never to contact him again. Who does that? I blamed myself for being so blind. He totally fooled me. He told me over and over again that he loved me, and I believed him. I was really stuck in my own misery."

"Jodi, please don't feel guilty. You needed time to regroup and bounce back. And when you did, we found each other. Now, I can't imagine getting along without you."

"I wish you were still living next door to me. I'll never find a friend like you here in Pittsburgh."

Hannah replied, "Well, you're not supposed to. I don't want to be replaced. We can't run next door to see each other, but we have emails, phone calls, and visits to look forward to. Lots of visits."

"Yes, but I still wish we were not so far apart. By the way, how are the people who bought my house, Cranky and the Flower Lady? What are they up to?"

"You and your nicknames. Last weekend, I almost referred to those two by your crazy names instead of their real ones. I have to keep reminding myself to call them Cranston and Lily. They like puttering in the garden, so I often see them working in their yard. We wave at each other. Although he's a little cranky, and she's a little flaky, they really are okay. By the way, you nickname people all the time, and I've never asked. Did you ever give me a nickname?"

"Oh, I gotta run. I just heard the doorbell. Must be my contractor. I'll call again soon. And, Hannah, it was easy to come up with a name for you. You're my best friend. You're my Cherished Chum," Jodi said and ended the call.

* * *

Hannah sighed. She did miss Jodi. Yes, talking on the phone to her friend was nice, but it was so much better when she lived next door, especially after Hannah's husband died. Hannah picked up the family photo in the simple silver frame on the end table by the sectional. It was a good picture. The twins were juniors in high school at the time. They both looked like their father, tall and slim with wide smiles and masses of dark, wavy hair. Hannah stood in the middle of the group, dwarfed by her husband Aaron and their children; her blond head of curls barely reached Aaron's shoulder. She had a grin on her face, too. They were at a water park that day, and everyone had a glorious time. None of them suspected that, just one month later, a drunk driver would slam into Aaron's car and snuff out his life. Hannah bit her lip, determined not to cry, and returned the frame to the table.

"Aaron," she said aloud. "I do miss you. What am I going to do in two years when the children graduate college? They'll be leaving me, too."

Hannah walked into the kitchen, fixed herself a cheese and tomato sandwich, poured herself a tall glass of iced tea, and put her simple dinner on a tray she carried to her deck. It was still warm but cooling down, and sitting outside was pleasant. Hannah relaxed. She put aside the week and let her thoughts slide back, fourteen years back, to when she moved into this home in Parkerville.

She remembered how excited Aaron had been about moving to Lancaster County from Minnesota. He had claimed it would be a great adventure; they would leave behind their old lives in the Twin Cities and strike out on their own. Hannah did not share his enthusiasm. It wasn't easy to part from friends, relatives, and all that was familiar. But Aaron, a cardiac surgeon, could not wait to join an up-and-coming practice specializing in heart and vascular surgeries. After accepting the position, Aaron immediately left Minnesota to take care of the "big things," buying a home for the family and settling into his practice. He left Hannah in charge of the "little things": arranging for a moving van, packing up the contents of their house, driving two active six-year-old children to Pennsylvania on her own, and settling everyone and everything into their new home. Afterward, a physically exhausted and frazzled Hannah told her husband that he would have to seriously rethink his definition of "little things." And then there was that awful morning.

Chapter 8

That awful morning had become part of Hannah's story, part of her history. It was just a week after their move into their new home. Hannah still had not found the bath towels, and she was tired of dabbing at herself with a small hand towel after she showered. She rationalized that the family could always use extra towels and was determined to go shopping for some big, fluffy ones. Hannah was thinking about bath towels when she opened her front door and walked outside to look for Aaron and the twins. She was surprised to see a small crowd of people in the street. And two Parkerville police squad cars were parked in the quiet cul-de-sac, too. Aaron was snapping pictures of their circular driveway with his camera while talking to a short, round police officer. The policeman was listening to Aaron, nodding and writing notes on a pad. Hannah was startled and confused. Then, she looked at the chalk markings on her driveway and understood why the police were there.

Hannah couldn't believe it. There were anti-Semitic chalk cartoons, crudely drawn, up and down the driveway. One was of stick figures entering an oven, and the words written underneath the picture were *Jew you must be murdred*. There was an assortment of swastikas, *Heil Hitler* upraised arms, and body parts pierced by knives and dripping in blood. Most of the captions under the drawings were misspelled. Hannah's automatic reaction was to reach for her two children, who were standing beside Aaron, and pull them to her. What in the world was going on? They had just moved in. Who knew they were a Jewish family? Why did someone want to scare them?

Hannah looked around. She noticed that another police officer was taking photos of neighboring driveways. She walked over to see what was written on them, holding firmly onto the hands of her children. She pivoted and shielded the twins with her body. The other driveways had chalk drawings on them, too, but theirs were of a sexual nature. There was a poorly drawn picture of a woman with large breasts on one driveway, and the words *Big Bobbies* were written across her chest. A man with a large organ between his legs was sketched on another driveway, and the words *Big Peenus* were written beside the figure in block letters. The driveways of all ten homes in the cul-de-sac had chalk pictures scrawled on them. Hannah assumed that the people looking at the graffiti lived nearby. However, she wasn't sure as she had not met any neighbors. Hannah heard someone say, "This is just a silly kids' prank." Several remarked that no real damage had been done, that the chalk drawings could easily be washed away. Folks seemed to be enjoying this time together. The atmosphere was festive.

Hannah and the twins walked back to their front yard. The policeman Aaron had been talking to was now next door, helping an attractive, stylish woman with long red hair unload a heavy suitcase from her car. Later, Hannah would meet and bond with her redheaded neighbor named Jodi; however, on that morning, Jodi was focused on flirting with the policeman, cajoling him into unloading bulky objects from her convertible. Afterward, the officer and Jodi walked down to the end of Jodi's driveway and looked at the chalk drawing there. They both laughed. Their laughter magnetically drew others to them. Soon, many people were laughing and pointing at the picture. Hannah couldn't see it from where she was standing, but she heard one man call out to another that it was very funny that the word next to the cartoon couple was *Intercurse.*

Hannah was numb. Something like this had never happened to her before. What did it mean? She would have preferred if her driveway had the same type of graffiti as the rest. Yes, the sex drawings were sick and tasteless, but they did not scare her the way the Nazi symbols on her driveway did. Hannah looked at Aaron. He was upset, too. They quickly hustled their children into the house and locked the door. After sending the twins to another room to play, Hannah turned to her husband and said, "What have you gotten us into? You said this was going to be a friendly, safe, and quiet place to raise our kids."

Chapter 9

Saturday, June 15

Hannah was up early on Saturday morning. She was bound and determined to do some gardening. Last week, she noticed that her next-door neighbor Cranky had been looking disdainfully at her weeds. Whoops! She really would have to be careful. His name was Cranston, and he was retired and took meticulous care of his yard. The least she could do was get his name right and control her pesky weeds. However, the cool morning air beckoned, and Hannah correctly reasoned that if she took a nice walk, the weeds wouldn't care. They would still be waiting for her when she returned.

Hannah quickly donned a loose, faded sundress, plopped a wide-brimmed straw hat on her head, and slipped into a comfortable pair of sneakers.

Hannah thought, *Jodi would never wear such an outfit. She would, at the very least, put on designer sweats. But, as usual, I don't have the time to bother. Nor do I own anything with a designer label.*

Hannah grabbed a pair of sunglasses and her keys, locked the door to her house, and started off on her habitual neighborhood walk. It always started with a turn around the cul-de-sac.

When Hannah came to the farmhouse in the curve of her horseshoe-shaped street, she paused to admire it. The house was over one hundred years old. It was a sprawling and stately red brick home with ample acreage, a pond, and a barn in back of it. It was an enviable property, the pride of the neighborhood, and nothing had deterred the Henley family from purchasing it when it went up for sale, not even the fact that a triple murder had occurred in its kitchen and a rape in its barn. Hannah still thought of it as the Baker house and probably always would. Whenever she passed it, she always thought of Helen Baker.

Helen Baker was the only neighbor who had stopped by after Hannah's driveway was desecrated. Helen came over the very next day. She brought cookies, the gooey type with a superhero on the packaging, and Hannah's children had been delighted. Hannah made coffee, and the two women chatted while the twins watched a cartoon show on the TV in the family room and munched on some of the cookies.

As she continued her walk, Hannah thought about her conversation with Helen Baker that day. She knew she could not accurately recall every word, but she would always remember most of what was said. And Hannah would never forget Helen's fear. Over the years, Hannah had replayed the exchange many times in her mind, always chastising herself afterward for not doing something about it.

* * *

Helen had said, "I'm sorry I didn't stop by before now. I saw the moving van and all, but my husband and I have been grappling with some troublesome family issues. However, when I saw what those vandals did to your driveway, I had to come over and let you know how upset we are. That was not right. Bruce, my husband, said I shouldn't wait to bake anything, that I should just come over. I'm sorry the cookies are store-bought and nothing much."

"But just look," Hannah had replied, "my kids are very happy. They would gobble up the whole package right now if I'd let them. And I do appreciate your concern. Frankly, I was shocked, and I'm still scared. I keep the kids close now; they can only play outside when mom or dad is with them. I don't understand why someone would write such hateful things on our driveway."

Helen looked like the stereotypical spinster librarian. She was very skinny and plain, wore her hair in a tight bun, and her tortoiseshell eyeglasses slid down to the base of her long narrow nose. Helen sighed and then said, "I hate to say this, but I'm afraid we have a local gang of high school dropouts who like to play pranks. I think they marked up all our driveways. Of course, I can't prove it, but I do know a few things. You understand."

"I'm not sure I do," Hannah said.

"You see, my son Matthew is only fourteen, and he's really a good boy but going through a difficult stage. Just the regular teenage defiance sort of things, but it's hard on Bruce. Matthew was never at the top of his class in school, but he did all right. Recently, his grades have plummeted, and things have gotten really bad at home, too. I can't tell you how exhausting it is to be arguing all the time. So, I spy. I know that sounds terrible, but a mother has to know what her son is up to. I pick up the extension and listen to his phone conversations when someone calls him on our house phone, and sometimes I follow him to see if he really goes where he says he's going."

Hannah was confused. She didn't know what to say in response. She wasn't sure how Helen's troubles with her son related to the anti-Semitic messages on her driveway.

"You do understand now, right?" Helen asked.

Hannah shook her head to signify that she did not.

"Well, my Matthew likes this group of dropouts who sell drugs, and I think they're responsible for what was written on your driveway. They aren't the brightest bunch, and I bet they didn't realize that this house had been sold and a new family had moved in. Last week I overheard one of those hoodlums tell Matthew on the phone that the teenage daughter of the Jewish family that used to live here wouldn't go out with him. He said he was determined to put that 'snobby bitch' down. Please forgive my language, but that's what he said. So, I think all those terrible drawings were meant for her and not for you."

Helen's shoulders slumped. She relaxed. "I'm glad to get that off my chest. It makes everything better for you, right?"

No, Hannah thought, *it does not make everything better for me and my Jewish family. The hateful words and drawings were real, and even though we may not have been the intended target, I'm not comforted. I'm upset that such ugliness exists here.*

"Now," Helen continued, "let me tell you about my church, the Parkerville Mennonite Church."

"Wait, maybe I should tell you first that we are a Jewish family."

"Oh, no wonder those driveway drawings scared you so much. I guess I should've waited a bit to know you better before mentioning my church, but I do enjoy bringing it up right away. Our lives revolve around the church, and I'm always anxious to share what it has to offer. However, lately, even the church hasn't been enough to sustain me. Matthew's problems have taken over everything."

And then, Helen Baker broke down and cried and apologized for crying and cried some more.

Hannah instinctively reached for Helen's hand. The act must have been comforting because Helen hiccuped and stopped sobbing.

Helen dabbed at her tears with the tissue Hannah offered her and said, "I've been nervous and not sleeping well. Bruce and I can't control Matthew. What are we to do? We can't lock him up in his room forever. And I'm so afraid. I think there's a prowler who enters our house when we're not at home. Bruce says I'm imagining things because nothing is missing. But I know objects have been moved; they're not in the right places. My home doesn't feel safe. I know it's silly, but I'm really afraid something bad will happen in my house."

Chapter 10

By the time Hannah had finished her walk, she had also concluded her "Meeting Helen Baker Memory." The police never did find out who marked up the driveways on her street when she first moved in. For Hannah and Aaron, the incident had been a hate crime, but, fortunately, nothing more related to it occurred. For her neighbors, it had been a harmless, childish joke. The driveways had been easily cleansed. After being sprayed with water, the crude sexual messages and the Nazi threats had been washed down the drain. Two weeks later, when Helen Baker, her husband Bruce, and their daughter Dara were murdered, and Helen's niece was raped, those horrendous crimes took center stage. Everything else paled in comparison.

After the Baker family had been killed, Hannah had trouble processing that three people had been violently murdered just a short distance from her home. Murder and rape were not supposed to touch the lives of people living in quiet suburban neighborhoods. Hannah had wanted to go to the police to tell them what Helen Baker had said about the teenage gang and the possible prowler, but Aaron had talked her out of it. He reminded her of an article printed in their local paper three days after the Baker murders. With the Baker crimes taking over the front pages, the news that swastikas had been painted on the doors of their synagogue in downtown Lancaster was buried in the middle of the newspaper. Their driveway graffiti and the damage to their temple frightened Aaron. He insisted that it was not a good time for Hannah to become involved in a police matter, not a good time to shine a light on their family and jeopardize their safety. He was also worried about his new practice and did not want their names linked with the heinous acts of Matthew Baker. Besides, the police did not need anything more. The Baker boy was guilty. The case was closed, and Hannah would not be helping anyone. Hannah understood and decided to accept her husband's reasoning. Above all else, Aaron was interested in protecting her and the twins. But a nagging doubt remained.

Jodi echoed Aaron's sentiments. She also believed Hannah had no reason to get involved in the Baker case. The boy had a fair trial and had been found guilty. Justice was served. But the itch of doubt persisted, and over the years, Hannah couldn't help herself; she just had to scratch at it.

Chapter 11

Sunday, June 16

Sunday morning was just right, comfortably warm with a golden glow, and Hannah Stein's morning was moving along at a smooth, predictable pace. She had eaten a light breakfast, chatted on the phone with her daughter Sophie, and now was ready for the final part of her Sunday morning ritual; she would correct student papers. She was prepared when she walked onto her deck. She had her coffee cup in one hand, and with the other, she carried a basket containing a green felt tip pen, a yellow highlighter, and a stack of class exercises. She placed everything on the outdoor table and collapsed into a comfortable deck chair. It was not long before Hannah was immersed in her work, and she was surprised when a shadow fell across the student paper she was reading. She looked up. Her neighbor Lily was standing on the other side of the table. Good. She remembered to greet her as Lily and not Flower Lady, Jodi's fun nickname for her.

Oh, no, Hannah thought. *I should've done a better job when I was weeding yesterday. I wonder if she has come over to complain.*

"Hi, Hannah," Lily said. "I saw you out here. Looks like you're busy. I promise I won't take up but a minute of your time. I just want to let you know that Cranston fell on Thursday. He's going to need surgery on his hip. Luckily, our son Ethan was able to drop everything and come for a visit. He's going to help us out. I just wanted to let you know. So, if you see a tall, dark stranger hanging around the place, don't call the police. It's not a stalker or thief. It's just Ethan."

Lily turned her head and scanned her back yard. "Why, there he is. He just walked out of the house." And then she called, "Come on over, Ethan. I want you to meet my neighbor."

Hannah stared. The guy walking toward them was gorgeous. It was as if Superman had materialized out of a comic book and taken actual human form. The shiny dark black hair, the piercing blue eyes, the handsome face, and the clearly defined muscles on his tall frame were all, definitely, Superman material. Hannah guessed he was in his mid-thirties as he sported a few laugh-line wrinkles, but there were not many.

Suddenly, a bell clanged loudly. "That's Cranston," Lily said. "I left the windows open so I could hear him while I was working in the yard. He rings a bell to call me. I better go in and see what he wants. Ethan, why don't you be neighborly and say something nice to Hannah while I'm gone." And then Lily quickly jogged back to her house.

"Well," said Ethan, "I guess I should say something nice and neighborly, but I have no idea what." He grinned and then chuckled. He had a wonderful deep voice and a great laugh.

Hannah smiled. She was at a loss for words. She suddenly wondered if she had remembered to comb her hair this morning. Her blond curls were always frizzing in the summer, so she usually just gave up and let them do their own thing when she was at home. Looking at Ethan, she also wished she had dabbed on a little make-up.

Ethan drew up a chair and sat down at the table across from Hannah. "Hope you don't mind, but we might as well talk for a little while to please my mother. I no longer know many folks in Lancaster, so I'm happy to meet you. I've been working for several years in Philadelphia. I'm a police officer. Mom told me you teach at Buchanan College. What are you working on?"

Hannah said. "Right now, I'm correcting some composition exercises."

"That's right. Mom did mention that you are an English teacher. Well, I must admit that English wasn't interesting to me when I was in high school. But I do find books interesting now. In high school, I couldn't understand why people made such a fuss about that boy floating down the river. You know the one, Huck Finn. And that rich guy. Gatsby was his name. I never could figure out what was so great about him. But now I wish I could go back and tell my English teachers that I've seen the films based on those books, and I liked them. I actually went back and read the books. And now I like the books, too. I think they speak to me now because I'm older, lived more, and thought more about life. You don't think I'm crazy, do you?"

"No," Hannah said. "I think people relate to novels in different ways at different points in their lives. I think that's especially true for the classics."

Ethan said, "I do think it's funny that we have to get old to appreciate something that was presented to us when we were young. That's been right in front of us for a long time."

Hannah stood up. "I'm sorry, Ethan. I have to leave now. I do hope your dad's surgery goes well and that he'll feel better soon. I also hope we'll be able to talk again. I really do. But I've just thought of something, and I have to go inside and look at a novel to see if I'm right. I can't wait."

A short time later, Hannah, with a classic novel in her hand, smiled. Sometimes it paid to think like an English teacher.

Chapter 12

Monday, June 17

On Monday morning, Hannah was pleased to note that Brad, Gina, and Frank had all signed up to meet with her during her afternoon office hours, and they had chosen consecutive appointment times. It was not surprising that the trio showed up together for the first scheduled meeting and said they wanted to pool their allotted times and get right to work.

Gina was beaming. "I was so afraid I'd have nothing solid to share. But, finally, things are progressing. I'm going to talk to Sandra Metzler, the girl who was raped, tomorrow. And Frank deserves all the credit."

Frank said, "Actually, I didn't do much. I just asked my mom to talk to Sandra Metzler's mother. The two have been friends since they were in kindergarten together. And then Sandra's mom spoke to Sandra. Luckily, Sandra agreed to the interview."

"And I don't want to blow it," Gina said. "I came up with a list of questions, but first I want to run them by you to make sure they're okay. I really don't want to embarrass or hurt Sandra."

"If you're able to, ask her a question for me. I want to know why the rape charge was dropped," Brad said. "That'll help me with my end of our investigation, the legal part."

Frank said, "And I'd like to know if her friends, her church, and the police offered her the right kind of support. If you can, find out how being raped by her cousin affected both her and her family. It's one thing to know your rapist, but I'm guessing it must be much worse to be related to him." Frank paused. Then he said in a rush, "I know. I'm bouncing all over the place. Violent crimes affect a community in so many ways. I keep telling myself that I have to narrow my focus, that I can't cover everything in a ten-page paper. But I can't make up my mind. Everything seems important."

Gina was typing quickly on her keyboard. "I'm adding your questions to my list. I'll try to work them in. I just hope Sandra Metzler will feel comfortable talking to me."

The group went over Gina's questions. They tweaked a few; however, there were no major changes. Hannah advised Gina to record the conversation so she could accurately quote Metzler later in her paper.

It was Brad's turn next. He reported that he would have pages from the Baker trial transcript on Wednesday. In the meantime, he had been looking into how other teen murder suspects had been treated and charged in Pennsylvania.

"I haven't had time to compare our state with the rest of the country yet. But get this; I found out that a twelve-year-old kid was charged with first-degree murder for a murder he supposedly committed when he was eleven. That's the law in Pennsylvania. If you are charged with murder, you are charged as an adult. It doesn't matter how young you are. However, this was an unusually young suspect, and the courts argued about what to do with him. The boy was eventually tried in juvenile court, found guilty, and kept in a detention center. He was imprisoned for almost ten years before the Pennsylvania Supreme Court overturned his conviction due to a lack of concrete evidence linking the boy to the murder. It blew my mind. Why are kids, who have so little control over their emotions, treated this way?" Brad asked.

Hannah said, "It sounds like you'll be arguing against the status quo in your paper."

Brad nodded. "I think I will, Professor Stein. I never expected to discover what I'm finding."

Frank said, "I've some good news to report. Apparently, Mr. Chambers was really rattled after Friday's video call with Matthew Baker. I know this because he immediately got in touch with several church elders, including my dad. Well, word leaked out to the congregation that

Baker is now insisting that he's innocent. Believe me, people were talking about it, both before and after the service on Sunday. So, Mr. Chambers has arranged for an emergency video chat tomorrow to get everything straightened out. And guess what? Baker asked Chambers to include me. Apparently, Matthew has gotten it into his head that my research will help clear him. I really don't think I can do much for him, but I'm glad I'll get the chance to ask him some more questions."

"Another interview with Baker. That's great, Frank. By the way, did you learn anything about PCP, the drug Baker had in his system on the night of the murders and the rape?" Hannah asked.

"Oh, yeah," Frank said. "I did some online research. PCP is known by a few names, including angel dust. I learned it makes you feel like you're detached from reality and distorts what you see and hear. Wait. Let me check my notes, and I'll tell you more."

Frank shuffled through some papers he had brought and pulled out a sheet. "I wrote down some things that went along with what Baker said on Friday. PCP can cause blurred vision. He did mention that things were blurry on the night of the murders, and it can alter your mood and make you feel strong and powerful. I remember that Matt said that the drug he took enabled him to feel better and not small and weak. Some experts claim that if you use PCP you will become violent. Others say it doesn't cause you to be violent, but it might make you more aggressive if you are a violent person. Oh, one last thing, its effects can last four to six hours, so it's important to learn when Baker took the drug."

Hannah said, "Good work, Frank. Before you three leave, remember to frequently check the class research handbook. It explains how to properly quote someone you've spoken to and how to cite online research."

Brad sighed. "Just when things start to get really interesting, you have to remind us of stuff like that."

"Well, you can't forget why you're doing this research," Hannah said. "I want to be able to give all of you A's on the quality of your research and the quality of your written papers. And, one last thing, sign up for these same appointment times on Wednesday afternoon. We'll be able to discuss what Gina and Frank learn from their interviews, and Brad will be able to share some of the trial's transcript pages. Will that work for everyone?"

The three students nodded and agreed.

"And, Frank," Hannah added, "I have a feeling when you ask Matthew Baker about finding Stevenson in the library that he is going to tell you that Stevenson's first name is Robert, and his middle name is Louis. Do let me know if I'm right."

Chapter 13

Hannah had just finished plopping a hamburger patty on the hot grill on her deck and entered her kitchen when her cell phone chimed. She fished her phone out of the pocket of her jeans. She glanced at the name on the screen and smiled. The call was from Jodi. She quickly answered the call.

"Hi there, friend. What are you up to?" Hannah asked.

"Nothing much," said Jodi. "I'm having my usual Monday night dinner, a Chinese take-out meal. I also plan on gorging myself on ice cream for dessert. How about you?"

"You'll be impressed. I'm barbecuing a hamburger. Right now, I'm heading into the kitchen to make myself a salad. My day was good. How was yours?"

"Good. But I hope I didn't make a mistake with my contractor. After our date on Friday night, I think he likes me far more than I like him. This could become a problem. What do I do if things get sticky? What if he messes up the work on my house if I want to cool things down? What if things don't click between us, and he just disappears?"

Hannah laughed. "Jodi, how in the world can I advise you? You know I dated very little when I was young, and I married Aaron right after college. What do I know about such things? Besides, you're the world's most prominent expert on dating. Or so you led me to believe."

"I know. I do like to project that image, but sometimes even someone as experienced as I, a true dating maven and goddess, has trouble with men. Not often. But sometimes. Seriously, do you have any ideas? I thought I was really falling for this guy, but now I'm not so sure. Say, I haven't asked in a while, is there a new man in your life? Four years have passed since Aaron died. You really should start dating."

Hannah put her phone on the kitchen counter and turned on the speaker. She could hear Jodi while she gathered ingredients for her salad and sliced a cucumber. She listened as Jodi, once again, advised her to get out in the world and date, but she knew, in her heart of hearts, that was impossible. She was Mrs. Aaron Stein, the doctor's wife and the twins' mother, and nothing, not even Aaron's death, was going to change that. Still, it was strange that she had worried about her appearance when she met Ethan yesterday. Very strange.

"Jodi, I think I've fallen under your spell. I met my neighbors' son yesterday. And you know what? I immediately came up with a nickname for him. It was easy. This guy is Superman personified. Just picture the Man of Steel. That's exactly what he looks like. I couldn't get over it."

"And?"

"Jodi, there's nothing more. I met him, we talked for a few minutes, and that's all. He's staying at his folks' place, your old house, to help his dad through hip surgery."

"And?"

"Jodi, please. I think the guy's in his mid-thirties. Much too young for me. And, besides that, he's way out of my league. Trust me. If you saw him, you would nickname him Superman, too."

"Hannah, first of all, you're only forty-three years old. You're in your prime. Second, you're a professor at Buchanan College; that tells the world that you're really smart. Third, as my grandmother used to say, you're as cute as a bug's ear."

Hannah laughed. "Hey, that's a really old expression and usually describes cute little kids. Besides, bugs' ears are peculiar. Grasshoppers have hearing organs in their knees."

"See what I mean about you being smart."

"Oh, no," Hannah said. "I gotta go. Superman is banging on my kitchen door, and there's smoke everywhere. I think my deck may be on fire."

Chapter 14

"Hannah. Hannah," Ethan was shouting, "your grill's on fire."

Hannah opened the door which led from her kitchen to her deck and saw smoke billowing from the open grill. There were neon blue and yellow flames shooting up into the sky. She quickly scooped up a box of baking soda and a potholder and then ran outside. She used the potholder to help her grasp the hot knob and turn off the grill. Next, she poured the whole box of baking soda over the flames and lowered the grill's lid.

"That should do it," said Ethan. "I'm impressed. You moved quickly."

"Well, I'm embarrassed," Hannah said. "I was grilling a hamburger while I was in the kitchen talking to a friend on the phone. I lost track of the time. Thank you so much for noticing the fire."

"I was just getting ready to eat my pizza on my folk's patio when I saw the smoke and flames. I ran right over to let you know."

"Thank you for coming to my rescue," Hannah said. But what she was thinking was, *You really are Superman!*

Ethan lifted the lid of the grill. "The fire's out, but your hamburger is really burnt. It looks like a lump of coal."

"There goes my dinner. Luckily, I have the salad I was cutting up."

"Is it a big salad?" Ethan asked.

"Yes. I'll be fine."

"I have a better idea. Dad had his surgery this morning, and Mom and I were at the hospital all day. He's doing fine, but Mom wanted to stay on. She sent me packing. She told me to go back to the house and relax. I stopped at Mario's Pizza. I ordered a Mario's super-large with the works on it. I was hungry and was thinking big, but you should see the size of it. There's no way I can eat it all by myself. Come join me. You bring your salad, and we'll share."

"But I don't want to put you out. Really, I'll be fine."

"Come on. I've been sitting in a hospital waiting room for most of the day. Take pity on me. I'd like to talk about something other than surgery and rehab exercises. Please come," Ethan said, and then he smiled.

His smile was so warm and welcoming that Hannah, much to her surprise, agreed to join him. She grabbed her salad bowl and crossed the short distance from her home to Cranston and Lily's patio. On the table was a Mario's pizza, cheesy and delicious. Hannah was on her second slice and Ethan on his third when they noticed a black cat with bright green eyes staring at them.

"Hello, Audrey," Hannah said.

"Is that your cat?" Ethan asked.

"No. She lives on a farm about a quarter of a mile from here. But the farmer doesn't consider her a pet, just a barn cat. He doesn't feed his cats as he wants them to eat the mice in his field. But this cat likes to roam. So, everyone in our neighborhood knows Audrey. We give her table scraps. She always gobbles up what I put out, so I think she's decided it's easier to beg for food than to hunt for it."

"She's a beauty, but how do we get her to stop staring at us?"

"Oh, that's easy," Hannah said.

They had finished the salad, so Hannah tore up a slice of pizza and put the pieces in the empty bowl. The cat's eyes never left the food. When Hannah put the bowl on the ground, the cat slowly and cautiously approached it. In less than a minute, the food disappeared, and after that, so did the cat.

Ethan laughed. "That was quick."

"Yes, she must have been hungry. I, actually, don't know her name. I just call her Audrey, and she seems to like it. At least, she doesn't object. With her long, elegant neck, she reminds me of that classic film star, Audrey Hepburn. I sometimes wonder if my neighbors have their own names for her, too."

"Tell me more. Besides feeding stray cats, what else is there to know about Professor Hannah?"

Because he seemed genuinely interested, Hannah told him about her marriage, her children, her work, and a little about her childhood in Minnesota. Ethan reciprocated and told her about growing up in Parkerville, joining the Parkerville police force, and then feeling the need to move to Philadelphia, where he could be an officer in a big city. He also casually mentioned that he had impetuously married in Philadelphia, regretted his decision, and divorced.

It was getting dark. Hannah and Ethan had devoured a good portion of the pizza. They sat back and relaxed in their chairs, apparently in no hurry to end the evening and separate.

"I've been waiting," Ethan said.

"Waiting?" Hannah asked

"You know. You left me abruptly yesterday and said you had an important matter to check out in a book. I've been waiting to hear if you found what you were looking for. So, were you on the right track? Were you correct?"

"Oh, that," Hannah said. "Yes, I do think I'm right. Actually, I'm almost positive I am. But I have to wait till Wednesday to know for sure. One of my students will have the answer for me then."

"And then you'll tell me and explain?"

"Yes, I promise,"

"Good. Then we have a date for dinner on Wednesday," Ethan said.

Uh-oh, Hannah thought. *How did that just happen? A date? Really? He's Superman, but I'm no Lois Lane! I don't know what to say.*

Hannah was too stunned to reply. She didn't say anything, but as she didn't object, Ethan interpreted her silence as agreement.

He said, "I'll meet you on your deck at seven on Wednesday evening. Wear casual clothes and comfortable sneakers."

So many reasons to refuse were swirling in Hannah's mind. If she wanted to, she knew she could manufacture at least six plausible excuses. But that would take some effort. Right now, Hannah was feeling mellow and, if she dared put a label on her emotions, happy. So, she said, "Okay." And found it very easy to do.

With a dinner date pending, Hannah desperately wanted to ask Ethan a few more questions about his personal life, but she resisted the temptation. Instead, she added the years of his professional life in her head.

"Ethan, I just realized something. You were probably part of the Parkerville police force when the Baker murders and rape occurred. Is that right?"

"Yes. I remember the case well. It was unlike any other crime scene I've ever seen. There was so much blood. It was splattered everywhere. It turned my stomach to see that young girl, Dara was her name, all cut up. And the mother and father were slashed in multiple places, too. And that poor girl who was raped. She was in really bad shape."

"Were you on hand when the son, Matthew Baker, was caught?"

"Yes. I'll never forget that either. We found him hiding in the family's barn, in the loft. He was covered in blood, waving around a bloody knife, and babbling nonsense. Boy, was he guilty. There was no way he could wiggle out of it."

Hannah was quiet, trying to connect what Ethan had just said to what she already knew about the case.

"I'm sorry. I didn't mean to spoil such a nice evening by talking about such horrendous things. Have I upset you?" Ethan asked.

"No. I'm not upset. I guess I should explain why I asked."

And Hannah did. She told Ethan about her students and explained why they were interested in the murders and the rape. She also mentioned how startled both she and her students were when they recently heard Matthew Baker claim that he was innocent. Ethan was quiet. He looked worried.

Hannah said, "Now, it's my turn to ask. Have I said something that's upset you?"

"Of course not," Ethan answered. "It's just that sometimes it's better to leave well enough alone. Matthew Baker is guilty and belongs in prison. That's all there is to it. The case is closed. Trust me, Hannah. There's nothing more to find out."

Chapter 15

Tuesday, June 18

The following day at three in the afternoon, Gina and Sandra Metzler were sitting on the couch in Sandra Metzler's living room. After obtaining Sandra's permission, Gina put her phone on a nearby table to record their conversation. Sandra worked out of her home, and her business was called Sandra's Super Stitches. She was well known locally for her work as a seamstress. Clothes to be altered and hemmed were hanging on large racks lining the walls of the room.

"Gina, I hope you don't mind if I do some hand stitching while we talk. I had a rush order come in. I'm trying to please a good customer and get some repairs finished quickly, so she can take the garments with her on a trip. She's leaving tomorrow. Some people never think ahead."

"No problem at all, Ms. Metzler," Gina said. "I can't thank you enough for talking to me."

"Please, just call me Sandra, and I'm happy to help. However, if you had asked me to discuss the rape just a couple of years ago, I would have refused. For a long time, I couldn't deal with it. Not any part of it. It's something you never get over. But now I understand that it's something that happened to me in the past and not something that's still happening."

Sandra Metzler was only fifteen years old when she was raped by her cousin. She was now a twenty-nine-year-old woman but childlike. She was tiny, with small delicate features, and she had a high-pitched voice. Gina watched Sandra's fingers move a threaded needle nimbly in and out of the fabric on her lap.

"I wish I could sew like that," Gina said. "I struggle so when I try to sew on a button."

Sandra smiled. "Actually, that's good for me. I need people like you to bring me your clothes, so I can make a living. I had to find work I could do at home after the rape. I couldn't leave the house. Home was safe. For years I was a nervous wreck whenever I had to leave my house."

"Did you ever suspect Matthew Baker was capable of hurting you?"

"Never saw it coming. Not any of it. I felt so comfortable in my cousins' home. Dara and I were the same age. We weren't just cousins; we were best friends. And Matthew was only a year younger, so he was always hanging around. He was just Dara's little brother to me, a bit of a pest at times but generally sweet. And then he changed. Drove my aunt and uncle crazy. When Matthew got involved with drugs, I thought they'd explode. They were worried sick about him. And they were embarrassed. People at church were beginning to notice."

Gina said, "If you're able to, can you tell me what happened on that terrible night."

Sandra kept sewing. Her stitches were still small and evenly spaced, but she began to shove the needle into the material with more force as she spoke.

"It was the Saturday night before Labor Day. There was a concert on the back lawn of our church. It was fun; there were singing groups and ice cream. Dara and I shared a blanket with our friends. When the event ended, I went back to Dara's house for a sleepover. As usual, Dara and I went up to her room to talk. We were fussing with our hair and talking about the boys we liked. Nothing unusual. It was around ten-thirty when Aunt Helen called to us and told us to get ready for bed. Dara went into the bathroom to brush her teeth, and I was pulling a nightgown over my head when we first heard shouting. Dara came out of the bathroom and was angry. She said she was sick and tired of Matthew arguing with her parents and getting into trouble. She begged me not to tell my parents. Dara didn't realize that they already knew. Then we heard really loud screams. Awful screams. And loud crashes. And more screams. Dara ran out of her room. I tried to follow, but I was wearing fluffy slippers. They were old and stretched out. I was moving quickly, and one of my loose slippers fell off. The one on my right foot. I was halfway down the hall when I realized it. I went back for the slipper, picked it up, and put it back on my foot. There were more screams. Then more horrible screams. So many screams."

Sandra's hand was shaking. She put her sewing down. "It's odd how that simple, everyday thing, a bedroom slipper, may have saved my life. Would I have been killed if I had entered the room with Dara? I'll never know. By the time I reached the bottom of the back staircase, it was all over. The screams had scared me, so I hesitated and just peeked into the kitchen. There was blood everywhere, and bodies were on the floor. And I saw the back of a figure holding a bloody knife in the air. That's when a voice in my head shouted at me to run. Run! I opened the side door off the hallway and ran out of the house. But I heard someone running behind me. I didn't turn to see who it was. I just ran for my life. My slippers flew off my feet and into the air as I ran through the yard. I ran to the barn. I don't know why. Dara and I often hid there when we were little, and the barn door was open. That voice in my head told me to go to the barn. I had just gotten through the door when I got tackled from behind."

Sandra paused and took a deep breath to steady herself.

"Are you okay?" Gina asked. "It's okay to stop. It must be very difficult to talk about all this."

"Yes, it is," Sandra said. "But at this point in my life, I won't let it control me. Don't worry. I can control it now."

Sandra continued, "I don't remember the rest very clearly. I remember that my forehead hit the floor. Hard. It dazed me. Hands roughly turned me over and ripped my nightgown apart. Then a heavy body was on top of me. I felt smothered. I tried to hit and claw, but I was punched in the face. That hurt a lot, too. I felt a strong pull on my ponytail, and then my head was repeatedly banged against the floor. My legs were pried apart, and after that, there was a jabbing pain inside me. Pain and more pain and more pain. It seemed to go on forever."

Sandra gulped for air and swallowed. "I was so dizzy. My body ached. I remember that I tried to sit up, but I felt like I was going to pass out or throw up. At some point, Matthew covered me with a blanket. I do remember that. But he didn't say anything, and neither did I. I cried. I don't know how much time passed. I just know that I half-crawled and half-walked over to the neighbor's house. I clung to the blanket and tried to wrap it around my body. I rang and rang the doorbell, and finally, someone answered, took me in, and called the police. An ambulance came. Then the nightmare continued. The medical exam. The police questions. The newspaper accounts. The gossip. All the time, there was gossip. I felt like I was being assaulted over and over. Over and over. People kept telling me that I should thank God that I was only raped and not killed. They told me that I should feel grateful. Grateful? It was a dumb thing to say. It made me so angry."

* * *

Gina was unsure how to proceed. She wanted to be considerate and respectful, but would she be if she asked more questions?

Meanwhile, Sandra picked up her needle and continued to sew. After a short time, Sandra cut the thread and then put her needle in a nearby pincushion. Gina carefully examined the garment Sandra had repaired but could not see Sandra's stitches.

"That's incredible," Gina said. "No one will ever know the fabric was ripped."

"That's the whole idea," Sandra said. "If only lives that are torn apart could be so easily mended."

"May I ask you a few more questions about yours?" Gina asked. "About your life after the rape. Is that okay?"

"Go ahead. As I said, I'm much stronger now. I get out; I'm no longer afraid to leave the house. And I joined a support group to help other rape survivors. Best of all, I found a wonderful man. I'm engaged and will be married in the fall. It's hard to believe my life has changed so much. So go ahead. Ask your questions. I can handle them."

Sandra added, "But before you start, I might as well answer the one question everyone, sooner or later, always asks me. The answer is 'yes.' I still have nightmares about the rape. Thank goodness, far less often than I used to. Some things in my dreams are clear, but many things shift and are hazy. I know it's weird, but when I dream about my attacker, sometimes there are brown eyes floating above my face and sometimes blue ones. I wish I knew why."

Chapter 16

Wednesday, June 19

On Wednesday afternoon, Gina, Brad, and Frank were standing outside Professor Stein's office, waiting for her office hours to begin.

Hannah was winded when she rushed up to them. "So sorry I'm late. I was in a meeting on the other side of the campus that ran long."

Brad said, "No problem. Actually, we were early. We couldn't wait to get started."

Hannah unlocked her office door. Her students followed her in, and they plopped down on the couches by the imitation fireplace. Hannah's desk chair had wheels. She rolled it over to where her students were sitting and joined them.

"Okay," Hannah said. "What's up? What have you uncovered since we last met?"

Gina told the group about her interview with Sandra Metzler.

Gina said. "I was worried about the interview. I didn't know what to expect. But Sandra was really nice. She's a survivor, and now she helps other women who have been raped. After talking to her, I think I'd like to focus my paper on what she feels most passionate about, the need for better support services for rape victims. Would it be okay if I went in that direction? I know Frank has been looking into the ways communities respond to violent crimes. I don't want to get into an area he's already researching."

Hannah said, "No problem there. How you choose to define and support your arguments will make your paper your own. Go for it."

"That's good to hear," said Gina. "And I recorded the interview. Wait till you hear it. I have to tell you that it really freaked me out when Sandra described the murders and the rape. It was also hard to hear her talk about what happened to her afterward. Sandra said she tried to cooperate with the prosecutor, but she couldn't recall things clearly; details kept shifting as she had a head wound and was groggy during the attack. Also, she only saw the back of the killer in the kitchen for an instant. She never saw his face before she ran from the house. As the prosecutor couldn't get a consistent story of the rape out of Sandra, nor could she identify the killer, he decided to just go with the triple murder charges and not have her testify. He was afraid her muddled memories would be ripped apart by the defense attorney and might end up hurting the prosecution's case. Her parents were relieved. They wanted the rape charge dropped. They were confident that Baker would be found guilty and severely punished for killing three people. And the Metzler family knew that if they were not satisfied with the verdict and the sentence, they could always go after Baker for the rape later because Sandra was a minor at the time. Sandra's parents wanted to protect her. They wanted to keep her out of the spotlight so the gossip would stop."

Brad said, "I sure am glad Sandra Metzler told you why Baker was never charged with the rape. I'm not sure right now if there will be a good place for all of that in my paper, but I really did want to know."

"When you listen to the interview," Gina said, "you'll hear the whole story from Sandra's point of view. And Frank, Sandra talks a bit at the end about how uncomfortable she felt at family gatherings after she was raped by her cousin. She knew she had conservative relatives who didn't like the fact that she wore shorts in the summer and sleeveless tops, so she thought her relatives avoided talking to her because they blamed her for leading her younger cousin on. Much later, she found out she was wrong. Her relatives had been distant because they were afraid. Afraid of saying the wrong things. They thought the best thing to do was to pretend the rape never occurred, so Sandra could forget all about it and feel better. Sandra said she was miserable. She didn't know how to ask for help, and her family didn't know how to give it."

Gina added, "I think a rape within the family must be the worst type of all. I hope you can use some of that in your paper, Frank."

"Thanks, Gina," Frank said.

"Frank, tell us about Matthew Baker now," Brad said. "Did you get the chance to ask him questions during yesterday's video chat? Did you learn why he now believes he's innocent?"

Chapter 17

Frank said, "Yesterday, I was lucky. There were only three of us on the video chat, so I had time to talk to Baker. With Matthew's permission, I put my phone next to my computer and recorded most of the call." Frank tapped his phone, opened the recording app, and located the spot he wanted. "Here's where Matt talks about the night when his family was murdered. I've replayed it several times and have been going over it a lot in my mind. Listen and tell me what you think."

Frank hit the play button, and the group heard Frank's voice asking, "Can you tell me what happened that night? What do you remember?"

And then they heard Matthew Baker's response. "Well, we came home from that church thing. I didn't want to go. And I was right. There was nothing for me there. My folks were with their friends, and Dara was with hers. No one cared that I was on my own. I just walked around; I had nowhere to settle. No one I wanted to talk to. I was relieved when the whole thing ended. We were home a bit before eight-thirty. I remember the time because my folks went into the living room to watch this TV show that came on at eight-thirty. Dara and Sandra went upstairs to Dara's room to talk their girl talk. I grabbed an apple and some cookies from the kitchen and then snuck out to the barn. Went up to the loft. I wanted to get away from my family. I'd been fighting with my dad all day, and I just wanted to be left alone. I knew I'd feel better if I got high. And why not? My folks didn't care about me. The real me. They only wanted a good little son to parade about at church. They never once asked me what I wanted. So, I went for my stash. I kept my drugs hidden in the loft because I was pretty sure my mom searched my room. She'd say she was just cleaning or putting clothes away, but she was always going into my room. Snooping. She thought I didn't notice, but I did. After I smoked some weed that was sprinkled with PCP, everything stopped being so bad. I felt calm, relaxed, and happy."

Frank paused the recording and said, "Based upon what you just heard, I think it was around nine o'clock when Matthew started to feel the effects of the drugs. Now, PCP can affect people in lots of different ways, including causing hallucinations and memory loss. I don't know if any of Matt's memories can be trusted, especially those after he was high on drugs. I'll play the last part for you now."

Matthew Baker's voice continued, "I heard loud voices coming from the open kitchen windows. I was glad I was safe in the barn. I figured my folks were arguing over what to do with me. I didn't want any part of it. The noise hurt my ears, so I curled up in the hay and tried to block it out. Then, I heard screams and more screams I could not block out. I stood up but found that I had trouble walking. Somehow I got down from the loft and ran to the kitchen door. The screams were terrible. I felt that I had to do something. I had to silence those screams. I opened the kitchen door. The room was too bright. The overhead light was on. I saw blood everywhere and a knife going up and down. Up and down. Over and over, it went into my father, into my mother, and then into my sister after she ran into the room. Unbelievable. The kitchen tilted and looked blurry. I turned my head away to clear it. I looked out the window. I saw Sandra. She was running toward the barn, and a figure was running after her. I stumbled into the kitchen and slipped on the bloody, sticky floor. I fell. Fell into the blood. My right hand landed on a knife. I clutched it tight. I shook the bodies on the floor, but they didn't move. Their eyes were open, but they didn't see me. I yelled at them to talk to me, but they didn't respond. I remember I was still holding the knife in my hand as I moved toward the barn. I wanted to find and kill the Angel of Death. The Angel of Death had killed my family and deserved to die. But I had trouble moving. My legs were out of sync and slowed me down. When I reached the barn door, I felt nauseous. That's all I remember before I found a blanket to cover Sandra. She was whimpering. Her nightgown was ripped apart. It was important to cover Sandra. Afterward, I went back up into the loft.

Time floated again, and things slowed down. When the police came, I tried to tell them about the Angel of Death, but all they wanted was my knife. I put the knife down for them, but they still didn't listen to me. I was so angry. They wouldn't listen to me. And then there were handcuffs. They put handcuffs on me. The handcuffs hurt my wrists. Sometime after that, I was in the police station. That's where the words kept zapping me over and over. Killer. Murderer. Rapist. Killer. Murderer. Rapist. Killer. Murderer. Rapist. Such terrible words repeated over and over."

Frank stopped the recording. The group was silent, absorbing what they had just heard.

"Hey," Gina said. "Is Baker right? He said he was in the loft when he heard his parents' voices. But Dara and Sandra thought they heard him arguing with Bruce and Helen in the kitchen. Was he in the loft or in the kitchen? If he was in the loft, then who was in the kitchen fighting with Matthew's folks? Did Baker or some other person repeatedly stab Bruce, Helen, and Dara and then run after Sandra? And if Matthew was not the killer and was just a witness, as he now claims, then who committed the three murders?"

"It would have to be someone with a motive," answered Brad. "Why would someone want to kill the Bakers? And why didn't that person kill Matthew, too? Matthew said he was standing in the doorway, and the light was on in the kitchen. If there was a killer in the room, the killer must have seen him. Why was Matthew spared? This wasn't a robbery gone wrong. The papers reported that nothing of value was missing. Baker was the one with a motive; he was high on drugs and angry. How could he not be the killer?"

"I know. I know," said Frank. "These are the same questions that have been going round and round in my brain. But Matt was very convincing yesterday. He said that his memories are clearer now. He's worried that the real killer is still on the loose and could strike again. I'd like to believe him. But then I circle back to the big problems. He was high on PCP at the time. And he and his dad were at each other's throats. Why should I believe he's got it right now? What do you think, Professor Stein?"

Hannah thought, *Oh, boy. How do I navigate this? The idea was to help the kids find interesting research topics, and, I must admit, after reexamining*

Matthew Barker's crimes, I wanted to be reassured that justice has been served. I never intended to drag Frank into my sticky morass of doubt.

Hannah said, "I think Brad's right. Unless these violent murders were committed by a deranged person, and the Bakers were simply unlucky, random victims, logic would dictate that the killer had to have a motive. Did the police consider other suspects and motives? Was there anyone who hated the Bakers so much that he or she would violently murder three of them and then arrange for Matthew to be blamed for their deaths? Or could the murders be related to some business transaction? Bruce Baker was a real estate developer. He must have dealt with large sums of money. Did someone he did business with harbor a grudge? And what about Matthew's link to illegal drugs? Did someone become violent while attempting to steal Matthew's drugs? Or did Dara have a bad break-up with an old boyfriend? Or maybe the motive was related to something in Helen Baker's past?"

Hannah stopped. She was flustered. She realized that she had let her mind race and had said too much. Instead of reining Frank in, she had just opened up whole new fields of possibilities for him. There was no reason for her to be speculating. The police must have looked into all the motives she just rattled off and more. Surely, they must have.

"Please remember, Frank," Hannah said to regain control, "your job is to write a research paper. There are experienced lawyers who will help Baker with his legal woes if there are grounds for an appeal or a reason for the verdict to be overturned."

Frank said, "I know. I envy Gina and Brad. They've used the Baker case as a springboard to find their topics. They're focused. But now I can't stop thinking about the whole case. Matthew may be in prison for something he didn't do. And if he is, I'd like to help get him out."

"But don't forget that Baker savagely raped Sandra Metzler and messed up her life for a long time. Don't expect me to have any sympathy for him," Gina said.

Brad said, "And there were good reasons why he was convicted. There was physical evidence."

"Brad, did Matthew Baker's lawyer come through for you? Did you get some pages from the Baker trial transcript that you could use?" Hannah asked.

"Yes, she chose well for me, and early this morning, I made copies of the most interesting parts for all of you." Brad rummaged in his backpack and took out four packets of paper. He gave one to Hannah, Frank, and Gina and kept the thick one for himself. Brad grinned. "There are no bombshells here, but there is a surprise."

Chapter 18

Hannah was impressed. Brad, her lanky, tattooed student, had immediately stood up and taken control of the room. He succinctly summarized large portions of the transcript and made all the testimony he referred to, even the parts that were just procedural, sound interesting and compelling.

"Now turn to page twenty-four in your packets," Brad said. "This is where the prosecuting attorney starts asking questions of the first police officer to respond to the 911 call. You'll notice how the prosecutor's questions guide the local cop, an Officer Ethan Clark. Clark explains, in a step-by-step manner, what the police saw, said, and did. A female officer was the second officer on the scene. She remained by Sandra Metzler's side and was with Sandra during the ambulance ride to the hospital.

"Meanwhile, after calling for additional back-up, Clark went over to the Baker home. He cautiously walked around the house. The back door was open, so he entered the well-lit kitchen. He could see everything in the room clearly. He found three slashed bodies in a room splattered with blood. He checked for signs of life but found none and believed all of the people in the kitchen were dead. When more officers arrived, they spread out and went through the rest of the house, and they also went to the barn in back of the house, where they found Baker hiding in the loft. Clark was among the group of officers who approached Matthew, and Matthew was, in Clark's words, 'acting wild, flailing his arms and screaming that the Angel of Death was on the loose.' Clark told Baker that the only way to avoid the Angel of Death was to put down the large bloody knife he was holding, and then Matthew could come with them to the police station where he would be safe. Baker was shaking and crying, but after a few minutes, he put down his knife. After releasing his weapon, the officers thought Matthew was going to be compliant, but then he suddenly started shrieking, 'No! No! No!' and ran toward the officers. They knocked Baker down, cuffed him, and scooped him up. They read him his rights. The police officers then half-dragged and half-carried Baker from the loft to the back seat of one of their cruisers. Clark testified that Baker had a lot of blood on his clothes, his hands, and his face."

Hannah asked herself, *Why didn't Ethan tell me that he had testified at the trial? Did he forget? Not think it was important? Or was there some other reason?*

Brad paused and took a deep breath. Then he added, "If you read on, you will learn that Baker's clothes were saturated with blood, blood that matched his family's blood types. Those blood types were also on the knife Baker was holding, and Matthew's bloody fingerprints were on the knife and all over the kitchen. An Amish cleaning girl had thoroughly washed and cleaned the floor and all the surfaces in the kitchen the day before. No one else but the family and Sandra Metzler, according to the police report, had entered the home after it was cleaned. All the fingerprints were accounted for, and there was no sign of forced entry."

So, nothing indicates that an intruder entered the house and committed the crimes. Everything points to Matthew Baker, Hannah thought.

"Now turn to page forty-two. You'll see a copy of a note that was entered into evidence. The police found this crumpled note in a desk drawer in Matthew's room. In the note, Baker lists all the reasons he hated his father. On the bottom, he lists ways to kill his dad. Notice that Matthew includes decapitation, drowning, crucifixion, and stabbing. The prosecution claimed this note showed that Baker had been planning on murdering his father. He may not have wanted to kill his mother and sister, but, the prosecutor contended, he definitely planned on killing his dad."

"Wow," said Gina. "That's sick. I mean decapitation and crucifixion. Really?"

"I know. It's weird. I did say there was a surprise in the transcript, and this is it," Brad said.

Chapter 19

Frank leaned forward from his place on the couch and said, "Should we take this note of Baker's seriously? All kids have fantasies. Sure, some say they'd like to kill their folks when their parents punish them, but they don't really mean it. Matthew was fourteen years old. Maybe writing such things down was just his way to get his anger out. Nothing more than that."

Brad nodded in agreement. "That's exactly what Matt's lawyer said in her closing argument. She told the jury not to pay any attention to the note. She claimed Matt was just behaving like a typical, frustrated teenager and never planned on hurting anyone. Instead, she asked the jury to focus on the diagnosis of the psychologist who testified for the defense. This psychologist maintained that Matthew was not in control of himself at the time of the murders, that he was suffering from a form of post-traumatic stress disorder. The psychologist believed that Matthew, who had been adopted by the Bakers when he was five years old, had been abused by his birth parents. His lawyer insisted that Matthew had physical and emotional scars and that these had to be considered. The term she used to describe his condition was 'diminished mental capacity.' She argued that he was a troubled child who needed medical treatment and should not be tried and sentenced as a dangerous adult."

I remember the heated editorials in the paper at the time, Hannah thought. *And the neighborhood was divided into camps, too. Opinions regarding the appropriate punishment for Baker ran the full gamut, from sending Matthew to a juvenile mental health facility to the death penalty.*

"What did Baker say when the police asked him about the murders and the rape? How did he explain what happened?" Frank asked.

Brad replied, "Well, the police didn't immediately question him when the officers brought him to the station. They waited many hours. They waited till he passed a drug test. They needed to prove that all the hallucinogens were out of his system. When the detectives did talk to Matthew, they were careful to follow all the rules for dealing with a minor. Baker always had his public defender by his side to protect his rights. If you look at pages thirty-two through thirty-nine in your packets, you'll see a portion of the police interrogation. Notice that the police kept asking Matthew about the knife. Baker was unclear about a lot of things, but he was always sure that he had picked up the knife in the kitchen; he felt the weight of it in his hand. He talked about the knife as if it were a living predator. He said the knife looked for his father first, then the knife went after his mother, and, finally, the knife found his sister and completed its job. After six hours of questioning, the detectives felt nothing more was to be gained from Baker. He always said the murders were committed by the knife and sometimes added that the knife was controlled by the Angel of Death. The knife and the Angel of Death were responsible. He was not. And he was sure that he never raped anyone. Especially Sandra. He said he loved Sandra and would never hurt her."

Brad looked at the others. "That's it for the trial. What's left from the legal end is how the jury determined the extent of Baker's guilt, if he had committed first-degree murders or not. And then there was the sentencing."

"I think we should save those for next time," Hannah said. "We've covered a lot, and I have another student scheduled to arrive in five minutes. So, did something click today, Frank? Are you closer to finding your topic?"

Frank shrugged his shoulders and sighed. After Gina and Brad had packed up and left, Frank remained behind, still tethered to his spot on the couch.

Frank said, "I just have to ask. Professor Stein, are you a psychic?"

"A psychic?" Hannah asked.

"Yes. Because you were correct. It was Robert Louis Stevenson. How did you know?"

Hannah smiled. "So, I was right. I thought I was on the right track, but it's good to know for sure. I'll explain how I figured it out after class tomorrow."

Chapter 20

It had been a long day, and after her office hours were over, Hannah Stein realized she still had to get home, choose an outfit, and get ready for a dinner date. Thinking about going out on a date made her blush. Was it really a romantic date? Come on. Probably not. Words carried many levels of meaning. Every English teacher knew that. When Ethan said they had a date, surely he meant they had a day and a time to meet and nothing more. Two neighbors sharing a neighborly outing. That was all there was to it. Right?

Hannah was about to lock her office door when she heard her cell phone chime. She quickly put a hand in her shoulder bag and rummaged for her phone. When she found it, she swiped at the screen to answer the call and said, "Hello."

What she heard in reply was, "Hi there, little sis. It's Michael. You remember me, don't you? Your big brother who hasn't seen you in ages."

Hannah did a quick calculation. Had it been nine months? Yes, she had last spoken to her brother nine months ago. Every time she called him, his phone went to voicemail, and she always left a message, but he never returned her calls. Instead, she would sporadically get cryptic emails from him. In the last one, Michael wrote, "Submerged in work and the work of finding myself. Can't talk now. My pain is your gain." She remembered the message because she had mulled over it for days, trying to understand what it meant. How could something that benefited her hurt him? It bothered her. It sounded ominous.

"Michael," Hannah said. "So good to hear from you. It's been so long. How are you? How's Dad? I check with the nursing home regularly. They say he's okay."

"Actually, I do want to talk to you about Dad. I'm going to be in Harrisburg on Friday to take a deposition for a case my law firm is working on. I could drive to Lancaster afterward and take you to dinner. I'd like to talk to you in person about Dad. How about it? Do you have time for me? I promise to behave myself. No teasing my little sister or pushing her down. Thank goodness we've outgrown that kid stuff. Would seven o'clock work for you for dinner?"

Hannah gasped. Something was wrong. Her hand shook. She felt cold, and her chest hurt. Hannah leaned against the door to her office to steady herself. What was going on?

"Hannah, are you still there?" Michael asked.

"I'm sorry. Something must be wrong with the connection," Hannah lied. She took a deep breath to regain her equilibrium and then calmly said, "Of course, I want to see you. It's been a long time. Let's meet in Hershey, so you won't have to drive all the way to Lancaster. There's a great Italian restaurant there. Pirandello's. I can give you directions."

"No problem. I'll find it. I'll call you for help if I get lost. Looking forward to seeing you, Hannah. I've missed you."

"And I've missed you, Michael."

But after Hannah ended the call, she wondered if that was true. Had she really missed her brother?

Chapter 21

As Hannah drove out of the campus parking lot and headed toward home, she checked the time. If she was lucky and Jodi was not busy at work, Hannah would be able to squeeze in a quick conversation with her friend before she had to get ready for her date. Darn it all. She still wasn't sure if it was, in the strictest romantic sense, a date. But with all her experience, Jodi would know.

Hannah gave her phone a voice command to call her friend, and a short time later, she heard Jodi's voice coming through the speaker system in her car.

"Hannah. Finally. I should be angry with you. Last time we spoke, you told me your deck was on fire. Naturally, my mind went to the worst. I visualized you in bandages in a burn unit. Then you sent me a text and told me not to worry. Just a small fire in your grill. But did you elaborate? No. So, did your neighborhood Superman save you? What's going on? Why didn't you get back to me?"

"Jodi, I really have been busy, and right now, I'm in my car driving home from work. First, forget about the fire. It was nothing. A small problem. I have a big problem now, and I need your help. I agreed to have dinner with Superman in an hour. And Jodi, I just had another panic attack. While I was talking to my brother on the phone. What's happening to me? Maybe this dinner, which may or may not be a real date, is too much for me to handle. Should I forget the whole thing?"

"Another panic attack? But you're okay. Right?"

"I seem to be."

"Good. So, for the time being, let's put that on the back burner. Now, did I hear you right? Did you say you have a date with Superman?"

"Well, he did ask me to have dinner with him. Does that mean he invited a neighbor to share a friendly meal, or is it a real date?"

"Oh, Hannah, there's only one way to find out. You definitely must go. Good for you, girl! It's about time you reentered the world."

"But Jodi . . ."

"Say no more. We have to discuss what you're going to wear."

By the time Hannah pulled into her driveway, her friend had given her the boost of confidence she needed to get through the evening. The teenage anxiety pangs in Hannah's stomach settled into anticipatory butterfly flutters. Jodi had also offered much-needed fashion advice as she was well acquainted with the meager contents of Hannah's closet. Hannah parked her car and felt ready for her next challenge. Could she still wriggle into her only pair of form-fitting black jeans?

Hannah opened her car door and sighed in relief. There was, as Jodi had pointed out, no downside in spending some time with a pleasant, good-looking man. Why did the reason for the encounter have to be defined? So, Hannah gave herself strict instructions, *Stop worrying. Just enjoy the evening.*

Suddenly, Hannah's sanguine thoughts were interrupted by high-pitched screams. They were coming from the house next door, from Lily and Cranston Clark's home. Their front door was open, and Hannah could not believe what she was seeing. Ethan Clark was dragging a howling woman out of the house. The pretty blond broke loose from Ethan's grip when they cleared the doorway and lunged at him. Her hands clawed the air, and her fingernails narrowly missed scratching Ethan's face. The woman was shrieking obscenities, and all the while, she kept trying to hit, slap, and kick Ethan. Ethan feinted and ducked to avoid the blows but did not retaliate.

Hannah asked herself, *What's going on? Should I call the police? But which one needs help, the woman or Ethan?*

Hannah did not know what to do. Suddenly, Lily Clark came running out of her house, waving a small piece of paper and shouting, "Stop! Here's your money. Just go home and leave us alone."

The woman kept screaming, "Liar. Cheat. Thief." Those were the words Hannah heard repeated, along with a few colorful expletives. The rest of what the woman shouted was lost in her piercing screeches and cries.

Lily shouted again, "Stop! Here's your money."

Finally, the woman terminated her persistent rant and turned to Lily. She snatched the paper out of Lily's hand and looked at it. Hannah guessed it was a check because she heard the woman yell, "Okay. It's for the full amount. I'll leave. But you're a fool, Lily. You won't always be around to save him. He may look good, but he's rotten. Rotten to the core. Save yourself before it's too late. The smartest thing I ever did was to walk away from this creep."

Lily looked stricken and ran back into the house. The woman picked up her purse, which had fallen to the ground in her struggle with Ethan, put the check inside, and then she sashayed over to her car, which was parked at the curb. She swung her body into the car, gunned the motor, and took off.

"Ethan, are you okay?" Hannah called.

Ethan turned. He gasped when he saw Hannah standing in her driveway by her car. He ran over to Hannah and then sheepishly asked, "Did you see all that?"

Hannah said, "You and that woman were really going at it."

"It was a simple misunderstanding. Feelings were hurt, and things escalated. But it's over now. Let's go ahead with our plans. I have a picnic basket packed for us. I promise to explain and answer all your questions over dinner."

"Well, I don't know," Hannah said.

"Please believe me. This was nothing. We'll go to Lake Keller. We'll have dinner and take a walk around the lake, and I assure you, after you hear my side of the story, you'll understand. You'll forget all about this unfortunate outburst. Why, just thinking about a nice evening with you is already driving it out of my mind. What do you say?"

Hannah hesitated, but what Ethan said sounded reasonable. She felt she should give him a chance to explain. And it would be dinner at Lake Keller, one of her favorite local spots. Another temptation. So, Hannah pushed aside her reservations and agreed.

Ethan grinned and then said, "Well, that's a relief. We'll have a great time."

Will we? Hannah wondered. *What kind of a story will I hear? Ethan, what in the world did you do to make that woman so angry? And why did your mother have to give her money?*

Chapter 22

"I don't care if people call them hoagies or subs or grinders. Hannah, you have to admit it. These cheesesteak sandwiches are terrific. Of course, not as good as the ones in Philly, but they are special. Right?" Ethan asked.

Hannah nodded in agreement. She was chewing and savoring every bite of her sandwich. On the way to Lake Keller, Ethan had stopped at Hoagie Heaven and picked up two cheesesteak hoagies to go, and they were delicious. Ethan's picnic basket contained cans of soft drinks, bags of chips, carrot sticks, and cookies for dessert. It was, as Ethan claimed it would be, a veritable feast. In addition, they were very lucky. They easily found a parking place in the lot next to the lake, snagged one of the shaded picnic tables, and, as a mild wind was stirring, were blessed with a meal free from mosquitoes.

Ethan swiped at his face with a napkin and then wiped his hands with another. It was impossible for anyone, even someone who resembled Superman, to eat a juicy cheesesteak neatly. Ethan took a sip of his Coke and said, "And now for the explanation."

Hannah listened carefully. According to Ethan, what she had witnessed was the result of a simple financial misunderstanding between Ethan and his former wife, Meghan.

Ethan said, "So, you see, when I found the old checkbook, I remembered I had put money in this joint checking account for an anniversary cruise. I saw no reason not to withdraw it. It was mine, and there's no way we'll ever go on a cruise together now. Well, Meghan hit the roof when she learned the money was missing. Thought the money was hers. I don't know why. When we broke up, it was a simple and fast divorce. We both agreed to walk away and only take what was ours. Nothing more. We each had our own savings accounts, so that part was easy. I never dreamed my withdrawing my own money from this checking account would cause my ex to go ballistic."

The explanation was plausible. But why the scene? Couldn't this problem have been quietly and calmly resolved? And why had Lily felt the need to pay the woman off if the money in question belonged to Ethan?

Hannah was tempted to ask those questions and more when Ethan, who was sitting beside her on the bench facing the lake, picked up her left hand, stroked it, and gave it a gentle squeeze.

"Hannah, thank you for coming here with me. I hate conflict, and it was a rough day. Your being here has turned everything around. And have I told you that you look great? Those black jeans say it all for you."

Hannah blushed and thought, *He's smooth. Probably has had a lot of practice. I'd better watch myself. Still, I'm glad he noticed the jeans. But I better not eat a cookie for dessert, or I might just pop the top button.*

"Glad to be of help," Hannah said. "That's what neighbors are for."

"Oh, but I think we're more than just neighbors. Don't you think so, too?"

Hannah blurted, "Ethan, we live in two different worlds. I'm a widow with two grown children. And I'm a lot older than you are."

Ethan chuckled. "What's a few years? They don't make any difference at this point in our lives. You're what? Forty, maybe?"

"Actually, forty-three. And you're only thirty-eight and a bachelor without children. There you have it. Two different worlds."

"Ah, but that proves you're interested in me. You figured out my age."

Hannah blushed again. "It was easy to do the math. When we shared the pizza, you mentioned the year you graduated from Parkerville High."

Ethan smiled. "Well, you're right about one thing. Not about the difference in our ages. That doesn't bother me at all. But we do come from two different worlds. Let's pack up our leftovers and put the picnic basket in the car. Before we take our walk around the lake, I want to show you something."

Ethan grabbed a cookie and munched on it as he put the remaining food in the basket. Meanwhile, Hannah folded the plastic tablecloth they had used and put it in the basket as well. It was a short walk to Ethan's car. Once the basket was safely stowed in the trunk of his vehicle, Ethan took Hannah's hand and led her to the far end of the parking lot. They crossed the road and walked down the shoulder till they came to the entrance of a trailer park.

"This is it," Ethan said. "This says it all. Everything anyone might want to know about my childhood is right here. This is where I grew up. A world away from the upper-middle-class home my folks live in now. A world away from what you're used to."

Hannah looked at the small houses jammed closely together on this small piece of land. Loud TVs and music leaked from the windows of the tiny homes. She wondered what it would be like to live in such a cramped, noisy area without trees for shade, without gardens. The whole area was paved in concrete. No wonder Lily loved her flower beds, and Cranston took such pains to keep his lawn lush and green.

"No space. No privacy," said Ethan. "Still the same. My sister and I hated living in this park. We both left as soon as we could. Let's find out if my family's tin can of a home is still here."

Ethan held Hannah's hand and guided her around one turn and then another. It was like moving through a maze. He stopped in front of a trailer with a bright red awning and said, "This is it. Someone's added a touch of color with that awning, but it's still a sad little place to live. Mom and Dad stayed on till they finally could afford their dream home. I thought living in a big house was just a fairy tale. And now, the fairy tale has come true for them. I just wish it hadn't taken them so long. Enough of this place. Let's get out of here."

Ethan quickly guided Hannah out of the trailer park and back to the lake. When they were at the starting point for the trail around Lake Keller, he relaxed.

Ethan said, "Now, this is better. I've spent a lot of time unwinding here. The lake and I are old friends. When I was growing up, I'd always say I lived near Lake Keller. I hoped people would assume I lived in one of those big houses on the hill overlooking the lake. I always was ashamed of the trailer park, but I wanted you to see it. Do you know why?"

Hannah replied, "Tell me why."

"I wanted you to see where I come from. I wanted you to know who I am, what drives me. I work hard with one goal in mind. I'm never going to live like that again. For some people, that is enough, and they are content. But not me. I want more. I want you to understand because I think we started something the other night. Maybe you didn't feel it, but I did. You're different. You're a woman I could fall for, and I want our beginning to be open and honest. I want it to be real."

Hannah was surprised. Not uncomfortable, but definitely surprised. And then she was surprised because she was not uncomfortable. She should be uncomfortable. This felt like a real date. Her first date since Aaron died. Things were moving much too fast.

"Hannah, you're not saying anything. Did I scare you? I promise not to rush you. Just tell me that we're okay, that I have a chance."

"We've just met. We need time. Time to get to know each other as friends. It's getting late. We'd better start our walk. It's a school night for me. I have to get up early."

"Of course, you're right. Nice and slow and friends first. And while we're walking, you can tell me about that matter you had to resolve when I first met you. Did you find out today if you came to the right conclusion?" Ethan asked.

"Ah, that's right. I did promise to tell you how that all turned out. Actually, you helped me. When you talked about classical books, I suddenly remembered an author named Stevenson. Robert Louis Stevenson. And he wrote *Dr. Jekyll and Mr. Hyde.* In this novel, drugs alter a man's behavior and bring out his evil side."

Hannah thought Ethan would be pleased that he had played a part in solving a riddle, but when she explained how the author and this book were linked to her students' research of the Baker murder case, Ethan did not look pleased. He was not pleased at all.

Chapter 23

Thursday, June 20

The next day Frank waited till class was over and the classroom had cleared before walking up to the front of the room and approaching his teacher.

"Is everything okay, Frank?" Hannah asked. "You look worried."

"I'd like to talk to you if you have a little time," Frank said.

"Tell you what. I'd like a cup of coffee to perk me up. Why don't we grab something from the stand down the hall and go outside and sit at one the of tables in front of the building? We can talk there."

A short time later, seated in the fresh air and fortified by several sips of coffee, Hannah said, "There. I'm alert again. What would you like to discuss?"

Frank said, "Let's start with Stevenson. How did you know Baker was talking about Robert Louis Stevenson when he said Stevenson turned his life around?"

Hannah chuckled and then said, "I can't take all the credit. I had help. A short time after I heard Baker mention the name Stevenson, a neighbor spoke to me about some well-known novels he had read in high school. Remember, Baker said he found Stevenson in the prison library. He didn't use the word 'met.' He said 'found.' That must've been lurking in the back of my brain. Classical books led me to think of classical authors, and then it dawned on me that Baker's Stevenson could be the famous author. Around the same time, a good friend and I talked about buried memories. I didn't know much about them, so I did a little research. I found out that a variety of stimuli can help someone recall a repressed memory, including reading a story about someone who has experienced a similar trauma. That's when everything came together and clicked. Robert Louis Stevenson wrote *Dr. Jekyll and Mr. Hyde.* Jekyll took drugs to turn into the evil and violent Mr. Hyde. Did Baker read that novel?"

"Yes. At the end of my last visit with him, Matthew told me he'd read that book."

"I thought so. That's why his memories came roaring back because Baker, like Dr. Jekyll, experimented with drugs."

"Yes. Yes. That's exactly what he said happened. And then he saw himself in the kitchen where the murders took place. But he was watching and not moving. That's how he knew he was not the murderer. But I . . ."

"But you're still not sure," said Hannah.

"That's right. I'm not sure. Are memories recovered this way accurate?"

"That's unclear. Memory is never perfect, and people often believe that they saw or heard things they never experienced. You're right to be skeptical, Frank."

"And, Professor Stein, I don't know what to make of Baker's defense. His lawyer said Baker became a murderer because he was abused before he was adopted. I'm worried about that, too."

"Why?"

"Well, I've been talking to people in my congregation who knew Matthew Baker when he was little. And everyone I've spoken to has said that he was just a normal kid. No one expected him to be a killer. That got me to thinking. You see, my folks adopted my sister Mary. After some distant cousins died in a house fire, we just picked Mary up and brought her home. She was seven years old at the time. I was nine and not too sure about sharing my parents with this little girl, but I found I liked being a big brother. Mary and I got along fine. Most of the time, we still do. But I really hated it when Mary had these horrible nightmares and would scream and scream and wake everyone up."

"Was she in the burning house?" Hannah asked.

"No, she wasn't. Mary was at school when her folks died in the fire. We thought she had those bad dreams because she missed her parents, but we found out later it was because she was afraid they hadn't died and would come back to get her. My mom and dad learned from Mary's pediatrician and therapist that Mary had been physically abused. And, I hate to admit it, she's acting wild now. She's snarky, defiant, and really quick to explode. I can't help but wonder if she has what Matthew Baker had. That post-traumatic stress problem. It's scary stuff. Do I have to put that in my paper?"

"No. First, you have to slow down and find your topic. Then you only need to put in your paper the research that supports your thesis. Not everything you stumble across along the way. Also, you have to remember that people are complicated. Researchers have never stopped debating the effects of heredity and environment. Lots of factors go into how people turn out. Matthew Baker's lawyer was fighting for his life and offering the jury a diagnosis to excuse Matthew's behavior. But post-traumatic stress may not be the right or the only explanation. Plus, don't forget, your sister is not Baker. Most teens go through a rough patch and act out, but the vast majority don't become killers."

"Okay. Good. Now, there's one more thing. I'm getting a lot of pressure at home to stop asking questions about Matthew Baker and his murder trial. I told you Mr. Chambers was upset when Baker turned around and said, 'I'm innocent.' Many in the church have put a lot of time and effort into getting Baker to accept responsibility for his actions and to turn to God for support and forgiveness. Folks have been complaining to my parents that my involvement is encouraging Matthew to backslide, to blame everything on others. It's been tough at home. My parents don't see why I have to pursue this. They don't understand why I don't drop it and just write a paper on a nice safe topic."

"Frank, this assignment is designed to help you learn research and composition skills, not to cause problems within your family. Please feel free to go off in a new direction. You won't disappoint the group, and you won't disappoint me."

"But I will be disappointed, Professor Stein. And I would be disappointing Matthew Baker, too, if he's innocent. Which I'll never know if I don't keep at this. Thanks for listening and offering me an out. But no. I'm going to stick with this. I know I have to narrow my research and find a specific topic. But it has to be a topic related to Matthew Baker. I'm in too deep to back out now."

Chapter 24

Frank is trying to be fair to everyone. To our investigative team, his family, his church, himself, and even Matthew Baker, Hannah thought as she tossed her empty coffee cup into a trash container. *I never intended to complicate a student's life. I just wanted to make this assignment more interesting. I hope I didn't make a mistake.*

As Hannah walked across the campus to her office, her mind drifted in and out of her conversation with Frank and then jumped to Michael, her adopted brother. But she never thought of him that way. He was simply Michael, her brother. He was ten years old when she was born. Her mother had told Hannah the "family story" many times when she was little. It was as familiar to her as "The Three Little Pigs." The "family story" began, as all good fairy tales do, with "once upon a time."

Once upon a time, her parents had wanted children, but for some unknown reason, they were not blessed with any. So, they adopted Michael. And then, ten years later, Mom gave birth to Hannah. That's when they found out that someone had been missing all along. When Hannah was added to the family, it was complete, and everyone in the family lived happily ever after.

Hannah remembered her mother always smiled and kissed her at the end of the tale. Hannah loved that story, but now she wondered what Michael had thought of it. He never showed her much affection when she was growing up. Was he happy when she was added to the family?

Just as Hannah reached her office, she heard her cell phone's ringtone. She barely got out a word of greeting before an impatient Jodi said, "Hey, you. You can't keep a girl hanging. What happened last night? Was it a date or not?"

Hannah laughed. "I was going to call you, so we could talk about it. Really, I was. "

"Well, I'm at work. I only have a tiny bubble of free time. Tell me something quick, and then you can elaborate later."

Hannah laughed again. "Okay. The short answer is that I think it was a date. A nice date. And I do promise to call soon. I'll share more details later."

"Good. But I need to know the real clincher. Did he kiss you goodnight?"

"Oh, Jodi, he gave me a sweet little kiss on my cheek at the door. Does that qualify?"

"It's a good start. I have to run. Talk to you later." And Jodi ended the call.

Hannah grinned and thought, *Yes, it was a good start. It was my first date after Aaron's death. And I didn't fall apart. What's more; I enjoyed it. I hate to admit it, but Jodi's right. As much as I want to, I can't reclaim my old life. I have to move forward, and I think I'm ready now.*

Chapter 25

Friday, June 21

After Friday's class, Hannah stopped Frank as he was heading out of the classroom.

"Just a quick word before you take off," Hannah said. "After our talk, I checked some sources. I wanted to find out if a significant number of serial killers were abused when they were children."

Frank said, "Then you learned what I did. That childhood abuse among serial killers is much higher than in the general population."

"Yes, it's an interesting fact. But the correlation doesn't offer us proof that one thing causes the other. There are killers who never were abused. Also, there are many people who have moved past their childhood traumas and have never committed a criminal act."

"I get it. But if Matthew Baker's guilty, why did he kill his whole family in such a brutal way? Did the abuse he experienced before his adoption warp his brain? Or was it the drugs he took that night, combined with his anger? Or a mixture of these reasons? Or something else?"

"You're asking a lot of good questions, Frank. Here's another possibility. Some psychologists believe that psychopaths murder because their brains aren't wired correctly and that no amount of loving nor stable family life nor therapy will change them. Would you like to explore this further? You could research why teenagers commit murders and what can be done to stop them."

"I'd like to look into this more. I think I've finally found the topic for my paper. I just wish I could make up my mind about Baker. I don't know if he's innocent or not. I don't think he's a psychopath, but I'm no expert. I could be wrong. I'm going to try to join another video chat with him. There definitely is more I'd like to know."

Chapter 26

The remainder of Hannah's day flew by in a blur. She attended a department meeting, met with two students, and chatted with another teacher about a new course they were debuting in the fall. Before she knew it, it was after six o'clock, and Hannah was in her car and on her way to eat dinner at Pirandello's Fine Italian Eatery in Hershey. Hannah gave Jodi a quick call after she pulled into a parking place in back of the restaurant. Hannah explained that she had been exceptionally busy and was now meeting her brother for dinner. Although Jodi moaned and groaned that she would perish if she did not hear Hannah's date story immediately, Hannah guaranteed Jodi that she would survive. Hannah also advised her friend to lower her expectations.

"Jodi, nothing earth-shattering happened. The story will keep," Hannah said. "I do promise to call you tomorrow."

When Hannah walked into the restaurant, Michael waved to get her attention. He was standing beside a small table by a window. Hannah noted that Michael was as handsome as ever. He was a big guy and had a commanding presence in his well-tailored suit. He was sporting a few more wrinkles since Hannah last saw him, but for a man in his fifties, he looked remarkably fit and trim.

After they both were seated, they looked over the menu, placed their orders with their jovial waiter, and exchanged the usual pleasantries. Michael asked Hannah about her classes and the twins, and Hannah asked Michael about the lawsuit he was working on and Susan, the woman in his life.

Michael said, "Susan and I are engaged. She's the real deal. I never thought I would marry, but now that I've found the right woman, I don't want to lose her."

Hannah said, "I'm very happy for you. I immediately liked Susan when I met her. I liked the way she looked at you. I just knew there was something electric between you two. When do you think you'll marry?"

"I'm going to leave that up to my bride. I like the sound of that. My bride. We may be getting married in Chicago. Susan was offered a great new job and will be moving there soon. And, lucky for me, I can relocate to my firm's Chicago office. I will officially be living in the Windy City in September. That's why I need to talk to you about Dad and what he needs right now."

"Go on. I bet you're going to say that I need to get more involved as you'll be leaving the Twin Cities. Don't worry. I'll pitch in. We'll make it work."

Normally, Hannah would have enjoyed her meal. She loved Pirandello's chicken piccata, but tonight she just picked at her food. Her throat tightened and her stomach clenched after Michael told her that her father had been battling lung cancer for months.

"Why wasn't I informed?" Hannah asked.

"I know this is hard to hear," Michael said, "but Dad didn't want you to know. He didn't want you to worry about him. You know how stubborn he is. Once he makes a decision, he won't change it. But he's deteriorated mentally, too. The doctors aren't sure if it's the result of the chemo treatments or dementia or a combination of both. Sometimes he talks to me and makes perfect sense, but sometimes his thoughts are muddled. Past and present get mixed up. He's not the same."

"Oh, no."

"His decline has been painful to watch."

"Michael, you wrote in an email that your pain was my gain. Were you referring to this?" Hannah said.

"Oh, that. I was frustrated that day. You see, I know you do the best you can, but I'm the one who's been monitoring Dad's doctors and health issues. And sometimes, he forgets who I am. But he always remembers you. However, he often thinks you're five-years-old, the age you were when Mom died, and he wants to set aside money for your care. Let's be honest. Dad's in a good nursing home, and it costs a lot. There probably won't be a lot of money left after he dies, but whatever there is, he wants it all to go to you. I don't know if he recently changed his will or could, considering his mental state, but it hurts to hear him say that he wants to cut me out."

"Michael, I'm so sorry. Believe me, if I inherit anything, I'll share it with you."

Michael nodded, but he looked skeptical.

"Don't you trust me, Michael?"

"It's just hard to walk away from our past. Dad's always favored you, and now at the end of his life, after all I've done for him, he's doing it again."

"I'm so sorry. What can I do?" Hannah asked.

"Nothing. It's not your fault, Hannah. We just fell apart as a family after Mom died. You were so little when it happened. Just five years old when Mom was killed. And you didn't speak a word for months afterward. Of course, you needed help. But Dad forgot that I needed comforting. I lost my mother, too. But what did he do? He packed me off to a military school. And, in the summers, to sports camps. But you got to stay home with Aunt Gail. You got the love and attention, and I got shipped off." Michael leaned back into his chair and sighed. "I was so angry back then. And it still hurts. Maybe Dad wouldn't have treated me that way if I'd been his real son and not an adopted kid."

"Michael, we've never really talked about any of this. I still don't remember our mother's death clearly."

"Do you want to talk about it now?"

Hannah stalled for time. She picked up her fork and pushed some food around on her plate. Thoughts were swirling in her brain. *I was five years old. I saw Mommy fall. Michael was adopted. He was fifteen years old when Mom died. No, when she was murdered. I saw someone push Mommy down the stairs.*

"Hannah, you look pale, and you're shaking. Are you okay? We don't have to discuss this old stuff. I've moved beyond it now. I finally feel free of the past, and I'm looking forward to my marriage and my new life in Chicago."

Hannah felt sick, nauseous, and lightheaded.

Hannah suddenly became aware that someone was laughing loudly. The guffaws and snorts were jarring. She looked up and spotted the source of the discordant laughter, a small elderly woman sitting in a nearby booth. Hannah wondered how such loud noises could come out of such a tiny frame. The woman rose and fussed with the lavender scarf she wore around her neck, and Hannah immediately felt that something was wrong. It was the same feeling she had when she saw the little girl in the parking lot. Danger. There was danger here. But where? Where was the danger? Certainly not from the teenage boy who slid out of the booth and retrieved a cane that was propped against the wall. He didn't use it as a weapon. No, he politely handed it to the elderly lady. She gripped the cane with one hand, and the boy supported her other skinny arm. Slowly, they walked toward the front door. Hannah was mesmerized. Her eyes remained on the couple until they left the restaurant.

"Hannah, what's wrong? You don't look well. Why are you staring at those people? Do you know them?"

"No. No, I don't."

"Well, you're scaring me. I remember how you looked when Mom died. I ran out of my bedroom after I heard your screams and saw you standing beside Mom's twisted body. You looked so small in your purple nightgown. You were pale and shaking then, too. What brought this on now? Is it because I mentioned Mom's death?"

Michael kept talking, but Hannah stopped listening after hearing the words "purple nightgown." Purple was Hannah's favorite color when she was little, and most of her clothes, including her nightgowns, were lavender.

Chapter 27

Saturday, June 22

Early the next morning, Hannah fulfilled her promise. She called Jodi and told her all about her evening with Ethan.

"I'm proud of you, Hannah," Jodi said. "You've discovered that being attracted to another man doesn't take anything away from Aaron. Plus, it doesn't hurt that the man looks like Superman and is attracted to you, too. You can't get much better than that."

Hannah did not reply.

"You're not going to argue with me. Are you?"

"No, not now. I've got something else to work out with you. Something happened last night."

"When you were having dinner with your brother?" Jodi asked.

"Yes, when I had dinner with Michael."

Hannah told Jodi that she had learned that her father had lung cancer and that he was exhibiting symptoms of dementia.

"I'm angry," Hannah said. "Someone should have told me that Dad is in such bad shape. I used to nag him that one day all those smelly cigars he always smoked would catch up with him, and now that day is here. I was planning on returning to the Twin Cities over Thanksgiving break, but I don't want to wait that long. As soon as this summer session ends, I'm going to visit my dad. I want to see for myself what's going on. And there's more."

"More?" Jodi asked.

"Last night, Michael brought up our mother's death. That surprised me. You see, we've never discussed it before. I know that's strange. It's the one event that totally changed our lives, but it's something my family has always danced around and never confronted head-on. My father always insisted that Mom would want us to move on and not rehash the painful past."

"You've never said much about your mother's death. Just that she died when you were very young. What did she die of?"

Hannah paused. It was still hard to say the words, "She didn't die of something. She was murdered."

"Really?" Jodi asked.

"Yes. I don't remember it clearly."

"My God, Hannah. Murdered? Who murdered her?"

"I don't know. Afterward, I went over everything with some nice police officers, but I knew I disappointed them. I saw, but I didn't see the murder. I told them I was asleep, and then something woke me up. I don't know what. I was upset because my stuffed rabbit named Bunny wasn't in bed with me. If I were to fall back asleep, I needed Bunny. I got out of bed and went downstairs. I found Bunny just where I left him, on a dining room chair. I was clutching Bunny and just about to go back upstairs when I heard angry voices and loud crashes. I was confused. I looked up. I saw my mother. She was on the second floor, at the top of the stairs. She looked frightened. She started to move down the stairs, but hands grabbed her around the waist and spun her around. Her back was to me. The hands were on my mom's shoulders. I screamed when I saw those hands fly into the air and then push my mother backward down the stairs. Her head bounced on the slate floor. I screamed and screamed. I don't remember anything more. I've tried and tried so many times, but that's all I can recall. When my father came home from his business trip the next morning, he asked me countless questions about those hands, but I never could attach them to a face nor a body. About a week later, I just couldn't answer any more questions. Not from my father and not from the police. I just stopped talking, and I didn't say another word for a very long time."

"Oh, Hannah. That's awful."

"For many years, I just blocked out that night. I couldn't deal with it. But when I was a teenager, I asked more questions. My father said very little. Claimed it was too painful for him to discuss my mother's death. He did tell me that several pieces of my mother's jewelry and her purse were missing, so the police concluded a thief had entered our home, killed Mother, and then made off with those valuables."

"Did you ever talk to a child psychologist about this?"

"A good question from a good therapist. No, Dad didn't get me any professional help. He insisted that getting back to normal was the best thing for us. But we never were the same. My father was an architect, and he wasn't home a lot. After Mom died, he traveled more and more. Michael was seldom at home; he was sent to a military boarding school. Dad sold the big house and bought a small rancher, one without stairs, and that's where I grew up with my Aunt Gail, my mother's sister. She came to take care of me. My father told me that she was my personal Mary Poppins and could cure anything with her hugs and kisses. And I guess he was right. Six months later, I was able to talk and play again. But I always knew I wasn't like the other little girls. I felt that I had been robbed of my mother and that there was a hole inside of me that nothing and no one could fill."

"Do you still feel that way?"

"No. I've filled up that hole with the people I love. First, there was Aunt Gail. Then Aaron, the twins, and my students. And, of course, you and other good friends. But, for some reason I don't understand, my dad always pushes me away when I try to get close. And my brother's not much better."

"Sounds like you're running out of time to establish a bond with your father. Better to try again now than live with regrets."

"Maybe. But first, I have to find a way to stop these panic attacks. Last night I had another one. And I've been thinking about it and the other ones I've had recently, too. I think they're connected."

"How?"

"By color. Last night, Michael reminded me that I was wearing a purple nightgown when my mother died. He said I was pale and shaking then, a real mess when he found me. When I had the panic attack in the parking lot, it was right after my students and I had been discussing the Baker case. I saw a little girl dressed in lavender clothes and sensed danger. The same thing happened in the restaurant after Michael mentioned our mother's death. My heart started pounding like crazy, and my stomach hurt when I saw a woman adjusting the lavender scarf she was wearing."

"Okay. But more is at work here than just seeing a color. Right before each of these attacks, you were thinking about death."

"Why, yes. Of course. That makes sense. But how do I account for my anxiety when I was making dinner plans with Michael? We weren't talking about death, and I didn't see anything lavender then."

"I don't know, Hannah. Look, you've been thinking about the Baker murders a lot lately. Perhaps hearing from your brother reminded you that there was also a murder in your family. Maybe it was just a case of bad timing. Too much doom and gloom for you to handle."

"Okay. Maybe it was just that and nothing more. Now, it's your turn. Tell me all your news. Entertain me with what's going on in your love life."

While Jodi chatted about the handsome guy who asked her to help him choose a watermelon in the supermarket, Hannah's mind wandered. She remembered her favorite color was purple when she started kindergarten. But after her mother died, Hannah refused to wear her lavender outfits. She recalled the battle she had with Aunt Gail over this. Finally, Aunt Gail had thrown up her hands in defeat and packed up all of Hannah's purple clothes and given them to a charity, muttering all the while about how Hannah's father was needlessly spoiling her and wasting good money on new clothes. It was strange. A few days ago, Hannah would have said that lavender was just an innocuous color. But now, that pale purple hue had become a malevolent force. It had the malicious power to prey upon her psyche and pull her back to the worst time in her childhood, the time when her mother was killed. What else had she buried in her brain? What other memories were waiting to be unearthed and resurrected?

Chapter 28

Sunday, June 23

Hannah stretched her arms above her head. She was sitting outside on her deck, and she was content. It was a good Sunday morning. Her son Seth had surprised her with a phone call, and she had enjoyed her weekly talk with her daughter Sophie. Both her offspring were healthy and happy. In addition, Seth had assured her that he was spending his money wisely in France and did not need additional funds. Hannah was relieved. It appeared that Seth, the twin who had always been lackadaisical about budgeting, had finally learned how to live within his means.

Hannah's computer was on the table in front of her, surrounded by stacks of books and papers. She finished her stretch, lowered her arms, and started typing again. She rapidly finished the paragraph she was working on and was thinking of revising a sentence when she was startled by a voice asking, "Are you a saint or a sinner?"

Hannah looked up. Ethan Clark was standing on the other side of the table and grinning at her. She had been immersed in her work and had neither seen nor heard him approach.

She smiled back. "Well, hello. That's an odd way to greet someone."

Ethan pulled out a chair and sat down across from her. "I figure you have to be one or the other. This is the second Sunday in a row that I've caught you playing hooky from church. So, if you're a sinner, you're avoiding church because you're bad and not about to change your sinful ways. But if you're a saint, you're so good that you can bypass church and get to heaven on your own. Well, which is it?"

"Wait a minute. If you're keeping an eye on me and not attending church yourself, are you a saint or a sinner?"

"You answer first. Which are you?"

"How about neither or maybe a combination of both? The reason I don't spend my Sunday mornings in church is because I'm Jewish," Hannah said.

"Really? No fooling?"

"Yes, really," Hannah said.

"Sorry about jumping to the wrong conclusion. I do know better. I hate it when people assume things about me. That's why I moved to Philadelphia. I wanted a fresh start. In a big city, you can be anonymous. You can leave your past and your family behind. You can experiment and find out who you want to be."

"Who do you want to be?"

"I'm still working on that. But right now, my mom and dad need me and appreciate my help. I like being here now. I like being with you."

Hannah blushed and then said, "Thank you. I enjoy your company, too."

"So formal? I thought since we are officially dating and on the brink of being a couple that you could say something a bit more intimate."

"Officially dating?"

"You bet. We officially had a great first date." Ethan grinned. "I must be losing my touch if you weren't convinced. I thought I made my interest in you very clear."

Hannah bit her lip and looked away. Then she said, "The trouble is I'm out of practice. It was my first date since my husband died. This is all so new to me. I don't know what to say. I don't know what to do."

Ethan smiled. "Just rely on me. If you have any questions, I'll answer them, and the answer to each will always be that I'm here for you. You're very special. You're beautiful, intelligent, and understanding. I think we've started something between us. Is that okay?"

Hannah found herself nodding in agreement but thought, *We've only had one date. Ethan moves faster than a speeding bullet.*

This Superman had incredible powers. He seemed capable of bending Hannah's will of steel with his compliments. Yes, Ethan was a joy to behold. But there was more. Much more. He made Hannah feel pretty and desirable. She hadn't felt that way in a long time, and she liked it. She liked it very much. Certainly, there was no harm in dating this incredible guy. She had been without a man in her life for four years and was entitled to a little romance. Still, Hannah was wary. What type of man was Ethan? Did he flirt with every woman he met? Hannah realized that she knew very little about him. She had answered his question, but he had not answered hers. Was Ethan a saint or a sinner?

Chapter 29

Hannah was tired and becoming exasperated. Jodi was prodding her to elaborate, but there was nothing more to say.

"Look, Jodi, I've had a busy Sunday, and I still have another phone call to make before I head to bed. Honestly, I've told you everything. Everything. Ethan came by when I was working on some lesson plans this morning, and we went miniature golfing in the afternoon. He was good at it, and I was dreadful. No surprise there. He had a chocolate ice cream cone afterward, and I chose cherry-vanilla. A pleasant, simple date. And he did say that we are officially dating. That's the word he used, 'officially.' Really, there's nothing more to add."

"Ah, but you didn't cover the final kiss at the door. There had to be a good-bye kiss at the door."

"Okay. Yes. There was. This time on the lips. Soft and sweet. Are you satisfied?"

"For the time being. I do sense you're leaving something out."

"No, Jodi, I've covered everything. Now, I have to call my Aunt Gail and wish her a happy birthday. I've never missed her birthday a single time in my life, and I'm not about to start now."

"Okay. Okay. But I expect you to keep me up to date. Dating Ethan is a momentous step for you. I just want to make sure he treats my best friend right. If he slips up, let me know, and I'll come over and bop him on the head."

Hannah laughed. "Right. My good buddy, the ultimate pacifist, is going to bop someone on the head?"

"Well, not really. But I would yell a lot. Give him a good tongue-lashing. Seriously, be careful, Hannah. I know I pushed you into dating, but this is new territory for you, and I don't want you to get hurt. Go slow, and be sure of this guy before you fall for him."

"Will do. Thank you. I promise to watch my step."

After Hannah ended the call, she thought about what she had not told Jodi, what she wanted to keep to herself. She had not lied. Ethan's final kiss at the door had initially been soft and sweet. What she had not said was that Ethan's lips had lingered, and the kiss had become more demanding. The passion had intensified. She felt dazed and breathless when they parted. To be honest, she had never been kissed like that before. It both frightened and excited her. Everything about Aaron's lovemaking had been just like her husband, good, warm, and dependable. But Ethan's kiss had been electrifying.

Hannah shook her head to clear it, to stop thinking of Ethan and that kiss. She forced herself to calm down before she called Aunt Gail on her cell. It would not do for her aunt, who could detect every one of Hannah's moods in her voice, to ask Hannah questions about this new man in her life. Hannah could not believe it. She once again had a man in her life. But for how long? In all likelihood, Ethan would move on to other women when he returned to Philadelphia. No, there was no reason to tell Aunt Gail about Ethan now.

Chapter 30

"Happy Birthday, Aunt Gail," Hannah said when she reached her aunt a short time later.

"Thank you, dear. You never forget. The bouquet of roses you sent is beautiful. How are you? How are Seth and Sophie? Sophie sent me the sweetest birthday card, and Seth mailed me a postcard from France. Can you believe it? They remembered me, too."

"Not surprising. You are their favorite great aunt."

Hannah smiled. She was proud. Without her prodding, her children had remembered Aunt Gail's birthday. Hannah made a mental note to thank them. The whole family owed a lot to this gentle woman who had raised Hannah and lavishly spoiled the twins with affection and a mountain of gifts from the moment they were born.

Aunt Gail was eager to hear about the twins' most recent exploits, but afterward, there was a lull in the conversation.

"Anything else happening in your life, honey?" Aunt Gail asked.

"Well, I had dinner with Michael on Friday night. He was in the area for work. Did you know that he's planning on moving to Chicago and that he's getting married?"

"Why, yes. I did. I didn't say anything because he wanted to tell you himself. I'm happy for him. I think he's finally found a keeper. Susan's a good woman. I like her very much."

"I liked her when I met her, too. But, Aunt Gail, during our dinner, Michael said something that bothered me. He brought up our mother's murder. No one in the family ever talks about it; however, Michael did on Friday. He's still carrying around a lot of hurt. He feels he was kicked out of our home at the worst possible time, right after Mom died. Why did Dad send him away to a military school?"

"Oh, my. Actually, your parents were arguing about that decision right before your mother was killed. I bet you don't remember how difficult Michael was when he turned fifteen. He had a growth spurt and was tall and hefty. He liked to flaunt his strength and taunt your mother. He disobeyed all the house rules, ignored his curfew, and started sneaking out of the house to drink beer with his buddies. He banged up your mom's car one night when he took it for a joy ride. Your mother couldn't control him, and your dad was seldom at home at that time. He was working round the clock to be named the architect for that art museum outside of Winnipeg."

"I don't remember any of this," Hannah said.

"No reason you should, honey. You were living in your own world, excited about kindergarten and learning how to read. I stayed at your house to keep your mom company when your dad went to Canada to push his building design. I was amazed at how bad things had gotten. Your mom cried a lot, and Michael was angry and defiant. One night, when your mom laid into Michael about breaking curfew, I saw him push her into a corner. She was really frightened. When your mom called your father and told him what happened, he decided, right then and there, that Michael had to leave the house and go to military school. Your mom was upset. She thought a better solution was for your dad to stay at home more and discipline Michael. But you know your father. Once he decides on a plan, no one can change his mind."

"I'm amazed. It's like you're talking about different people and not my family."

"Honey, you were just a little kid, and your mom and dad wanted you to be a happy, secure child. Also, your parents were not getting along very well at that time and were arguing a lot. They did so behind closed doors so that you and Michael wouldn't hear them yell at each other. Your dad was taking big risks with their money. Spending a lot to make a lot in the future, and your mom was scared he would end up losing everything, including the house and all their savings."

Aunt Gail paused and then stifled a sob. "I'm sorry, sweetheart. I went home to help my mother, your Grandma Carol, when she fell and hurt her back. The hospital called when we were finishing dinner, and I packed up and left. And later that night, your mother was killed. I've asked myself countless times if things would have ended differently if I had decided to wait and leave the next morning. Maybe I would've heard the intruder and been able to warn your mother. Maybe your mom and I would've been able to fight off the killer together. I wish I could turn back time and do things differently."

"Oh, Aunt Gail, don't. Don't blame yourself. You don't know how often I've wished I could link the hands I saw push my mother down the stairs to a shape and a face. I know I let everyone down. It took me a long time to forgive myself. You don't know what would've happened had you been there. You might have been killed as well, and then who would've saved me?"

Chapter 31

That night Hannah had trouble sleeping. Too much was swirling in her brain. It was as if her thoughts were revolving in a rapidly moving centrifuge. There was Michael, the adopted son who was out of control and sent away to a boarding school. There was Aunt Gail and all her regrets. There was her mother's murder, a wound that never healed. There was her father. She had wanted to ask Aunt Gail about her father's health but had opted to delay the discussion. They had covered enough weighty family matters during their phone call. It was, after all, Aunt Gail's birthday. And there also was that kiss from Ethan.

Hannah knew sleep would elude her for some time. She got out of bed, went to the kitchen, poured herself half a glass of white wine, and then grabbed a mystery novel off a bookshelf in her family room. The book was supposed to be, according to the blurb on the cover, "riveting," but it did not grab her. The hard-boiled detective in it was a cliché, and when she found herself rooting for his nemesis, who was far more interesting than the hero, she gave up on the book.

Hannah looked at her laptop. She had left it on the end table beside her recliner. She knew opening it would be a risky move. If she gazed at her work emails, she would be bombarded with pleas for help from her students, adding to the list of concerns bouncing around in her head. But the temptation was too great. She opened her computer, clicked on the email icon, and then quickly scanned the long list of messages in her In Box. She paused when she saw that a student had sent her an email earlier that night, and "Urgent" was the only word on the subject line.

Dear Professor Stein,

Brad, Gina, and I must see you tomorrow, Monday. We think we are on to something important. Please make time for us.

Your student,

Frank Brubaker

Hannah sighed. What happened? Why was it crucial for those three to see her right away? Now, on top of everything else, there was this mysterious message. She knew it was going to be a long night with very little sleep.

Chapter 32

Monday, June 24

The next morning, after class was over, Frank, Brad, and Gina impatiently waited for the last straggler to leave the classroom, and then the three gathered in front of Hannah's desk.

"Professor Stein, do you have some time to talk to us now?" Frank asked. "We really need to talk to you."

Hannah nodded. She had rescheduled her morning meeting. She was curious and wanted to know what was so urgent that it could not wait.

The trio sighed in relief.

"Good. Very good," Brad said. "We have a lot to sort out."

Hannah waved her arm, the gesture inviting her students to sit down at the desks in the front row, and then she joined them.

"Now, what's going on?" Hannah asked.

Gina said, "You better start, Frank. You were the one who talked to Matthew Baker on Saturday night."

Frank said, "Matthew is entitled to a few phone calls a month, and he called me. I was surprised to hear from him. He said he needed help. He pleaded with me to continue to ask questions. To find some way to prove he's innocent and get him out of prison. I explained that I couldn't make any guarantees. Told him I'm just a student and not a private investigator or a lawyer. But he said that was okay as he was desperate. So, we talked. And I remembered to ask him about the money."

Brad interrupted, "The three of us have spent a lot of time discussing this case, and we believe that we have to follow the money. That's what they do on all the TV cop shows. All the detectives follow the money."

"And it makes sense," Gina said. "We wondered where a fourteen-year-old kid got the money to buy illegal drugs."

Frank said, "So, I started with that. I asked Matthew how he paid for his drugs. The answer was that he stole money from his parents all the time. His folks always kept cash in the house to pay their help and just replaced the stash when it was low. Never were too careful. And Baker earned more money by recruiting customers for Ken Graybill, his neighborhood dealer. Then Matthew brought up Friendly Fred's, the place where Ken Graybill and his gang hung out when Matthew was in middle school. Baker said that's where he went to score drugs, and he often brought along rich kids who also wanted to get high."

"And," Brad added, "get this for a coincidence. Friendly Fred's came up again after Frank left church yesterday."

"You see, Professor Stein," Frank said, "church on Sunday was really uncomfortable. Some people were giving me dirty looks. I didn't like it one bit. And after church, this one lady started yelling at my folks in the parking lot. She told them they hadn't raised me right. That the Good Lord had punished the wicked Matthew Baker and that I shouldn't meddle with the Almighty's decisions. I wanted to tell her that Matthew Baker had been judged by people, not by God, and that people can make mistakes. But I couldn't get a word in. She kept shaking her fist and screaming. Then she abruptly turned and stomped off, but not before she told my folks to keep me away from Friendly Fred's Lanes. She said the sinners who corrupted Matthew Baker hung out there, and if my folks weren't careful, then those sinners would corrupt me, too."

"So, what did you do?" Hannah asked.

Brad said, "Actually, he called me and suggested we get in touch with Gina. Frank thought we should all go to Friendly Fred's. Everyone knows it. It's the only place to bowl in or near Parkerville. Professor Stein, you probably know it, too."

Hannah said, "I do. I took my children to many bowling birthday parties there when they were small."

Brad said, "Then you know how the building is arranged. Leagues and families stick to the right side of the place, where the alleys are. That side is safe and tame. The side with the pool tables and bar has always had a bad reputation. Fights break out there late at night on weekends. Been that way for as long as I can remember."

Frank added, "I can't remember the last time I went to Fred's, but I wanted to go back and check out the place. I figured there was a chance that this Ken Graybill character, who got Baker hooked on drugs, might still hang out there. And I thought it best to be prepared. So, I called my cousin Steve."

Gina beamed. "Oh, I do like this part. I'm so grateful Frank is so well-connected."

Frank said, "Well, sometimes it does help to have a large family, all living in or near Parkerville. I called Steve because Graybill went to Parkerville High. Steve's around Graybill's age, and even though Graybill was a drop-out, I thought Steve might know him or, at least, know about him. And my hunch paid off. Steve was able to tell me a lot about him."

***

Although Frank meandered a bit as he related what he had learned from his cousin, Hannah was able to piece together the salient points. The shocking part was not that this Ken Graybill was a "bad dude." You would expect that description to cling to a guy who sold illegal drugs to minors. But how, Hannah wondered, had Graybill, renowned for his shady dealings, avoided being charged as a drug pusher? And what was jaw-dropping was that Graybill was also known for publicly vowing that one day Bruce Baker, Matthew's father, would pay for what he had done to Ken's family.

Hannah's thoughts were racing. *Did Bruce Baker really harm the Graybills? Was Ken Graybill all bluster and talk, or was he a revengeful killer? Had the police looked at Graybill? Did the detectives question him and determine where he was at the time of the murders and rape? Or had the police been too quick or too lazy? Had they just accepted the easy answer and failed to dig deep?*

Hannah's thoughts picked up speed and were now galloping toward a dismal finish line. *Now I am more convinced than ever that I should have shared what Helen Baker told me with the authorities. I wish I had known about Ken Graybill years ago. What have I done by not doing anything?*

Chapter 33

"Professor Stein," Gina said, "you look like you're a million miles away."

"I'm sorry," Hannah said. "Please, go on."

Brad said, "Well, here's what happened at Fred's. We asked the guy working the refreshment counter if he knew Ken Graybill. This fellow said that Graybill had recently returned to the Lancaster area and often played pool on the weekends at Fred's. He mentioned that Graybill had come in earlier with some friends. Lucky for us, the guy took one look at Gina and said he would be happy to personally escort us back to the poolroom and point out Graybill. And he did."

Gina said, "I hate to flirt to get what I want, but sometimes it's for a good cause."

"We just stood in a corner near Graybill and watched and listened," Frank said. "We could not believe what we heard."

Hannah's students overheard a wobbly, obviously intoxicated Graybill boast to his friends that he was smarter than everyone in the room because he was set for life. He had his own personal banker, someone he called Sorry Face. Graybill claimed that it was easy to get money, big money, out of Sorry Face. All Graybill had to do was keep quiet about his past drug deals and the Baker case. Nothing easier than that. Ken Graybill scoffed that he could not understand why Sorry Face was worried about some silly college kids who were asking questions and stirring things up.

Frank said, "Actually, everyone in the room heard all that. The place was noisy, but Graybill was really loud. Then a huge man grabbed onto

Graybill's arm and hustled him out the back door. I heard someone call the big guy Moose, and the man had a tattoo of a moose on his upper arm."

"After they left, we left, too. Which was fine with me," Gina said. "I'm not that fond of bowling, and I have absolutely no interest in playing pool with the thugs at Fred's."

"But what should we do now?" Brad asked. "What do you think, Professor Stein? It sounded to us like Graybill knows something about the rape and murders. Something someone pays him a lot of money not to divulge. Should we tell somebody what we heard? The police? Baker's lawyer? Or do you think everyone will say we just heard the ramblings of a drunk guy and that they don't mean anything at all?"

Hannah took a deep breath and then replied, "I understand why you think this may be important, but Matthew Baker's case is closed. There has never been an appeal, and so far, no one has questioned the verdict or the sentencing. I think you'll probably need something more, like a solid piece of evidence, to have the authorities take a second look, but I may be wrong. Tell you what I'll do. My neighbors' son is a police officer. He used to work for the Parkerville police. Let me run all this by him tonight, if I can get a hold of him, and see what he recommends. I'll try to have an answer for you tomorrow. Fair enough?"

Three heads nodded in assent.

Oh boy, Hannah thought, *this is getting complicated.*

Chapter 34

Late that afternoon, Hannah was ready to head home. She was making a mental list of the questions she wanted to ask Ethan about the Baker case as she organized the papers on her desk in her office. After she divided the papers into two stacks, she slid the larger pile into her computer bag and put the smaller one into a folder that she deposited in her file cabinet. She sighed. It had been a long day.

Hannah was surprised when she heard someone knock on her office door. She was not expecting anyone to stop by, and there were not many people left on campus at this time of day.

"Come in," Hannah said.

Hannah was startled. Dr. Eileen Balinkowsky walked into the room and perched herself on the edge of Hannah's desk. Dr. B, the name everyone called Hannah's department head, was a tiny, birdlike woman who was famous on campus for her wit and intelligence, as well as for her propensity to flit from place to place when she spoke. Dr. B was always in motion, and her lectures were always overflowing with students who wanted to hear "the great one speak" and watch her animated presentations. She was in high demand; students, professors, and other department heads all clamored for her time. Dr. B never spontaneously dropped in anywhere and had never visited Hannah in her office. Hannah had no idea why Dr. B had suddenly materialized before her. What was going on?

Hannah blinked. Yes, Dr. B really was in her office. And Dr. B was neither speaking nor moving. Not good omens.

"Uh, hello, Dr. B," Hannah stammered. "How are you?"

"I'm good, but, apparently, you are not, Hannah."

"I don't understand," Hannah said.

"Well, all afternoon, our college president has been trying to reach you. And when he couldn't, he resorted to calling me. Several times every hour. Perhaps you can tell me what's going on. If I'm to lend you my support, I need to know why Dr. Daniels is angrily demanding that he see you immediately."

"But I've no idea. Really, I don't," Hannah said. Hannah pulled her cell phone out of her bag. "Ah, that explains it. No power. I forgot to recharge it last night. That's why I haven't gotten any calls. But why does Dr. Daniels need to talk to me? Is it a family emergency? Has something happened to my children?"

"No. No need to worry about your family. Dr. Daniels was very clear. He wants to talk to you about your summer class. Think, Hannah. This is most unusual. Have you said or done anything recently in your class that would warrant concern?"

"Well, I have allowed my students to choose their own research paper topics. One wanted to take the position that having a brothel on campus would be great for student morale and a good source of revenue. But he dropped the idea. Instead, he's arguing that we should legalize prostitution all over the United States, as it is legal in parts of Nevada. I know it's a controversial topic, but he's accumulating a lot of data to support his position. Do you think that's it? Do you think Dr. Daniels got wind of this and is upset?"

Dr. B smiled. "Actually, I hope so. I hope all this ruckus is about that and nothing more. But there is only one way to find out. Dr. Daniels wants to see you in his office. And, Hannah, after you talk to him, email me. I'll call and let him know you're on your way."

Dr. B slid off the desk and quickly walked toward the door. She turned when she had her hand on the doorknob and asked, "Hannah, what would you have done if your student hadn't changed his mind and wanted to write a paper in favor of having a brothel on campus?"

"As the topic directly relates to the college, I would have brought the matter to you."

"Good answer." Then Dr. B left the office and closed the door behind her.

Chapter 35

Hannah took a deep breath to calm herself. She was in the office of the President of Buchanan College, the legendary inner sanctum. Daniels was not known for his warmth nor his hospitality. Instead, he was famous for being a recluse. He seldom left this office, and, to Hannah's knowledge, no one at her pay scale had ever been invited or summoned to this imposing, dark place. Paneling, furniture, and carpet were all dark brown, and the heavy brown velour curtains admitted little light.

Daniels' secretary had said very little to Hannah before he left for the day. He just murmured, "You're expected, Professor Stein. Walk right in."

Dr. Daniels' office door was wide open, so Hannah obediently followed the instruction. She walked right in. Now she was standing in front of the president's mammoth desk. Daniels was seated on the other side; his back was to Hannah, and he was on the phone. Hannah impatiently rocked from foot to foot, waiting for Daniels to finish his conversation, but he droned on and on. His voice was low, and Hannah only heard random words.

Should I cough, clear my throat, or make some noise to let him know I'm here? Hannah asked herself. *Or would that be rude? I haven't been invited to sit down, so I don't think I should. Is this part of his strategy? Am I to stand here like a naughty student waiting to be chastised by the principal while he talks to someone on the phone and prolongs my agony? This is crazy! I just wish I knew why Dr. Daniels wants to see me.*

After five long, harrowing minutes had elapsed, Daniels ended his call and swiveled his desk chair around to face Hannah.

"You must know why you're here, Professor Stein, if you read the editorials in Sunday's paper." Daniels pointed to the open newspaper on his desk.

"Actually, I had a busy day yesterday. I never got around to reading the paper," Hannah said.

"Well, Julian Adams read the editorials and had plenty to say about them this morning. At Buchanan College, pleasing Julian Adams is of paramount importance. Your students need his scholarship money, and this college benefits from all his generous donations. But just look at these editorials." Daniels snatched up a page from the paper and thrust it toward Hannah. "Your reckless behavior has jeopardized the whole community outreach program. Adams is threatening to pull the plug and end it all."

Hannah quickly grabbed hold of the page and scanned the Letters to the Editor. Two of them were blistering indictments.

In the first letter, the writer questioned why a teacher was corrupting the minds of students by asking them to overturn the laws of man and God. Why were students in the Adams' scholarship program doing research that might help a convicted killer? Why was Buchanan College stirring things up and embarrassing a local church? In the second letter, the writer lambasted the college for straying into New Age methods of education and tarnishing its fine reputation. Why were Adams' scholarship students studying such distasteful topics as murder and rape? The writer reminded the college that Lancaster County is a God-fearing and conservative place and recommended that teachers who do not share the community's values be dismissed.

Hannah gasped. *I can't believe this,* Hannah thought. *I just wanted to make an assignment more interesting. But was I being selfish? I discussed the Baker murders and rape with my "stubborn three" because the case interested me. Have I done Frank, Brad, and Gina a disservice? I didn't expect to see letters like these. But maybe I should have seen them coming. Frank did say that he was getting static from church members. Oh my, such strong reactions to my students' research. However, there are just two letters of complaint. Why is Adams so upset? There hasn't been time to clarify things and write rebuttals.*

I came in here thinking Daniels was concerned about the brothel topic. Does he know about that, too?

"Well?" Dr. Daniels' question interrupted Hannah's thoughts.

"Let me explain," Hannah said.

"Please do. Take a seat and tell me how we got to this place."

Hannah sat down. She nervously cleared her throat. Then she told Daniels that she was following the curriculum for the study skills course, with only one exception. She had allowed her students to choose their own research topics, and she was pleased with the results. Her students were motivated and had eagerly embarked on their research. In addition, they had all learned how to properly cite sources and were on schedule to complete their papers and pass the course. She described how the Baker case had intrigued three of her students and enabled them to branch out from it and discover topics of their own. Hannah described the topics that had evolved from the case.

Daniels sat back in his chair and sighed. "Professor Stein, I understand. Your intentions were good, but you have upset people in the community. You have upset Julian Adams. He will pull his money out of the scholarship program for your students if I don't do something about all of this. I think there are some things you need to understand. Can you keep a confidence? If I tell you something personal about Julian Adams, do you promise not to share it with anyone else?"

"Yes," Hannah answered, but her voice quavered. She did not like committing herself to keeping a secret before she knew if it was something she should divulge.

Daniels then proceeded to tell her a sad story. A very sad story, indeed.

Chapter 36

Dr. Daniels' story started out innocently enough. Two young men, Daniels and Adams, became friends when they were freshmen at Buchanan College. After they graduated, they went off in different directions, and their friendship waned. Daniels earned a doctorate degree at a college in the Midwest, while Adams remained in Parkerville and became a local real estate mogul. When Daniels returned to Buchanan to teach, he and Adams rekindled their friendship, and Daniels met Conrad, Adams' son. Conrad had been a chess champion at the age of seven. However, the clever boy with so much promise grew into a surly teen with a wild streak. He did not do well in school. By the time Conrad was a barely-passing senior at Parkerville High, Daniels had moved up in the ranks at Buchanan and had become the college's president. Adams begged Daniels to overlook Conrad's low grades and test scores and admit him to Buchanan College. Adams felt his son, who had a high IQ, would do well if he was properly stimulated and learned how to study. Daniels pulled some strings, and Conrad was admitted to Buchanan. All was in place and going as Adams planned.

But Conrad never got the chance to change the trajectory of his life. One night, just a month before his high school graduation, Conrad swallowed a cocktail of illegal drugs and died. Adams fell apart, and his wife was devastated. Adams was so depressed that he did not see what was happening to his wife. She became withdrawn and brittle, mired down by grief and guilt. She blamed herself and her husband for not recognizing that their son had a drug problem. She went through the motions after her son's death, but she was never fully alive after that. She felt she had to be punished, and two years later, she committed suicide. Her death shattered Adams. Once again, he had not been able to save someone he loved. He immersed himself in business ventures, working incredibly long hours. He turned down social invitations and avoided family and friends. He kept up that lifestyle for years. Daniels reached out and tried to help his friend, but Adams rejected all his efforts. However, after surviving a mild heart attack, Adams reluctantly agreed to see a counselor. It took time, but Adams slowly learned how to deal with his grief. Then, Adams searched for a meaningful way to honor his wife and son and appealed to Daniels for help. Daniels came up with the Conrad Adams Scholarship Fund, free tuition for local students who, like Conrad, had promise but had not excelled in school.

"So, you see," Dr. Daniels said, "this scholarship program means a lot to Julian Adams. He read these letters in the paper and felt that he had been slapped in the face. He's a wonderful man, but he does have a fragile ego. He wants to be loved and admired and not have his name nor his son's name tied to anything unsavory. He's also a man of action. I must be one, too, if I'm to appease him."

Hannah said, "I could talk to him. I could explain. I could …"

"Stop. Adams will not listen to anything you have to say. He wants this to end now. The drugs that killed his son were tainted and were purchased from one of the drug pushers in the group that Matthew Baker hung out with. In Julian Adams' mind, everyone in that gang, including Baker, is responsible for killing his son. Adams has been rewriting history, linking his son's name to philanthropy and burying the story of Conrad's drug use. He simply can't deal with this. I need to help my friend. I also need to help the twelve scholarship recipients from last year and the students in your class now and the students who will follow, year after year. I must preserve the Conrad Adams Scholarship Fund."

Hannah was silent. She was stunned.

"Let's see if we can work something out to help our students. You were teaching at Wrightsville Community College before you joined us two years ago, right? And, from all accounts, you did good work there."

Uh oh, Hannah thought. *He's just reminded me that I don't have tenure yet. This can't be good.*

Daniels continued, "You're doing good work for us here, too. I looked at your file, especially at the end-of-the-course evaluation forms your students filled out last semester. You have a high rating; your students like you. Your department head speaks well of you, too. Yes, I think you're the type of teacher who puts her students first, above and beyond all else."

Daniels leaned forward and put his palms on the desk. He was ready to dictate his terms. "Professor Stein, each of your students will find more than enough material to fill a ten-page paper. They don't need to bring up the Matthew Baker case to support their arguments. Right?"

"Yes. That's true."

"Then your students have nothing to complain about. Agreed?"

Hannah found herself slowly nodding. But all the while, she was asking herself, *What will Dr. B think of this? Is Daniels trampling on my students' first amendment rights?*

Hannah wondered if Daniels was a mind reader because he said, "I anticipated that the formidable Dr. Balinkowsky might raise some objections. I've already discussed the matter with her. I apologize for keeping you waiting while I tied things up with her on the phone. Dr. Balinkowsky understands my position. Although she has some reservations, she will support me. Too many lives are at stake. I just can't yank scholarships away from needy kids. Can you?"

Hannah did not reply. It had to be a rhetorical question.

"Professor Stein, I will level with you. No one wants to infringe on your academic freedom or your students' rights. But the truth of the matter is that I have no way to fund your students' program if Adams pulls his money out. That means everything ends. No money for the whole community outreach program, for the scholarships and your position. Ask yourself what's really important here. I'm relying on you. Convince your students to drop the Baker case."

Hannah could not, for the life of her, remember what she said right before she left Daniels' office. It must have been satisfactory as Daniels shook her hand and thanked her for her cooperation. But she had not been asked to cooperate, to help resolve the problem. No, she had been pushed into a corner. It was a long walk from the Administration Building to Parking Lot B, where Hannah had parked her car, and she had time to dissect what had just occurred. Daniels had told her the true story behind the Adams' scholarship fund, and Hannah felt the weight of that confidence. And then he had added more pressure. If she refused to bend, her students would suffer, and her job would end. At least, Buchanan's president appeared to have his priorities straight. He seemed to genuinely care about her students, but not enough to "man up" and personally talk to the three who were investigating the Baker case. No, he delegated that job to Hannah.

I dread tomorrow, Hannah thought. *After revving up my students, I have to tell them to revise their papers and eliminate everything in them related to Matthew Baker for the sake of the scholarship program. I hate the idea, but what else can I do?*

Hannah spotted a nearby bench under a tree. She sat down, pulled out her computer, and quickly emailed Dr. B. The message was short, *Talked to Dr. Daniels. Understand what must be done.*

By the time Hannah reached her car, the pounding around her eyes and the knots in her neck could not be ignored. She had one giant, throbbing headache. She had been very tense in Daniels' office, and now all she wanted to do was go home, take a couple of aspirins, and lay down. Hannah unlocked her car and was about to slide onto the driver's seat when she noticed a white paper underneath one of the windshield wipers. She hurriedly plucked it out, thinking it must be a circular for a nearby store. When she read the words on the paper, her hand shook.

I can't believe this, Hannah said to herself. *I can't believe someone is threatening to murder me.*

Chapter 37

Three hours later, Hannah was sitting at her kitchen table. She had her head in her hands and was exhausted. Her head still hurt, but two aspirins, a little food, and a bottle of water had taken the sharp edge off the pain. Ethan was sitting across from her. Like Superman, he had swooped into her home and rescued her after she called him on the phone and uttered the word "help."

"You look bushed. Is there anything else I can do for you before I head out?" Ethan asked.

"No," Hannah answered. "You've been great. I appreciate all your help. You rushed right over and made me a sandwich and listened. It was an incredibly bad day, but I feel better now."

"Hannah, I'm worried about you. I don't like the idea of some crackpot threatening your life."

"Ethan, I do appreciate your concern, but there's no need to worry about my safety. I promise to be more vigilant, and I will remember to turn on the house's security alarm. And, yes, I will put your number and 911 on speed dial on my phone. Plus, I can shout really loud and call you for help if anyone should try to attack me in my yard. Which I still think is highly unlikely."

"Unlikely or not, I want you to be cautious and alert, Hannah. Tomorrow I'm going to get you some pepper spray to carry in your purse. I don't like this whole situation. Not one bit."

Hannah looked again at the paper that had been placed on her windshield. It was now lying on her kitchen table. Ethan had told Hannah to put it in a clear plastic bag to preserve any incriminating fingerprints.

The words on it had been scrawled with a black marker. The message was brief and misspelled. *Baker is a murdrer. Stop looking or you will be murdred!* The harsh note reminded Hannah of the anti-Semitic chalk drawings and misspelled words that were on her driveway when her family first moved to Parkerville. Just looking at this threat was depressing as it brought back bad memories. Hannah's first instinct was to burn the note or rip it to shreds, but Ethan said it was important to show it to the police. He insisted on taking it himself to the Parkerville police station in the morning. Hannah agreed. That did make sense.

"Please remember, Ethan, to tell the police about the hateful graffiti on my driveway. The misspelling of the word 'murdered' is the same. I know it might be a million-to-one shot. I know lots of people make spelling mistakes. But just in case it's significant, I want them to know."

"I will. But, Hannah, how can you be sure the misspellings are identical? Many years have passed since someone wrote on your driveway, and a spelling error is such a small thing."

"Those threats on my driveway scared me. I feared for the lives of my children. That incident is something I will never forget. And an English teacher remembers a misspelling."

Ethan threw up his hands in defeat. "Okay. I believe you. And while I'm at the police station, let me take care of that other matter for you, too. I'll report what your students overheard Ken Graybill say."

"Good. But should I personally tell the police what Helen Baker said to me before she was killed? I feel so guilty. Helen believed that someone had broken into her home before the murders. What do you think? Could it have been Graybill?"

"I don't know, Hannah. Graybill had a reputation. He was a teenage punk, always spouting off and getting into fights at school. Still, the Parkerville cops tried to give him a break as his father was a gambler and an alcoholic; the kid didn't have an easy life. However, when Ken Graybill started selling drugs to kids, he crossed the line. We wanted him off the streets. We'd pick up Graybill on one charge or another, but he always got off on a technicality. His attorney was clever, from a big Philadelphia firm. We never could figure out who paid for her. You may not know this, but Ken Graybill grew up in the Baker house.

The Graybill family had lived there for generations until Ken's father lost everything, the house and the land, to Bruce Baker in a high-stakes poker game. That's why Ken Graybill hated the Bakers. Ken believed his dad had been cheated, and Ken was noisy about it. Claimed he'd avenge his father. Of course, we looked at Graybill for the murders and rape, but he had an alibi. And besides, we caught Matthew Baker holding the murder weapon. It was obvious. Baker killed his family."

Hannah sat back in her chair. *Talk about irony. On the same day that I'm told to abandon the Matthew Baker case, I learn about Ken Graybill from my students and Ethan, too. Graybill had a motive to commit the murders.* Hannah wondered, *What else is out there, hiding in the shadows, that I don't know about these crimes?*

Ethan added, "Tell you what. I really don't think it's important, but I'll make sure the proper detectives also know that Helen Baker thought someone was sneaking into her home right before the murders. If they want to follow-up, they'll get in touch with you. Fair enough?"

"Thank you. I think that covers everything."

"Happy to help. Oh, one more thing. Is Will Dotlish still in charge of campus security?"

"Yes," Hannah replied. "But he's getting ready to retire. He's only working part-time this summer. Why, I should have thought of him. I can't believe it. I should've called the campus security office immediately after I found the note."

"Hey, it's okay. You had a scare and were rattled. I'll take care of notifying the campus force for you, too. I know Will. He's been around forever. I'll tell him what happened and sound the alert. Leave all police matters to me."

"Oh, I can't thank you enough, Ethan."

"Now, you've had a long day. I recommend you get some sleep. Listen to President Daniels. He's got your students' best interests at heart. Follow his advice, and move away from the gruesome Baker case. I want you to be safe and out of the line of fire."

"I know that sounds reasonable, but ..."

"Oh, Hannah, stop. We've talked enough tonight."

Ethan stood. He circled the table, scooped Hannah into his arms, and pressed her against him. He gave her a long and passionate good-night kiss.

"Hannah, promise me you'll forget all about Matthew Baker. Promise to think only of me."

And Hannah, savoring the warmth of the embrace and the kiss, whispered in response, "I promise."

Chapter 38

Tuesday, June 25

On the way to work the next day, Hannah smiled. She remembered how her body tingled when Ethan held her in his arms. It was a nice feeling. It was wonderful to be desired. But now, in the light of day, she also realized how foolish she had been.

Hannah thought, *There's no way in the world I can fulfill that promise. I love and cherish many people. And if Ethan understood me at all, he'd know that my children will always come first, ahead of everyone else. That was such a line. He said, 'Think only of me.' And I looked into those deep blue eyes of his and agreed. I don't understand it. I don't think straight when I'm with Ethan. There must be something I can do to counteract his sexy superpowers.*

Hannah made herself a promise. She had a full day ahead of her. She would concentrate on work and not spend another minute thinking about Ethan Clark. There would be time for that later. In the evening, after dinner, she would treat herself to half a glass of wine and a long conversation with Jodi. Jodi would help her sort things out. Having settled the "What to do about Ethan" question, Hannah focused next on what she was going to say to Frank, Gina, and Brad. She had a feeling they would rebel and not quietly accept what President Daniels proposed as a solution, and Hannah wanted to be prepared.

Hannah was right. Later that afternoon, during her office hours, three students exploded when Hannah explained that it was vital that they eliminate any mention of the Baker case from their papers and drop their investigation. Her students were angry and loud. The words "unfair" and "censorship" repeatedly circled the room and bounced off the walls.

"Okay, settle down. I hear you. I really do. There's no need to shout," Hannah said.

"But . . . but . . . but . . . ," Frank sputtered. "This is wrong. This is very wrong."

"The college can't do this to us," Gina said. "I owe a debt to Sandra Metzler. She trusted me. I have to tell Sandra's story. Everything in my paper revolves around her rape."

"And what about all the lawn mowing I have to do for my Uncle Bob?" Brad asked. "Remember, that's how I'm repaying him for helping me get those Baker transcript pages. Frank's right. This is so wrong. The three of us have worked too hard and come too far to just give up and back out now."

"And there's something more," Frank added. "My cousin Steve remembered that Graybill and his gang were known for doing their drug deals at various spots. On Saturday nights, it was at a picnic pavilion at Lake Keller. It was handy. Graybill lived in the trailer park just down the road. We need time to accumulate more of these bits of information. I keep going back to the drugs and the money. I found out how Baker paid for his drugs, but who was Graybill's supplier? I just feel there's more to uncover."

Ken Graybill lived in the trailer park near Lake Keller. Ethan's parents still lived there at that time. Did the police know about the drug deals at the lake? What did Ethan know? Hannah's thoughts were tripping over each other. Suddenly, she had more questions, too.

Brad said, "And don't forget about Sorry Face. Graybill claimed that Sorry Face is paying him money to keep quiet. It sure sounded like Graybill knows something important."

Hannah said, "I know you're all disappointed and have unanswered questions. At least I can report that last night I spoke to my neighbor's son, the police officer I told you about, and he was eager to help us. He's agreed to report all you heard Ken Graybill say at Friendly Fred's to the proper Parkerville detectives. And he's promised to follow-up on something for me, too. Shortly before the murders, Helen Baker told me that she thought someone was breaking into her home and moving things about. So, you see, by the end of the day, the police will have two new leads to pursue if they think they're important. We have to let them do their jobs. You have jobs to do, too. You have to write your papers and pass this course. You each have found more than enough source materials for your papers. You do not need to cite the Baker case. Each of your papers will be solid without it."

"But what about Matthew Baker?" Frank asked. "What if he's right? What if he's innocent? Are we to just let him rot in jail?"

Hannah said, "Matthew Baker had his day in court. He had a competent lawyer who put up a good fight for him. The prosecution pushed for the maximum, three first-degree murder convictions, but Baker's lawyer convinced the jury to take into account the boy's traumatic past."

"Yes. What Professor Stein just said is true," Brad told Frank and Gina. "I never got to the verdict and the sentencing when we were going over the transcript pages. The jury accepted Baker's lawyer's argument that he was not in full control of his actions at the time of the murders. The charges were reduced, three third-degree murders. Third-degree is less severe than first, but he still got a lot of prison time. Ten to twenty years for each of the murders. Matthew was just fourteen years old when his family was murdered. When the trial ended, he was fifteen. That's when he heard the judge say he'd be in a prison cell for thirty to sixty years."

"So, what do we do now?" Gina asked. "I'm confused. I feel I should stand up for Sandra Metzler and fight to keep her story in my paper. And if Matthew Baker's innocent of the murders, then I guess I should fight for him, too. But what if the jury was right, and he's guilty? And what about the rape? I don't want to work to free a rapist. And I have to think about my mom and dad. They're proud that I'm in this program. They never dreamed I'd get into a college like Buchanan. I'd hate to have to tell them that I lost my scholarship."

Brad said, "I need my scholarship, too. I can't afford this place. And without the support program, I wouldn't last a day here."

"Same for me," Frank said.

Hannah hated being manipulated by Dr. Daniels, and now she hated manipulating her students. But she played the guilt card because saving the scholarship program was so important.

Hannah said. "I think we all know what we must do. We can't be selfish. A Conrad Adams Scholarship is a life-changer. You may disagree with your benefactor, Julian Adams, but he's paying for the program. He's giving you and your classmates and so many more over the years to come an incredible gift. Adams feels he should be able to direct how his money is spent, and he wants to put some distance between this college and a murderer. Yes, it's good to stand up for free speech, but is this the right fight? Is it worth the cost?"

Reluctantly, three unhappy students agreed to alter their papers and not protest. Hannah sighed in relief when her students left her office and trooped down the stairs. She was not proud of her part in this maneuver, but she had pulled it off.

After Frank pushed open the door to leave Drake Hall, he turned to Gina and Brad, who were right behind him, and said, "We all got the message. Officially, we no longer will have anything to do with Matthew Baker. But there's more I want to know. No, I should say, more I have to know. How about you two? We can still investigate quietly. Unofficially. Do you want to join me?"

Brad and Gina simultaneously said, "Yes."

Chapter 39

Hannah was tired. On her way home from work, she decided that she would make a lousy international diplomat. Peacekeeping was exhausting. When she pulled into her driveway, she spotted a sheet of paper taped to her front door. She fervently hoped that whatever was written on the paper would not plunge her into further turmoil.

Hannah got out of her car, hesitantly walked up to her door, and grabbed the paper.

Oh, thank goodness. Nothing's wrong, she thought after she read these words, *I'm waiting for you on your deck. Meet me there. Love, Ethan.*

Hannah could feel the heat burning in her cheeks. She knew she was blushing. She rushed into her house and quickly ran upstairs. She ran a comb through her hair and quickly smeared on some lipstick.

Not a makeover, but at least I look a little better. Hannah gazed critically at her reflection in the mirror. She frowned. *I wish I had time to change into something more flattering. But Ethan must know I'm here. He must have heard me drive up and park, and I have no idea how long he's been out on the deck. Wouldn't be fair to keep him waiting. Guess this "old reliable" faded sundress will have to do.*

Hannah took a deep breath to calm herself and resolutely marched down the stairs. Much to her amazement, when she walked out onto her deck, Hannah found that Ethan was not alone. Audrey, the neighborhood black cat, was contentedly sitting in Ethan's lap and purring as Ethan absently stroked her back. His attention was focused on the computer screen in front of him.

"How did you do that?" Hannah asked. "I've been feeding Audrey for three years, but she's always been skittish and never has allowed me to pet her. How did you get her to sit in your lap?"

Ethan looked up and laughed. "Hey there. I've been waiting for you for some time. In fact, after I finished my beer, I thought a second wouldn't hurt. When I went back to my folks' house to grab another, I picked up a package of nuts from the counter. Got back here, and the next thing I knew, I was being watched by this feline. Well, I had my computer on the table and checked if cats could eat unsalted peanuts. When I read that they could, I thought it was only fair to share. So, I gave her a few. The next thing I knew, this cat was rubbing my leg, but I was intent on doing a little online research. Guess she wanted to be closer to the nuts on the table because she jumped up and suddenly was in my lap. I fully expected her to leave after we finished the nuts. I'm surprised she's still here."

After Ethan finished talking, Audrey languidly stretched, jumped off his lap, meowed once, flicked her tail, and then ran off. Hannah and Ethan both laughed.

"Sit down, Hannah. I'll be right back," Ethan said. He closed his computer, tucked it under his arm, and jogged next door.

A few minutes later, Ethan returned holding a large tray. On the tray were half a glass of white wine, paper plates, napkins, chopsticks, and a large brown paper bag.

"What's all this?" Hannah asked.

"It's what's left of my folks' Chinese take-out meal. They ordered way too much and suggested I share the leftovers with you."

"Oh, it smells great. You'll have to thank them for me. How's your dad doing? How's his recovery coming along?"

Ethan said, "He's getting grumpier every day. Has no patience with his doctors or therapists. Which I guess is good. Means he's feeling better. He's anxious to get back to his gardening. Soon he won't need my help. Soon things are bound to change around here."

Oh, Hannah thought, *that means Ethan will be heading back to Philadelphia. Oh, well, all good things do end, and this "whatever we have" was not meant to last.*

Ethan emptied the bag and arranged an assortment of white containers on the table. He used a spoon to place dumplings, Lo Mein, and several vegetable dishes on two paper plates.

"Gave you a bit of everything, but there's still more left. So, eat up. And there's half a glass of white wine for you. But I've got to ask. Why only half a glass? You told me on our walk around the lake that you only drink half a glass of wine at a time. You sure are a disciplined lady. I could never stop and drink just half a bottle of beer."

Hannah smiled. "I'm surprised you remembered. I've never been much of a drinker, and half a glass is just the right amount for me when I splurge and have a little white wine. I hate to admit it, but I gain weight easily. So, I'd rather eat my calories than drink them. And I do love to eat. Now when it comes to a chocolate candy bar, there's no way I could stop at half and save the rest for later. Thank you so much for dinner. I had a bad day, and I really appreciate this treat."

"Glad to help. I wanted to see you tonight. Wanted to tell you that everything's been taken care of with the Parkerville police and campus security. They both have all your information now. You can relax. You can forget about Matthew Baker and everything related to those grisly murders. And tell your students that they can safely move on, too."

"Thank you, Ethan. I'm so relieved. Thanks for helping me out."

But how could Hannah just move on when she had more questions. Frank had piqued her interest in Ken Graybill. Graybill was known to be a drug dealer, yet he had never been arrested. If high school kids knew where Graybill had conducted his shady deals, then why hadn't the police caught on and nabbed him? Would the Baker family be alive and well today if their son had not become dependent on the mood-altering drugs he bought from Graybill?

"Ethan, may I ask you a few questions?"

"Wait a sec. I've got something for you." And then Ethan pulled a small object from his pocket and slid it across the table. It was a key chain.

Ethan said, "You now own a pepper spray key chain. Carry it with you and be safe. No reason not to take that threat you got yesterday seriously. The Parkerville police have the note, but I don't think they'll learn much from it. You've got to be careful and alert."

"Okay, I promise," Hannah said.

"So, why was it a bad day? Did your students give you a hard time?"

"Well, the three who have been researching the Baker case were upset when I told them they had to revise their papers, eliminate everything related to Matthew Baker. They exploded. But I wasn't angry with them. I was angry with myself. My students complained that it's unfair to censor them, and they're right. I wish I could have fought for them. Instead, I caved for the good of the program."

"And you did the right thing. Hannah, life is unfair. People have to do what they must to survive. You know the old saying. It's a dog-eat-dog world."

"That's harsh from the man who just fed a hungry cat."

"Okay. You got me there. But bending a bit can't hurt you or your students. They did agree to back away from Matthew Baker. Right?"

"Yes, they did."

"Good. Now just concentrate on that, on all the good you did today. On how many people you helped. And the day's not over yet. There's more good to come."

"Ethan, what are you talking about?"

"Well, I was going to wait till we finished our meal. But I think you should open your fortune cookie right now."

Hannah thought, *That's weird. What's going on?*

Hannah picked up the fortune cookie Ethan offered her, cracked it open, and pulled out the paper message. It said, "You are charming and influential. Someone close to you will alter his life just to please you."

Hannah was confused. She read the fortune again. She still was confused.

Ethan reached for her hand and grinned. "I hope you like your fortune. It took me forever to wiggle it into your cookie with a tweezers. Believe me, with my big hands, it wasn't easy. So, do you get it? Do you understand what it means?"

What tiptoed to the front of Hannah's mind was, *A proposal. Oh, no. Please, no.*

Ethan said, "Let me tell you how you changed the course of my life."

And then he did. And Hannah lost her opportunity to find out more about Ken Graybill.

Chapter 40

Hours later, when Hannah was talking to her friend on the phone, Jodi squealed, "How romantic! He actually inserted his own message into a fortune cookie. Oh, Hannah, what further proof do you need? This guy has it bad for you. Ethan went to a lot of trouble to show you how much he cares. I'm impressed. Now tell me, what were you wearing when all this was happening?"

"Oh," Hannah said. "I was afraid you would ask that. Now, in my defense, I didn't expect to see Ethan tonight, and it was a very hot day."

"Oh, no. Don't tell me. You were wearing that baggy blue and yellow checked sundress. You know I've told you a million times to retire that old thing."

"I know. But it's very comfortable, and I'm attached to it. Please, forget about my clothes. There are more important things to talk about. I have a confession to make. When I read that fortune, I thought it might be a proposal. Why did my mind go there? After all, I only met Ethan a little over a week ago. It's just that he's so intense and moves so fast. I feel like I'm on a tilt-a-whirl ride when I'm with him. I don't know if I like or fear spinning around. When I read the fortune and learned that Ethan was going to change his life for me, I panicked. Then, when he explained that his plans had nothing to do with marriage, I was both relieved and disappointed. Does that make any sense?"

"Hannah, no one ever said that dating at our age was easy. Divorced guys carry around a lot of baggage and can send confusing signals."

"But things have gotten more complicated. I thought Ethan would return to his job in Philadelphia when his dad no longer needed his help.

Instead, tonight he told me that he's moving back to the Lancaster area for good. For me. That's a lot of pressure. He's changing his whole life around for me. It's crazy. We know so little about each other."

"Did you tell him how you feel?" Jodi asked.

"I was about to, but then he said that this visit with his folks had made him realize that they are getting older and could use his help. He added that he was burnt-out. Tired of chasing bad guys in a dirty, noisy city and ready to return to Lancaster County."

"Sounds like he has good reasons to move back home. You may be one of them, but you're not the only one."

"Yes. But then why did he put it all on me in the fortune cookie message? He wrote he was changing his life to please me. Oh, and get this. Ethan no longer wants to stay in law enforcement. Remember I told you that he was working on his computer while he was waiting for me. He was researching how to become a real estate agent in Pennsylvania. Said he's always been interested in homes. Loves going to open houses and watching the housing market. And while we ate our meal, he spent the whole time telling me what my house would sell for and asking me questions about my mortgage."

"A bit odd, but maybe he was just practicing his real estate skills."

"But I couldn't help him. Aaron paid off our mortgage years ago, and I have no idea what the current rates are."

"Wow. You had an interesting evening. And from what you told me earlier, quite a day. I know it was rough, but I'm happy to hear that your students will keep their scholarships and that you'll keep your job. Hang in there, my friend. Tomorrow is bound to be calmer. Both with your students at Buchanan and the romance taking place in your own backyard."

Jodi was right. Hannah had experienced a roller coaster of a day. However, before she ended the call, Hannah told Jodi that Ethan had gone to the Parkerville police on her behalf. There was nothing more for Hannah to do. Hannah felt she could finally relax and stop worrying about the Baker murders. Or could she?

Chapter 41

Wednesday, June 26

The next afternoon, Brad, Gina, and Frank were huddled around a small outdoor table at a coffee shop a few blocks away from campus. Frank's computer was in front of him on the table, and on the screen were two columns. One was titled "What We Know," and the other, "What We Don't Know."

Brad said, "I was blown away when Professor Stein let it drop that Helen Baker had spoken to her before the murders about an intruder coming in and out of the house. Why didn't Professor Stein tell us that earlier?"

"Yeah. That bothered me, too," Frank said. "Do you think Matthew was just acting goofy and playing tricks on his family? Or was it someone else? Could it have been the real murderer?"

Brad said, "I don't know. What do you think, Gina? You've been awfully quiet today. Anything wrong?"

"Sorry," Gina said. "I'm really tired. Didn't sleep well. I agreed to keep at this because I didn't want to disappoint you guys. I like being on your team. But late last night, I got a call from Sandra Metzler. She was in tears. Said she'd been having nightmares about the eyes ever since she spoke to me. She thought she had worked past her rape, but my questions set her back. I feel terrible. Sandra pleaded with me not to use her name in my paper. Not to reveal her identity. I, of course, was able to say 'no problem' as we'd agreed to no longer cite the Baker case. I explained all that to her, and now, here I am. Talking about her with you two. Am I a terrible person or what?"

Brad drummed his fingers on the table. "I do remember there was something about eyes in your taped interview."

"Yes," Gina said. "Sandra said that sometimes she remembered blue eyes and sometimes brown ones floating above her when she was raped. But remember, her head was bleeding, and her thoughts were muddled."

"Still," Frank said. "Two sets of eyes. Could that mean …"

"Two people. Possibly two rapists," Brad finished for him. "And, maybe, neither one was Matthew Baker."

"Or he might be one of the rapists," Gina said, "if there were two. Frank, you saw Baker. Do you remember if his eyes are blue, brown, or some other color?"

"Blue," Frank said. "They're definitely a bright blue."

Brad said, "I wonder if Sandra told the police about the eyes right after the rape, or did she remember them later."

"Oh," Gina said. "I bet the police looked into the matter. They must have. But, even if they didn't, what can we do about it now?"

Brad said, "Sandra never filed charges, but maybe the police saved something in an evidence box just in case Sandra changed her mind. Something with DNA on it. Something that could tell us if Matthew Baker really raped his cousin."

"If they found some evidence," Gina said, "the police should have it stored somewhere. Sandra was just fifteen years old when she was raped. In Pennsylvania, there isn't a statute of limitations for raping or sexually assaulting a minor. I found that out for my paper."

Frank said, "We've got to find a way to learn more."

"Frank," Gina said, "what about your cousin network? You seem to have relatives everywhere in Lancaster County. How about in the Parkerville police? Do you know anyone who could fill us in? Let us know if the police ever considered that there might have been two rapists?"

"Hmmm," said Frank. "Can't think of anyone."

Brad said, "My Uncle Bob may be able to help us. He has clients of all sorts, and he's in and out of the Parkerville station all the time. I bet he could hook us up with someone who'd be discreet. Unfortunately, Uncle Bob will be in his cabin in the Poconos till the end of the month. It's in this crazy valley, a dead spot for cell reception. There's no way to reach him till he comes home."

"I hate to wait," Frank said. "What about that neighbor of Professor Stein's? The cop who talked to the Parkerville police for us. Maybe Professor Stein could ask him to help us out. She said that he'd been a Parkerville cop. He might know something. Might have been around when the Baker murders took place. Maybe we'll get lucky, and he'll be able to help us himself. Or maybe he knows someone who can quietly look into things for us."

Gina said, "Professor Stein may refuse to help us. We're not supposed to be doing this."

"I know," said Frank, "but what else can we do? If we go to the Parkerville station and talk to the police ourselves, it may get out that we're still asking questions, that we haven't given up on Baker. Then we'd be in trouble, and the whole scholarship program could tank. We can't let that happen. But I really have to find out if those two sets of eyes are important."

"Okay," Gina said. "I get it. I want to know, too. We'd better head over to Professor Stein's office right now before I lose my nerve. I just hope we won't regret this."

Chapter 42

Thursday, June 27

Hannah collapsed into her office chair. One thing after another had filled her day. Now she realized she had to make a decision. She had resisted doing so for hours, but now it was time. There was nothing else to distract her. Nothing else to do. She simply couldn't put it off any longer.

Yesterday, late in the afternoon, Brad, Gina, and Frank had spoken to her in her office. They explained why they needed her help.

Eighteen-year-old kids, Hannah thought. *They swing back and forth. First, they behaved like responsible adults. They agreed to do what is best for themselves and the program. And now they act like – well, like kids. Curious, willful, and determined. And reckless! Everyone could lose. And then there's Ethan. What will he think of me if I ask him for more favors? He was so eager to please me, to help me, but this may be asking too much. I guess, like it or not, I've made my decision if I'm worried about Ethan's reaction to it.*

Hannah rubbed her neck. It hurt and was rock hard. She knew what she was about to do would not ease the tension. She picked up her cell phone and tapped the speed dial number to connect her to Ethan.

"Hey, beautiful," Ethan said when he answered. "Is everything okay? Are you in trouble?"

"Everything's fine. This is not a 'come save me call.' Rather it's an 'I've been thinking about you call.' You've been very generous. Since we met, you've treated me to several meals and helped me out in so many ways. I'd like to repay you. I'd like to cook a meal for you to say thank you.

Do you have plans for tomorrow night? Are you able to come over to my house for dinner?"

"Now that sounds great. I'll be there. And I'll pick up a bottle of Thorn Hill white wine. I know that's your favorite. Maybe I'll find a way to get you to drink a whole glass while we're eating dinner."

Hannah laughed. "I don't know about that, but I'm happy you can come." Then she added in a more serious tone, "And, Ethan, would it be out of line for me to ask you for another favor? You've been so good about contacting the local police for me and my students. I know it's asking a lot, but would you be willing to help my students just one more time? Let me tell you what they need."

There was a long silence after Hannah finished speaking.

"I wouldn't ask for myself," Hannah said, "but I'm afraid if I don't help my students that they may do something rash and irresponsible. Something that could ruin everything."

"Hannah, I don't understand. This is supposed to be over. Closed. Finished."

"I know. I thought so, too. But my students are insistent. They want to know if it's significant that Sandra Metzler remembers both blue and brown eyes. They won't back down."

"But this is ridiculous. You're their teacher. Just tell them there's nothing more to find. If you have to, just make up some plausible explanation."

"I can't do that, Ethan. I can't lie to them. And, maybe, just maybe, they're right. Maybe this is a question that needs to be asked."

Ethan's response was a long, exasperated sigh.

Ethan said, "Okay. I'll look into this for you. Tell your students to leave it to me. Tell them to stay far away from the police and the station. This has to be done right, or it will come back to bite us all. I'll take care of everything."

"Oh, Ethan, thank you. I really do appreciate your help."

"But I may not be of much help. After the murders, I, along with most of the force, focused on gathering evidence that would prove that Baker was guilty. I didn't have anything to do with Metzler. She was a rape victim and a minor. Our female detective, Erin Summers, privately questioned Metzler and did her best to shield the girl from the media. I heard that Erin left the Parkerville force after she married, but I think she still lives in the area. I'll try to track her down. She may remember if Metzler mentioned two different sets of eyes. But don't get your hopes up. All this happened fourteen years ago. Sandra Metzler never went after Baker for the rape, so the rape wasn't a priority."

"I know you'll try your best. I owe you so much."

"I'm hoping you'll move on. We have better things to talk about than this grisly case. I, for one, would much rather concentrate on us and our future than these murders from the past."

Oh my, Hannah thought, *a future involving Ethan. Is that something I want? Am I ready for that?*

Chapter 43

Friday, June 28

The following evening, Hannah admired her dining room table. She smiled. It took some doing, but she had pulled it off. Although she had not formally entertained in some time, she had not lost the knack. She had washed and ironed her white damask tablecloth, set the table with her wedding crystal and china plates, and cooked her old reliable, "company-pleasing" recipes. The house was clean, delicious aromas emanated from the kitchen, and the table looked pretty and welcoming. And Hannah looked pretty and welcoming, too. She had left work early to perform some magic in the kitchen and on herself. Hannah was relieved that her wayward curls had obeyed her commands and had not frizzed, and she was wearing a "Jodi-approved" outfit that was becoming. She was ready for her dinner with Ethan.

Her meal was ready for Ethan, too. Hannah had learned early in her marriage that she had neither the time nor the patience to be a gourmet cook, so she always relied on simple, hearty recipes. She had put a roaster chicken and potatoes in her crockpot that morning and covered them with a mushroom sauce. The rest was easy and quick to assemble. She had whipped up a simple appetizer, combined colorful vegetables to make a salad, and warmed up a loaf of Italian bread. Dessert was an apple pie from the local bakery. So, all was ready. There was nothing more to do. And that is when Hannah's heart started to flutter.

Calm down, Hannah gave herself strict orders. *It's just a dinner.* But she was worried. *Was Ethan just flirting when he spoke about our having a future together? Or was he serious?*

When the doorbell rang, Hannah gulped. Ethan was waiting on the other side of the door. There was no turning back. Hannah opened her front door and admitted her guest. Ethan greeted her with a dazzling smile. He was wearing khakis and a pale blue button-down shirt, and he came bearing gifts, a bottle of Thorn Hill's Pinot Grigio and a bouquet of colorful flowers bound together by a bright yellow ribbon.

"Hi," Ethan said. "Mom wouldn't let me leave the house without flowers. You know how fussy she is about her gardens. She must really like you to part with these. She said I was to tell you to put them in water right away."

"Oh, Ethan, they're lovely. Do thank her for me. And you brought wine, too. Thank you."

"Yes, ma'am. I deliver as promised."

"Well, make yourself at home. Dinner is ready. I'll just pop into the kitchen and put the flowers in a vase. Wine goblets and an opener are on the table. Why don't you open the bottle and pour some wine into our glasses? I'll bring out the appetizer platter."

"Sounds good. And how's this for a plan? Let's enjoy dinner, and afterward, we'll talk about the Baker case and finally put that ugly matter to rest."

"Really, Ethan? You have answers for me. That was quick."

"As I just said, I deliver as promised."

One hour and forty-five minutes later, Ethan sat back in his chair and contentedly sighed.

"That was one great meal. My mom is many fine things, but she's definitely not a good cook. I really enjoyed the food. And I've missed this. Leisurely enjoying a dinner and having a good conversation. This has been so relaxing. Everything was delicious," Ethan said.

Hannah smiled and thought, *Yes, it was nice to have dinner with you. You're great company and a wonderful storyteller. But, please, tell me what the police had to say about that horrible note and Sandra Metzler's rape. I can't wait a minute longer. Darn it all! I'm as bad as my students.*

Hannah raised her cup to her lips and finished her coffee. "Thank you, Ethan. I'm glad you enjoyed the meal. Now, I don't mean to rush you, but I'm dying to know what the police told you. Did you find out why Sandra Metzler remembers both blue and brown eyes?"

Ethan said, "Why don't we move over to your deck? I can tell you what I learned there. What do you say?"

Hannah wanted to say, *No. Just start talking.* But instead, she agreed to his plan. After all, he was her guest.

After they were comfortably ensconced on the deck, Hannah turned to Ethan and said, "Okay. Begin. No more delays."

"I'm afraid there really isn't much to tell. First, nothing came of the note that was on your car. You slid the note into a plastic bag, and yours were the only prints on the note. So, that was a dead end. The note was written on ordinary paper. No marks on it. Nothing unusual to track down. Same for the marker used to write the note. It's the type commonly sold in discount, stationery, and chain stores all over the country. We don't have a handwriting sample to compare to the note, so the lettering, phrasing, and misspelling don't help us either."

"Okay," Hannah said. "And the rest?"

"I found out there was a small fire in the basement of the station three years ago. That's where the evidence boxes are stored, and the sprinkler system flooded the place and made a mess of everything. A lot of boxes and files were destroyed. I had a friend look this morning, but he couldn't find anything down there with Sandra Metzler's name on it. Sorry about that. Guess anything that might have been saved related to the rape was either ruined by the fire or by water damage."

"What a shame," Hannah said. "My students were hoping there would be some DNA evidence that would prove who really raped Sandra. Anything else?"

"Nothing significant. I tracked down Erin Summers, the detective who dealt with Metzler. Gave her a call. She remembers the case. Erin spent a lot of time with the girl. Erin felt really sorry for her as Sandra was so young and scared. The problem for Erin was that Sandra's story changed with each retelling. Probably due to Metzler's head wound. Erin did say that Sandra was worried about eyes."

"She did?"

"Yes. Sandra talked about them a day or two after the rape. Brown and blue eyes looking down at her. Erin said she was stumped. Then she solved the riddle when she happened to visit Sandra in the hospital during a shift change, a time when Sandra's day nurse and night nurse were both in her room at the same time. The nurses regularly monitored Sandra and changed the bandages on her head. While examining Metzler, they would have been looking down at their patient. One nurse had brown eyes, and the other had blue. Easy to understand Sandra's confusion. I think that covers everything. Now we can talk about other matters."

"Hold on. Helen Baker believed someone was moving things about in her home before the murders. What did the police say when you told them that? And what did they make of Ken Graybill's boasts that someone is paying him not to talk?"

"Hannah, I did inform the proper people. But no one is going to consider these things as leads unless there is more to substantiate them or something more happens. There's nothing more we can do."

Hannah hesitated. Ethan had just closed the book on everything related to Matthew Baker, but she still wanted to know more about Ken Graybill. One opportunity to quiz Ethan about Graybill had already slipped through her fingers, and she did not want that to happen again. Graybill was part of the Baker murder mystery drama. But how important was he? Was he just a despicable dealer, a supportive actor, or did he play a more prominent role?

"Ethan, I've been meaning to ask you a few questions about Ken Graybill."

"Good grief, Hannah. Why? How can you possibly have more questions?"

"One of my students happened to mention that Graybill lived in the trailer park near Lake Keller. At that time, your folks were living there too. Did you ever run into him? Did the police know what Graybill was up to? Why wasn't he caught if it was well known that he made drug deals at Lake Keller?"

"Really, Hannah? You want to talk about Graybill now? I told you we ruled him out. He had an alibi at the time of the murders and rape. Why are you so fixated on the Bakers? Why can't you let this go?"

"I don't know, Ethan. My mind keeps spinning around Ken Graybill. Especially after you told me that he thought Bruce Baker cheated his father. A teen with a grudge who had lived in the house, knew it inside and out, could have figured out a way to sneak into the place and move things about to upset the Baker family. Maybe, on the night of the murders, the family came home and found him there, and things got out of hand. Maybe way out of hand. What do you think?"

"I think you have a vivid imagination. Probably comes from reading and teaching so many novels. Most of the time, the simplest explanation is the right one. Matthew Baker was an angry kid, and we found him covered in blood and holding the murder weapon. Hannah, a lot of people were and are convinced that Baker is guilty: the police, the prosecutor, the jury, and the judge. They can't all be wrong. Let it go."

"Okay. But just one more thing."

"All right, Hannah. Just one more. And then we stop. This has got to stop."

"Ethan, if high school kids knew where Graybill sold drugs, why didn't the police? Why didn't they just go there and arrest him?"

"Well, I don't want you to think we didn't try. Because we did. We even set up a sting operation that went sour. I don't know how he managed to elude us. Graybill wasn't clever. So, there had to be someone who tipped him off. No matter. Graybill stopped dealing when the Feds and the Pennsylvania Drug Enforcement Agency guys swooped in and grabbed a couple of his underlings selling drugs in a club in Reading. Caught them with a big cache of illegal substances. A real drugstore. But they wouldn't deal. They wouldn't give up Graybill. I don't know why. I don't know how Graybill pulled that off. But he must have been worried, unsure if they'd remain loyal, because he immediately left Parkerville. The last I heard, he was living somewhere in Colorado, so I was surprised when your students spotted him at one his old hangouts, Friendly Fred's. I have no idea why he's back. Now, are you satisfied? Can we just enjoy the sunset and talk about something else?"

"Oh, forgive me, Ethan. I have to do something in the house before the sun sets. I'll be right back."

Ethan mumbled, "Now what?" after Hannah left. The door to the kitchen was open, and he saw Hannah lighting candles. He smiled. Perhaps things were about to take a romantic turn after all.

Hannah returned to the deck and settled into her chair. She said, "I bet we have a pretty sunset tonight. Last night the colors were so vivid and . . ."

But she did not have the opportunity to finish her sentence. Ethan reached for her. His arms tightly circled her body. He pulled her over to his chair, which he had lowered to a reclining position. Suddenly, he pressed his mouth harshly against hers. His kiss was rough, persistent, and demanding. Ethan crushed Hannah with his body. Hannah felt smothered. She tried to wriggle free, but she was trapped beneath him. When the kiss ended, Ethan loosened his grip on Hannah and began to run his hands over her body, oblivious to the fact that she was struggling to move away from him.

"Stop. No," Hannah cried, pushing hard against his chest to put some distance between them.

"Why? What's wrong?" Ethan looked confused. "Isn't this what you want, too? Are you worried someone will see us? Do you want to go inside?"

Hannah was upset and shaking.

"I don't get it, Hannah. You were married. You're not some naive kid. You know the score. We're two grownups that are attracted to each other. I can feel it, and you gave me all the right signals. Dinner, wine, and the candles."

"Oh, Ethan, dinner was just a 'thank you' meal. Nothing more. And the wine, you might recall, was your idea. I didn't realize drinking some wine would send you some sort of romantic signal. As to the candles, I should've explained. It's Friday night. Remember, I told you I'm Jewish. I lit two candles to welcome the Sabbath. I also lit a candle for my husband. This is the anniversary date of his death, so I lit a special *Yahrzeit* candle for him."

Ethan sighed. "I'm sorry. I read this all wrong. Look, Hannah, you know where we're heading, and I'm very ready to go there. You're beautiful and smart and everything I want, but you can't keep a guy waiting forever."

Chapter 44

After Ethan left, Hannah went back into the kitchen. Suddenly, she was very tired. She took one look at the dirty dishes piled in the sink and groaned. She did not have the energy to clean up. Instead, Hannah locked the doors, turned off the lights, and climbed up the stairs to her bedroom. It took every bit of her willpower to resist immediately collapsing into bed. She quickly changed into a nightshirt, washed off her make-up, and brushed her teeth. However, after she settled her head on her pillow, she could not sleep. She replayed the evening in her mind, over and over. She thought about everything she had said and done.

What happened? Hannah asked herself. She was embarrassed. *Did I lead him on? I didn't mean to, but did I? I feel like I'm on a runaway train. Should I apply the brakes or rush down the track? What do I really want? And the timing. Of course, Ethan didn't know that this is the anniversary of Aaron's death, but I did. Why did I invite Ethan over tonight? And why am I thinking about another man now, on this night of all nights, when all my thoughts should be focused on Aaron?*

Hannah punched her pillow. She moved from her back to her side, but neither position was comfortable. She was now too wide awake to sleep. She turned on the lamp on her bedside table and grabbed a book from the stack beside the lamp. It was a romance novel. Not the type of book she usually read, but Jodi had insisted on passing it on to her because it "sizzled."

When Hannah's alarm clock buzzed the next morning, the book was lying on Hannah's chest.

I'll have to tell Jodi that what sizzled for her fizzled for me. But I must admit, the book did have one redeeming virtue; it helped me fall asleep.

Hannah pushed herself out of bed. *It's strange,* she thought, *I've read so many books in my lifetime, but not a single one has prepared me for meeting someone like Ethan. And I can't follow the example of the conflicted woman in this novel Jodi likes. I can't just run off to Nashville and turn into a promiscuous, middle-aged country rock star. That's not a viable option.*

* * *

Later that morning, Hannah attended the Saturday morning service at her synagogue and recited the traditional mourners' prayer, *Kaddish,* to commemorate Aaron's death. The nervous *Bar Mitzvah* boy reading from the Torah during the service reminded her of her children when they were thirteen years old and had stood in the very same spot. The twins had celebrated Seth's *Bar Mitzvah* and Sophie's *Bat Mitzvah* together. Hannah remembered that Seth had driven them crazy for weeks beforehand. He was worried his voice would crack at crucial points and cause everyone to laugh, and Sophie was no help at all. She kept teasing him, assuring him it would. But the two were well-prepared for their special day, and, mercifully, Seth's voice had been strong and steady. The twins had led the entire service and flawlessly sung and recited all the Hebrew prayers. Both Hannah and Aaron had been so proud of their children. It had been a wonderful and unforgettable day.

Oh, Aaron, Hannah thought when she drove home after the service, *why did you have to die? You were supposed to grow old beside me. I loved you, and I loved being your wife. I knew what was expected of me. I knew exactly what to do.*

After Hannah returned home, she cleaned up her kitchen and dining room. Normally, she hated doing household chores, but today she found the simple, ordinary acts of washing dishes and sweeping floors strangely soothing. They were mindless tasks, and her mind welcomed the mini vacation. When the rooms were, once again, clean and orderly, Hannah rewarded herself for a job well done. She polished off the remains of last night's dinner and scooped a generous portion of vanilla ice cream into a bowl for dessert.

Hannah poked her head out the kitchen door, and after she had ascertained that the coast was clear, no Ethan in sight, she walked out onto her deck with her bowl and spoon.

Coward, Hannah said to herself. *I'm a coward. But I don't want to see Ethan again until I figure things out. I just don't know what to say to him.*

Hannah sunk into a deck chair and then dove into her ice cream. Her mind wandered, and she found herself thinking first about Aaron and then about Ethan. Aaron had been so easy to understand. What you saw was what you got. Aaron was sweet, considerate, and steady. She always knew Aaron would never break her heart. Ethan was different. He was dynamic and exciting, but was he a man a woman could depend on? Hannah's thoughts were interrupted by a loud meow.

"Hello, Audrey," Hannah said to the black cat, who was licking her paws a few feet away from Hannah. "You came just in time. I still have some ice cream left."

The cat's green eyes followed Hannah's every move. Hannah placed the bowl on the deck, and the cat, true to form, licked it clean, meowed, and then ran off.

Hannah called to the retreating feline, "You're welcome, Audrey. See you again soon."

A moment later, Hannah was startled when she heard a female voice say, "That's one lucky cat. She ate a bit with us and then got to have dessert with you."

Hannah turned and blinked. Had Ethan turned into a woman overnight? The person talking to her, standing near the deck, looked exactly like Ethan, except the hair was longer and the waist was smaller. The figure was wearing gardening gloves and a flowered baseball cap.

"Hi. I'm Lydia. Ethan's sister. I'm helping my mom with the gardening today. It's a bit late to mulch, but Mom has been so busy taking care of Dad that she hasn't been able to keep up with the yard. I drove in from Delaware last night. Ethan's been good about helping out, but when he tries to work in the garden, he pulls out the flowers and leaves the weeds. Just can't figure out which is which. You must be Hannah, right?"

Hannah nodded.

"Well, I'm glad to meet you. All morning long, I've been listening to my mom talk about you. Hannah this and Hannah that. She's very pleased that Ethan is finally interested in a quality woman. I think she's exceptionally happy that you have two grown children. Her feeling is that since Ethan hasn't given her grandchildren that your children can provide her with great-grandchildren to play with. And your living right next door will make seeing them so easy and convenient. Of course, that's a ways off, but she likes to plan ahead."

Hannah did not know what to make of Lydia's news. But this was not a problem as Lydia was rattling off all this information at a very rapid pace. There simply was no opportunity to register a response nor interject a comment.

"And Mom is willing to overlook you're being Jewish because you're just what Ethan needs. A good influence. A stable person. Not at all like the type he usually falls for. Mom told me you saw Ethan fighting with Meghan over money. Meghan is wife number three. Ethan always chooses the same type; he never learns. He likes young shapely, blond beauties, but they can't control him. If he has a dollar in his pocket, he's just gotta make a bet. But you're different. Not at all like the ones he usually falls for. Mom thinks you'll be able to keep him in line and get him to Gamblers Anonymous. And now that I've met you, I think she's right. I think you're just what Ethan needs. Don't you agree?"

Hannah was speechless.

Chapter 45

When Jodi and Hannah talked on the phone later that afternoon, her flabbergasted friend said, "Ethan's sister really said that?"

"Yes," Hannah answered. "She said it was to my advantage that I was nothing like the beautiful, young women Ethan usually falls for and that her mom would overlook my being Jewish."

"And those were supposed to be compliments?"

"I believe so," Hannah answered. "I think Lydia just assumed I agreed with her. There was no time for me to get a word in. And, even if I'd been able to, I don't know what I would have said."

"Gosh, she dropped a lot on you. Three wives and a gambling problem. This superman of yours is complicated."

"Yes," Hannah agreed. "And there's more."

Hannah quickly summarized all that had occurred during her Friday night dinner with Ethan.

"So," Hannah said, "now I don't know what to do. I don't know what to think."

"Hannah, you do know more than you're willing to admit."

"What do you mean?"

"You were protecting yourself from yourself. Why else would you invite the guy over on the anniversary of Aaron's death? You knew you'd be safe. You could have chosen a different night, but you chose that one. You knew you would never let things get hot and heavy with Ethan when you were focused on remembering Aaron."

Hannah did not respond.

Jodi said, "Come on. You know I'm right."

Hannah sighed. "Yes, I think you are. I'm tempted by Ethan, but at the same time, I don't know if I'm ready to let go of Aaron and move on. I feel like I'm being unfaithful to my husband."

"We've been over all this. You know where I stand. I'm on the side of the living. Hannah, you gave your all to Aaron, and now it's time for you to think of yourself. It's sad that Aaron died at such a young age, but denying yourself the pleasure of male company will not bring him back. I knew Aaron. He loved you. He would want you to be happy."

"It would be easier if Ethan's folks weren't living right next door. What if Ethan and I become a couple and then break up? Would I still be able to pleasantly chat with his parents? Or would I fear running into them every time I walked into my back yard? And how do I get past Ethan's three ex-wives and his gambling problem?"

"I hear you. He's got a murky past, but, remember, people around our age are not newly minted. We all have baggage of one type or another. For example, the guy I'm going out with tonight has seven children."

"Jodi, another new guy? And, really, seven children? Where did you meet this one?"

"He's a mime. Actually, an actor, but he played a mime in a show I saw on Wednesday. It was theater-in-the-round and very intimate. We eyed each other when he was on stage and made a connection. After the play, the actors signed programs. As he was autographing mine, he asked me out for coffee, and over coffee, he told me about his two ex-wives and seven children. By the way, three of the seven are identical triplets."

"Oh, Jodi, your life is unbelievable. Are you really interested in this fellow?"

"I'll get a better handle on things after we spend more time together. Got to run. His name is David, and I'm meeting him for dinner at a restaurant across town. I'll see how this date goes."

"Wait, what about the other guys, the man from the grocery store and your contractor?"

"Oh, they're still in the picture. I like to keep my options open. You know me. I'm always open and honest with the men I date. But when I'm serious about a fellow and ready for sex, I drop all the others and remain faithful to my man. I do want to find a good man to marry. In the meantime, I see no reason not to go out and enjoy my life. I have to get a move on if I'm to get to the restaurant on time. Talk to you soon."

Hannah tilted her head back and closed her eyes after the call ended. She was sitting in an overstuffed rocker in her bedroom. She pushed the chair back and forth with her feet, and the rocking motion was soothing. She thought about Jodi, her beautiful, wonderful, and irrepressible friend. Jodi always rushed forward to take a big bite out of life. But that was not Hannah's style. Hannah hung back, weighing the consequences of her actions. Hannah nibbled and evaluated and was safe and secure, but was she missing out?

I wish I could be more like Jodi, Hannah thought. *But it would be such a big leap. No wonder Jodi enjoyed the romantic antics of that middle-aged country rock star in the novel she recommended.*

Hannah's phone pinged. There was a text. It was from Ethan. *Stopping by. Will see you in ten minutes.*

Hannah thought, *Just enough time to drive myself crazy wondering what he wants to say to me. And, after last night's debacle, what in the world should I say to him?*

Chapter 46

Nine minutes later, Ethan knocked on Hannah's front door, and after she opened it, he said, "I know I'm a minute early, but I couldn't wait. May I come in?" He held out a bouquet of red roses. "These are from a florist shop. Not my mom's garden. I want you to have something special to go along with my apology."

Hannah said, "They're beautiful. Thank you. Let's go into the kitchen. I'll put the flowers in a vase, and we can talk there."

Hannah turned and walked toward the kitchen, and Ethan followed her. He pulled out a chair by the kitchen table and sat down. Neither of them uttered a word while Hannah filled a vase with water, arranged the roses, and then used a kitchen towel to dry her hands. Hannah was flustered by Ethan's silence. She sat down on a chair across from him and impatiently waited. She did not want to be the first to speak. After all, he had initiated this encounter and said he wanted to apologize. But he did not say a word.

Finally, after another long, painful minute of silence, Ethan said, "This is tough. I don't want to blow it."

Hannah said, "Just start. I'll listen."

"Okay. First, I want to apologize for last night. I made a move, and you weren't ready for it. That's not what I do. That's not who I am. I don't know what came over me. I wasn't thinking straight. I promise you I can slow things down and move at your speed. Hannah, can you give a guy who's crazy about you a second chance?"

Hannah bit her lip. Her voice was soft and tentative. "I'm embarrassed. I'm sorry if I did or said anything that misled you."

"No. Don't worry. You just invited me over to share a meal. I read more into it because I wanted more."

"Still, last night was complicated. I wanted to cook for you and spend time with you, but another part of me was tied to my husband and his death. I should've explained."

"Why didn't you?"

Hannah hesitated. "I couldn't find the right words. My memories of Aaron are all I have left of him. I can talk to my children about their father, but I can't share him with anyone else. I'm scared because time is passing, and Aaron fades a bit every year. I need to cling to every scrap of him that I remember. I don't want to lose him."

Ethan reached for Hannah's hand across the table and held it.

"He must have been quite a guy for you to have loved him so much. But tell me, Hannah, why did you invite me to dinner last night of all nights?"

Hannah sighed. "It's a fair question. My friend Jodi thinks I was protecting myself. On some level, I must have realized that I would never succumb to a romantic impulse on the anniversary of Aaron's death."

Ethan smiled. "Then I do trigger a romantic impulse or two?"

"You do. But there's much to be considered."

"I bet you're referring to what my dear sister blabbed to you. She couldn't wait to tell me what she said. Lydia actually thought she was helping me out, clearing the air. But, look, I didn't lie. I told you about Meghan. I just didn't mention my other two exes. I didn't want to scare you off. You had a great marriage. I was afraid you'd turn your back on a guy who's made the same mistake three times. Doesn't say much for me, does it?"

"My friend Jodi believes that people around our age all have baggage of one type or another. I was one of the lucky ones. My marriage worked. Jodi says I can't expect everyone to be as fortunate."

"Now, that's a good way to look at things. I like this friend of yours. Sounds like she gives you good advice."

Hannah chuckled. "She's a force to be reckoned with. And most of the time, her advice is helpful."

"And Lydia also told you I like to gamble. Did Jodi give you advice about that, too?"

"Not yet. Do you have a gambling problem?"

"Of course not. Lydia's a drama queen. She blows everything up, way out of proportion. Yes, I bet a few bucks on sports games. Small amounts to make the games more exciting. Sometimes I win, and sometimes I lose. It's harmless fun. Nothing to worry about. Nothing I can't handle. I take it you're not a gambler."

Hannah laughed. "Me? No. I work too hard to take risks with my money. If I make a bet while playing gin rummy, it's small and harmless. Like loser buys the winner an ice cream cone."

"But it's still a wager. We all bet. It's natural. Buying stocks, joining the office pool to bet on the Superbowl, or playing bingo at church. Everyone gambles. You see that. Don't you?"

"Well, yes. But people have to be careful. They can become addicted to gambling and lose control of their lives and bankrupt their families."

"I agree. You're absolutely right, Hannah. But you don't need to worry about me. I only gamble a little for fun. Now, what you're doing is far riskier."

"What do you mean?"

"I checked, and the police still don't have a clue who wrote that threatening note you found on your car. You may be gambling with your life."

"But I've been careful. I do carry that pepper spray you gave me. Besides, nothing more has happened."

"And we have to make sure nothing will. Look, I've done my part. I've talked to the folks in the know and found out everything I could for you and your students. All your questions have been answered. It's time to move on and distance yourself from Matthew Baker. Then whoever threatened you will go away and stay away. I just want you to be safe. Okay?"

Always the pressure to stop investigating the Baker family murders. Why? Hannah asked herself. *And there's something else that's been bothering me. Ethan had an explanation for every one of my students' concerns. He tied up every loose end so quickly. Was that possible? He told me, just a short time ago, to make up answers to appease my students. Is that what he's done? Oh, I must be crazy. He says he's worried about me, and that's sweet. Why am I doubting him? It's silly.*

"Hannah, promise me you'll stop poking into this case."

"I do promise to talk to my students on Monday. I'll tell them what you found out."

"But that's not enough. I'm worried about you. I don't want you to get hurt."

"But Ethan . . ."

"Please, promise me you'll stop if there's any hint of danger."

"Okay. I promise. But nothing's happened since I found the note. I think it was just a prank, a bad joke."

"Maybe," Ethan said. "And maybe not."

Chapter 47

Sunday, June 30

Hannah felt a twinge of guilt when she looked at the alarm clock on her bedside table.

I can't believe it. It's 10:30. I never sleep this late on a Sunday morning, Hannah thought. *I'd better get a move on.*

Hannah swung her legs out of bed, stretched, and parted the curtains covering her bedroom windows. The sun was shining, beckoning Hannah to hurry up and get outside. She was content. Last night Ethan had assured her that he was willing to follow her lead, and that had eased the tension between them. It was one thing to share a meal and an evening with Ethan and quite another to share her bed. She needed more time. She had to believe, without any reservations, that she was important to Ethan and not just another conquest.

Yesterday, after Ethan apologized and promised not to rush Hannah, it was dinner time. As both of them were hungry, they raided Hannah's refrigerator and put together a quick meal of cheese omelets, toast, and sliced tomatoes. Afterward, they found an Alfred Hitchcock marathon on the classic TV channel, popped some popcorn, and settled in for a night of mystery movies. It was two in the morning when *The Maltese Falcon* ended.

As the film's credits scrolled across the TV screen, Ethan turned to Hannah and said, "I don't get that Sam Spade, the private eye in the movie. I'd be loyal to my lady love and protect her. I wouldn't turn her in to the police."

"But, Ethan," Hannah said, "she murdered Spade's partner. She had to be punished. Sam Spade knew that."

"No. I think they should have at least tried to make a clean getaway. They might have made it. In fact, I bet they would have."

Hannah was surprised and wondered why he said that. *Does he want me to think he's an incurable romantic, or does he mean it?*

Right before they parted, Ethan had been very chivalrous and had politely asked Hannah if he could kiss her goodnight. Hannah had shyly agreed, and Ethan had gently drawn her to him and held her close. A tingle had surged through Hannah when Ethan's lips softly touched hers. It was a sweet kiss, and she thought only of Ethan and forgot all about Sam Spade. However, this morning, as she was spreading cream cheese on her bagel, she puzzled over Ethan's odd reaction to the end of the movie.

Strange, she thought. *It's strange that Ethan, a police officer, would say it's okay for someone to get away with murder. Does he really believe that?*

Hannah sighed. She did not know the answer to her question because, truth be told, she really did not know Ethan that well. She took a small bite out of her bagel and looked out the kitchen window. She saw a ball of black fur curled on the edge of her deck.

Looks like I'm not the only one who snoozed away this Sunday morning, Hannah thought. *There's my favorite neighborhood cat, all curled up for a nap in the sun.*

Hannah poured herself a cup of coffee and added a dash of cream. She put the remainder of her bagel, her cup of coffee, and a bowl of cream for the friendly feline on a tray and opened her kitchen door. She walked outside. She carefully set the tray down on a table on her deck.

"Good morning, Audrey," Hannah called to the cat. "How are you today? You must be tired out. You're usually quivering with excitement when you spot me with some food. You're such a smart cat. You know I'm a soft touch. Look, I've some cream for you today."

Hannah put the bowl down on the deck and waited. Much to Hannah's surprise, the cat did not move nor respond with her customary, appreciative meow.

"Hey? What's up, Audrey? It's not like you to turn down a bowl of cream."

Hannah walked over to the cat, and what she saw made Hannah scream and scream.

* * *

A short time later, Hannah was sitting in her neighbors' kitchen, tightly gripping a cup of hot coffee.

Lily Clark was sympathetically clucking and patting one of Hannah's hands. Cranston Clark kept repeating the words, "Not right. What's this world coming to?" over and over while Ethan sat quietly next to Hannah. One of Ethan's arms was protectively draped over Hannah's shoulders.

Ethan's face showed his exasperation. He said, "Hey, Mom and Dad, you're not making things easier. You have to pipe down and let the officer get a statement from Hannah. Why don't you wait in the living room? Okay?"

Lily rapidly said, "Right. Of course. You know best. We'll be nearby if you need us," and then she and Cranston left the room.

"Now, go ahead, Officer Brown," Ethan said. He spoke to the young policeman who was standing near Hannah.

"Thank you," Officer Paul Brown replied. He wrote a bit more on the notepad in his hand. Then he turned to Hannah and said, "Let's see. I've got your name, address, contact information, and place of work. And you said you found the cat on your deck a little before eleven o'clock this morning. Correct?"

"Yes," Hannah said. "The cat and the note."

"And the note was next to the cat," the officer said.

The note said, *Stop Baker Investigation. Stop Or You'll Be Murdred Like the Cat!* It was printed on a sheet of white notebook paper. It now was in an evidence bag that the police officer had placed on the kitchen table.

Hannah looked at the note and shuddered. "It was such a shock. The lettering on the note is red and sticky. It looks like it was written in blood." Tears slid down Hannah's cheeks. "I can't get over it. Why did someone kill Audrey? And why decapitate her? She was such a sweet animal. I knew her and liked her and fed her bits of food. She was special, our neighborhood cat."

"I can't explain why some people are cruel to animals, ma'am. It sickens me, and it is a crime. I want to assure you that the Parkerville police will try to find out who did this."

Ethan looked at the officer and said, "Whoever killed the cat means to harm Hannah. This is more than just a warning. Hannah's in danger and needs to stop meddling with the Baker murder case. You agree; don't you? Right?"

"Well, sir, I do think Mrs. Stein needs to be careful. We'll have an officer drive by in one of our patrol cars several times a day over the next few days."

"And what about Audrey?" Hannah asked.

"I'll take care of that problem for you," Ethan said. "There are some services that will remove dead animals."

"Oh, that sounds so sad and impersonal," Hannah said. She looked at the officer and asked, "Can I bury Audrey?"

"You can bury a pet in your own back yard in Pennsylvania if you do so within forty-eight hours of its death. I'll check with the farmer who owned the cat. As he didn't do much for the animal when she was alive, I can't imagine he'd object if you want to take care of the cat's remains."

"Oh, thank you," Hannah said. "I know Audrey wasn't my pet, but I want to do what I can for her. I just can't believe it. She died because someone is angry with me. I'd like to bury her in my garden. It isn't much, but she'll be near the Clarks' flower beds, and they're beautiful."

"I'll call you after I talk to the cat's owner. Call the station if you have any questions or if anything further happens. And, of course, call 911 if there's an emergency." The young officer closed his notebook and added, "That should do it for now. I think I have all the information I need."

Hannah said, "I guess you'd better file this report with the last one. The one about the note on the windshield of my car. Both notes were handwritten and printed, and 'murdered' was misspelled on the other note, too. Maybe a handwriting specialist will find a connection."

"Ma'am, what are you talking about?" Officer Brown asked. "I checked before I left the station. There are no active reports related to you in our system."

Chapter 48

"I don't understand, Ethan. Why did the officer say he knew nothing about the other note? You told me you took care of that for me. Why, just last night, you said I had to be careful because the police didn't have any leads. What's going on here?" Hannah asked. She was pacing around the Clarks' kitchen, too agitated to sit down.

Ethan looked sheepish after the young officer left. He was leaning against the refrigerator. He turned, took a glass from the cupboard over the sink, opened the refrigerator, filled the glass with orange juice, and polished off half the juice in one big gulp.

"Oh, would you like some, too?" Ethan asked.

"No," Hannah said. "I don't need something to drink. I need to know what happened. Did you or did you not talk to the police for me and give them the note I found on my car?"

"Look, Hannah, I just wanted to help you. I did take the note to the Parkerville police station as I promised. But I was surprised when I got there because I didn't recognize anyone. The people I knew have moved on, and they have a lot of new hires. Like that young guy you just spoke to. I wanted to talk to someone who knew me, maybe owed me a favor. I learned that Joe, one of my old buddies, is still on the force. However, it was his day off. But I knew he did not live far from the station. So, I went to his house, found him at home, filled him in, and gave him the note. He said he'd take care of everything. And he was true to his word. Joe got back to me. He was able to answer all my questions. When I was on the force, I knew I could always depend on Joe. But the one part of the job Joe always hated was the paperwork. He got in trouble for being a procrastinator. I guess he hasn't changed. I bet the forms are still on his desk, waiting to be filled out."

Hannah frowned. She did not like what she was hearing.

Ethan hurriedly added, "I warned you that you'd have to be careful. And you've got to admit it; my instincts were correct. Someone's threatening you. Someone killed the cat, and that someone will hurt you, too, if you don't walk away from the Baker case."

Hannah stopped pacing, collapsed into a kitchen chair, and held her head in her hands.

"Oh, Ethan, this is all so overwhelming. So confusing."

"Please, Hannah, I just want to protect you. Everything I've done has been for you. I'll get in touch with Joe right away and get on his case to complete the paperwork and file a report. Yes, he should've done it earlier, but it doesn't change anything."

At that moment, Lily and Cranston Clark entered the kitchen. Sensing the tension in the air, Lily said, "I'm sorry to interrupt a serious discussion, but I want to give you this, Hannah. For the cat."

Lily held out a pale pink pillowcase trimmed in white flowered lace. "I know the cat meant a lot to you. I thought she should have a pretty shroud."

Hannah's eyes filled with tears. "That is very kind, Lily. Audrey was a beautiful cat, and it's appropriate that she be laid to rest in something pretty. If I get permission to bury her, she'll have a final resting place in my garden. I like the idea of her always being nearby. I'll miss her."

Hannah hugged Lily, thanked her and Cranston for helping her deal with that morning's calamity, and headed toward the back door.

"Wait," Ethan said. "Stay with us awhile. You've had a bad shock. I'll help you bury the cat later."

"No," Hannah replied. "I need to go home. There are things I need to do. My daughter phones me on Sundays, and I have work to do for my classes. I'd like to take care of Audrey on my own. I feel I owe it to her."

And, with that said, Hannah returned to her home. Normally, home was her haven, but now it did not feel safe and secure.

* * *

A few hours later, Ethan spotted Hannah digging in her backyard garden. Hannah swiped at some tears. Her hand was in a muddy gardening glove, so she left streaks of dirt on her cheeks.

Ethan walked over to Hannah and asked, "Need any help?"

"No. Thanks. I just finished burying Audrey. Her farmer didn't want to be bothered with a dead cat. He told the police that I could do whatever I wanted with her. Poor Audrey. I hope she knew that the folks who looked after her in this neighborhood valued her. I'm going to mark her grave with my bird feeder. I was just about to move it over here."

"I can help you with that," Ethan said. "It looks heavy."

"Okay. You're right. It is heavy. I guess I could use your help."

It took some wrangling, but the two managed to pick up the bird feeder and reposition it.

"It looks good here," Ethan said. "You've done everything you possibly could for that cat."

"I hope so," Hannah said.

"And soon, you'll be able to enjoy your back yard again, too. Put all this behind you, Hannah, and move on. You did promise me that you'd forget about Matthew Baker if you were in danger. Remember?"

"Yes. I do remember," Hannah quietly replied.

Chapter 49

Promptly, at nine o'clock that Sunday night, Frank and Gina met outside the entrance to Friendly Fred's Lanes. It was now fifteen minutes past rendezvous time, and Gina was impatiently pacing.

"Where's Brad?" Gina asked. "We agreed to meet at nine. I don't like hanging around out here waiting for him. The guys going in are eyeing us. I just know they're saying to themselves, 'They're not regulars. Who are they?' I don't like it. We shouldn't call attention to ourselves."

Frank laughed. "Gina, you'd think you'd be used to men staring at you by now. They're only looking at you because you're a pretty girl. No one's looking at me. But, hey, no worries. Here comes Brad. We can go in now. There's a good crowd in there, so we can blend in. Just stick with Brad and me. Don't make eye contact with anyone else. We'll move quickly around the place and see if Graybill's here. If he is, we might learn something. If he's not, we'll leave right away and come back another night. Okay?"

Gina nodded. "Right. I'm ready to spy on that shady drug pusher."

After Brad uttered a hurried apology for being late, the three entered the building and immediately headed toward the poolroom. That is where an intoxicated Ken Graybill had boasted that he was being well-paid not to talk about the Baker murders, so it seemed like the best place to start.

The pool tables in the backroom were all in use. The place was vibrating with loud piped-in rock music and the laughter and shouts of a raucous crowd. Frank quickly scanned the faces. He did not see Ken Graybill, but he did recognize three high school buddies standing in a dimly lit corner.

Frank pointed to the pinball machine and said to Brad and Gina, "Let's head over there. I see some friends. One has spotted me, so I gotta say 'hi' to them. Besides, they may know something about Graybill."

Frank led the way, and the other two followed. They slowly snaked their way through the crowd and, eventually, reached Frank's friends. A tall fellow and a short one, both wearing Phillies baseball caps, were loudly hooting and hollering whenever the pinball player racked up more points. Their cries echoed the machine's beeps. When the game ended, there was a lot of backslapping and high fives all around.

The tall fellow yelled, "Frank, look at this score. Dennis has set a new record."

Frank had to shout above the din but managed to introduce Gina and Brad to Dennis, the champion pinball player, and his cheerleaders. Promising to get in touch with Frank soon, Dennis peeled off from the group. He wanted to make sure his pinball score was posted on the leaderboard, and he wanted to collect his prize, a certificate for free food. The short Phillies fan followed in Dennis' wake, and that left the tall friend named Tom, who gestured toward an exit.

"It will be easier to talk in the parking lot," Tom hollered. The group left the poolroom through the back door and sidestepped the smokers clustered outside the building. Tom guided them to a comparatively quiet spot in the parking lot by a shiny, new red Corvette.

Brad blew out an appreciative whistle. "Wish this was my car."

Tom said, "Me, too. This beauty pulled into the lot as I was parking. Someday I'd like to own a brand-new Corvette. This one belongs to Ken Graybill."

Frank perked up when he heard the owner's name. "Say, Tom, do you know Graybill? Have you seen him tonight? Is he still here?"

"Why the interest?" Tom asked. "Graybill hangs out with a rough crowd. I heard he used to sell drugs. Don't know what he's into now, but it can't be good. He's someone you want to avoid, Frank. Not someone you want to look for."

Before Frank could respond, the back door to the poolroom popped open with a whoosh and crashed against the building. The loud noise startled Gina, and she jumped. She saw two men scuffling in the doorway and was surprised that she recognized them both.

"Look," Gina said. "Look who's being dragged out of the building."

A muscular giant was attempting to propel a small man out of the poolroom. The short fellow was staggering and shouting obscenities.

The large man screamed, "We gotta get out of here, Ken. You're drunk. You gotta shut up."

Frank looked at Brad and Gina and grinned. "We don't have to find Ken Graybill. It looks like he found us."

Graybill's huge companion spun Graybill around. Thick arms encircled Graybill's waist and held him close in a tight bear hug. The two men did an odd lurch-drag dance step through the parking lot till they ended up by the red Corvette.

"Why are you creeps standing by my car?" Graybill demanded when he spotted Frank, Brad, Gina, and Tom.

"Forget them," the big guy said. He reached inside one of Graybill's pants pockets and pulled out the Corvette's key fob. He pushed buttons; the car doors clicked open, and the engine began to purr. "Just get in the car. I'll drive you home."

"Oh, no, you won't. No one drives my car but me," Graybill said. The words melted together in a drunken slur. Graybill held on to the side of the Corvette to steady himself and then pointed at Frank. "Hey, you look like a college kid. Sorry Face told me all about the college kids. They're out to get me. I'm not supposed to tell them what I did. But I'm smarter than Sorry Face. I'm smarter than all you college kids, too."

"Shut up, Ken. Get in the car." The large man with the tattoo of a moose on his upper arm was pushing Graybill toward the passenger door of the sports car.

"No way," Ken Graybill shouted.

Graybill lunged and grabbed the key fob out of his friend's hand. Then he pivoted and jammed one of his elbows, with all his might, into the large man's stomach. The big fellow stumbled backward, bent over in pain. Graybill swayed but managed to remain upright. He wobbled over to the driver's door, opened it, and collapsed into the seat. After slamming the door shut, he released the parking brake, shifted into drive, and stomped on the gas pedal. The car took on a life of its own. It roared and raced out of the lot, barely missing two parked cars before it shot down the street.

The guy with the moose tattoo shook a fist in the air and let out an exasperated sigh. He turned and walked back toward the poolroom, muttering a string of foul swear words over and over.

"Well," Tom said. "That was weird and a little scary. Good to see you, Frank, but I've got to go back in and find Dennis. He rode with me, and I need to head on home. We never did get to play pool, but it's just as well. This place deserves its bad reputation. Next time, I'll just stick with bowling. Nothing happens on that side of the building."

After Tom left, Brad said, "Now what?"

"Now, we head home, too," Frank answered. "Nothing more to do here."

"Sounds good," Gina said. "Let's meet at our coffee spot tomorrow and talk. We can figure out what to do next and …"

Suddenly, there was a loud, rumbling noise. A set of headlights, attached to a fast-moving vehicle, was heading straight at them. Frank and Brad dove safely out of the way, but Gina slipped. Her head hit the pavement with a thwack. A red car sped past them, sending bits of gravel flying into the air.

Chapter 50

Monday, July 1

Hannah Stein was worried. She looked at the clock on the wall in her office.

Where are they? she wondered. Her mind flipped over possibilities, but she could not settle on one to account for the fact that Brad, Frank, and Gina had all been no-shows for class this Monday morning. And now, the three were late for their scheduled office hour appointments, and Hannah did not know why. None of them had emailed her or left an explanation on her office message unit.

What's going on? Hannah asked herself. *We need to discuss how they'll complete their papers after they delete all references to the Baker murders and the Metzler rape. I hope they haven't changed their minds. So many scholarships are riding on their cooperation.*

Hannah looked at the clock again. Her students were now fifteen minutes late. She had reserved the last appointment slots of the day for them in case they needed extra time. She nervously drummed her fingers on her desk.

How long should I wait? Hannah bit her lip, shook her head in frustration, and made herself a promise, *I'll give them five more minutes. If no one shows up, then I'll head on home.*

Hannah heard the quick, loud beat of feet pounding up the stairs. Her office door swung open, and seconds later, Brad and Frank, panting from their sprint, were standing in front of her desk.

"Sorry we're late," Frank said, "but we're sure glad you're still here."

Brad quickly added, "We've been chasing down leads all day. We had to do something. We had to find people who saw what happened to Gina."

Hannah was confused. "What happened to Gina?" she asked.

Before one of the boys could answer, there was a knock on Hannah's open office door. A tall figure in a police officer's uniform strode into the room. Hannah blinked. It was Officer Paul Brown. The same police officer who had interviewed her yesterday. He was now standing in her office and looking grim.

"Sorry to interrupt, Professor Stein, but I saw your open office door. I'm looking for Frank Brubaker and Brad Mason. Do you happen to know where I can find them?" the officer asked.

"Why are you looking for us? We haven't done anything," Brad blurted out.

"So, you're Brubaker?" the officer asked Brad.

"No, I'm Brad Mason. He's Frank Brubaker," Brad replied and nodded toward Frank.

Brown said, "Figured I might find you two on campus when I heard you're Buchanan students. And it made sense to look for you in this building. That junker parked outside in the no-parking fire zone is registered to Frank Brubaker. And if it's not moved right away, it will be towed."

"My car's not so bad," Frank said in defense of his ride. "It still takes me places."

"And that's the problem. You've been going to the wrong places. I should arrest you both. Right here and right now," Brown said.

* * *

A short time later, after being harshly lambasted for jeopardizing a police investigation, the boys looked crestfallen and quietly slunk out of Hannah's office. However, before leaving, Brad and Frank shared with the young patrolman the names and contact information for the people they had tracked down who had seen a fast-moving red car narrowly miss hitting them at Friendly Fred's. And two of those witnesses were positive that Ken Graybill was the driver behind the wheel.

Officer Brown shook his head and sighed. He turned toward Hannah after the boys left and said, "Now, I'll never admit this to those two, but those boys actually did the Parkerville police a service. I've been running around all day trying to find eyewitnesses, and those foolhardy kids found two. Folks I spoke to didn't tell me much, only that Brubaker and Mason had already talked to them. Darn it all. Questions have to be properly asked. Procedures need to be followed for us to make a case. And, what's worse, by poking their noses into things, your students might have been hurt. After all, by all accounts, someone did try to run those kids down."

"I still can't believe all this happened last night," Hannah said. She had quietly listened while Officer Brown interviewed Brad and Frank, and she had pieced together the story. "And Gina. Poor Gina. A concussion and a sprained wrist."

"The girl hit her head pretty hard when she slipped, but she was released from the hospital this morning. She's at home with her folks now, and they're keeping an eye on her. One of our detectives will interview her tomorrow, but I doubt she'll be able to tell us anything new. The kids instinctively jumped out of the way when the car came at them. Saving their skins was all they were thinking about."

"Amazing," Hannah said. "I knew my students were interested in Ken Graybill after they heard him say that someone is paying him not to divulge what he knows about the Baker murders. But I thought they had dropped the matter and moved on after we shared this information with the Parkerville police. I never dreamed Brad, Frank, and Gina had stumbled onto something that could endanger their lives."

"Let me get this straight. Someone at the station was informed?"

"Why, yes, of course," Hannah answered. "By the way, do you know a detective named Joe? Joe knows all about this."

"I just started, and I haven't met many on the force. Most of the time, I work nights and weekends. Today I'm covering for an officer who's on vacation. But I do remember meeting a detective last week named Jo. Short for Joanne. Was she the one you spoke to?"

"Actually, Ethan Clark, my neighbor, handled the matter for me and my students. Ethan used to work for the Parkerville Police Department, and Joe is a friend of his."

"Okay. I'll look into it. By the way, everything work out okay with the cat's burial?"

"What?" Hannah's mind was still focused on the red car and Ken Graybill. It took her a few seconds to change gears. "Oh, yes, and thank you. I buried the cat in my garden. I'm grateful the farmer gave me his permission. Thank you for your help with that."

"No problem. You know, I must admit this is a first for me. Talking to the same person about two different crimes two days in a row. It's strange, isn't it?"

"I guess so. It's certainly unusual for me," Hannah replied.

"But if the crimes are connected, it may not be so strange," Brown said. "We'll pick up this Graybill character. But until we have him safely locked away for trying to run down three teenage kids, I'd like you to be extra careful, Professor Stein. The violence circling around you is escalating."

Chapter 51

Hannah was running on automatic pilot after Officer Brown left her office. She mechanically pushed her computer and some student papers into her computer bag, locked her office door, and then left Drake Hall. She started walking and found, purely by habit, that she was headed toward the parking lot where she always parked her car.

What happened? Hannah thought. *I just wanted to make an assignment interesting for my students. I never dreamed I would be jeopardizing the scholarship program and putting my students in danger. Things have gotten out of hand. I need to accept that justice was served and move on. Matthew Baker killed his family and raped his cousin. Or did he?*

Hannah was lost in the maze of her thoughts. She was only vaguely aware of her surroundings and had not noticed that a stooped figure in dark clothes had followed her after she left Drake Hall. He had been a short distance behind her for some time. But now he was moving faster. Coming closer and closer to Hannah.

Hannah paused at the entrance of Parking Lot B and frowned. *Where did I leave my car this morning? I wish I had an assigned space. Which direction should I try first, to the right or to the left?* Hannah asked herself.

Suddenly, the dark figure was standing right beside her. He swung out his arm. Gnarled fingers tapped Hannah's right hand. Hannah looked down. What she saw startled her. There was an unusual watch on the man's wrist. There was a quick flash of recognition in Hannah's brain. She gasped in fear and started to shake. She swayed. The man put an arm around Hannah's waist to steady her and guided her to a nearby bench.

"Hey, pretty lady, did I frighten you?" the man asked. He was concerned and surprised by Hannah's reaction.

"Oh, my, you scared me, Will," Hannah replied.

Will Dotlish chuckled. "Well, I didn't mean to. I was just trying to get your attention. Never thought you'd react this way. You know, I'm going to retire when this summer session ends. So don't hightail it over to Human Resources and complain that I did anything wrong. You looked like you were off in space. I just touched your hand to bring you back to earth. And don't go fussing about me calling you pretty. I know they say it's not correct to say such things, but, darn it all, you are a pretty lady."

Hannah gave the head of campus security a weak smile. "No need to worry. You didn't do anything wrong. I'm flattered you think I'm pretty. I guess I was, as you put it, off in space. I was totally preoccupied. I also was trying to remember where I parked my car this morning." Hannah paused and then added, "I don't understand it. I saw your watch, and, suddenly, something clicked in my head and upset me. It's strange. I've never reacted like that to a watch before. Would you mind if I took another look at yours?"

Will held out his left hand, so Hannah could examine his wristwatch. He said, "It's a Casio C80. Boy, in the day, it was really something. A calculator watch. Wife gave it to me for my birthday thirty-eight years ago. She saved up to get me my heart's desire. Loved the watch then and still love it now."

Hannah quickly did the math in her head. Thirty-eight years ago, she was five years old. Thirty-eight years ago, Hannah saw two hands push her mother down a flight of stairs. Those hands killed her mother. Was there a watch on the wrist of one of those hands? Was it an unusual watch like the Casio C80? Hannah closed her eyes and concentrated on recalling the scene. Try as she might, the vision was blurry. Once again, truth was playing a game of hide-and-seek with her, and, once again, she was losing.

"You okay, Professor Stein?" Will asked. "You're awfully pale. Do you think you might be coming down with something? I bet there's someone over at Student Health Services who could check you out. I'd feel better knowing you're all right before you get behind the wheel and drive home."

"No, I'm fine now. I don't know what came over me. Your watch must mean something to me. I just don't know what right now. Maybe it will come to me later. Will, you did say you were trying to get my attention. Do you have news? Something to tell me about the note that was left on my car?"

"A note? No, I just wanted to make sure you knew about my retirement party. You're one of the good ones, Professor Stein. Not like some who walk around here with their noses in the air and think they're better than the ordinary workers. I hope you'll come to my farewell dinner."

"Yes, Will. Of course, I'll be there. I'm looking forward to it."

"Glad you can make it. I want to celebrate with my favorite Buchanan people. Now, why are you concerned about a note?"

Hannah was surprised. Ethan said he had contacted both the local police and campus security.

"Will, did Ethan Clark tell you about the menacing note that was left on the windshield of my car when it was parked in Lot B last week?"

"Ethan Clark. If I remember right, he left the Parkerville police force a few years back. Gosh, I haven't spoken to him in years. What's this? Something was left on your car? You'd better explain."

Hannah quickly told Will about the note that was left on her car and also about the one she found on her deck next to Audrey's body. When she finished, Will pointed to a security camera near the entrance to Parking Lot B.

"I forgot about the campus security cameras. I guess I've gotten so used to them being part of the landscape that I just don't think about them," Hannah said.

Will nodded. "Let's hope whoever left that note forgot about the security cameras, too. If you're sure you're okay, I'll head over to my office and sign into our security system. I'll check the footage from last Monday on my computer. Who knows? Maybe we'll have a picture of someone standing next to your car."

"Oh, thank you, Will. And please, call me on my cell phone and let me know what you find."

After Hannah reassured Will multiple times that she did not need further assistance, he reluctantly left her, with the promise that he would look into "this note matter" right away. Hannah remained on the bench a few minutes longer, trying to process all that had just occurred.

What is there about that wristwatch that frightened me? Hannah asked herself. *And why didn't Ethan talk to Will Dotlish? Did Ethan talk to someone else in the security office? Maybe that person forgot to tell Will about the note. Unlikely. Will is always on top of everything happening on campus. Will would've known about the note if someone had filled out a report. And I should've remembered there are cameras in the parking lot.*

Hannah sighed. *Enough!* She was exasperated with herself. *I don't know what to make of Ethan. Why would he lie to me? But the fact is, I don't need him. I'm not some damsel in distress. I used to rely on Aaron, but since he's been gone, I've learned how to take care of myself. I can work with the officials. I don't need an intermediary. What I do need are answers to my questions, and I'm going to get them. Oh, my gosh. Now I do remember where I left my car this morning. It's by the big oak tree on the left side of the parking lot.*

Hannah resolutely pushed herself off the bench. *It's time I headed home. And I need to talk to Jodi.*

Chapter 52

For twenty minutes, Jodi had been all Hannah could ever want in a sympathetic friend. She had quietly listened while Hannah had vented and poured out everything that had upset her over the past two days. Jodi's supportive comments had been a soothing balm, taking the sting out of Hannah's emotional scrapes and bruises.

"Okay, friend," Jodi said. "That's a lot to absorb. A cat murdered in your yard. A scary wristwatch. A deceitful boyfriend. Students plunged into danger. Unresolved issues about the Baker murders. Yup, that's some list. Now what?"

"What do you mean?" Hannah asked.

"What are you going to do about all this? What's next?"

"Well, first and foremost, I have to make sure my students are safe. The wristwatch question can wait. I don't understand why the watch scared me, but there's nothing I can do about it right now. Now, Ethan. That's a sticky problem. I feel very foolish when it comes to Ethan."

"No reason you should. You're not the first woman in the history of the world who's been taken in by a good-looking guy. It happens to the best of us. Besides, even if Ethan turns out to be a dud and isn't a superhero, you'll survive. And learn from the experience. Trust me."

"Trusting you got me into this mess. You're the one who told me to dive into the dating pool."

"Guilty as charged. But you're allowed to change your mind. You can go back to the shallow end and just dip your toes in the water. But before you retreat and give up on Ethan, maybe you should hear him out. Give him a chance to explain. After all, you were falling for him. There may be something to salvage here."

"I don't know if it's worth the effort. How do I determine if Ethan is telling the truth? How can I trust him?"

"Those are good questions. Which brings us back to Matthew Baker and the murders. Maybe Ethan does know more than he's revealed and is only trying to keep you out of danger."

"Oh, Jodi, I don't know what to think or believe. Everything keeps shifting with Ethan."

"Then you have to shift and adjust to keep up. You have to keep asking questions. Take your time, and then you'll know what to believe and what to do. You'll feel the truth in your heart as well as your head. But remember, sometimes love does involve a leap of faith."

"Hmmm," Hannah replied. "Maybe."

There was an uncomfortable silence, and Hannah decided it was time to steer the conversation in a new direction.

"Oh, Jodi. I didn't ask you about your new guy. You know, the mime with all those kids."

Jodi chuckled. "That didn't last long. We had a great first date. Over coffee, he told me all about himself, and he was really smart and funny. And then the second date. So boring. He was eating stuffed clams for dinner and ended up droning on and on about clams for forty-five minutes. I was ready to call it quits, but I decided to give him another chance. After all, the second date could have been an aberration. But it only got worse. Last night we went to a movie. Our third date. And afterward, I couldn't drag a word out of him. And believe me, I tried everything. I do mean everything. Can't explain it. He just fizzled out. I guess he gave me his all when he met me, and then had nothing left."

Hannah smiled and then said, "Well, at least you got another dating story to add to your collection."

"Yes, there's that. But too many men just pass through my life. It would be nice to want one to stay. And figuring out if a guy is Mr. Right isn't easy. Dating can be fun, but it's also exhausting. So, before you discard Ethan, find out more. Be sure you're making the right choice. Then you'll never regret your decision."

"Look," Hannah said. "I should go. I called my student Gina's number before I called you. I'm concerned. I'd like to find out how she's doing. No one answered her phone, so I left a message and my office phone number. I can retrieve messages left on my office phone. Maybe Gina or one of her parents called me back."

"Okay," Jodi said. "But I know you, Hannah Stein. You're going to hold yourself responsible for that girl's injuries, and that's not fair. Your students were investigating on their own, after you told them to stop, and some crazy driver tried to run them down. That's not on you."

"I hear you," Hannah said.

"Don't just hear me. Believe it. And, Hannah, listen to that police officer you spoke to. Be careful." Before Jodi ended the call, she made Hannah promise to keep in touch and call her again soon.

Hannah took in a deep breath and exhaled. She felt better after her conversation with Jodi, but she did not agree with her friend. She was the one who had brought the Baker case into her classroom, and afterward, Gina had been hurt. She did feel guilty. She quickly punched in numbers on her phone and connected to her office phone system. There was one new message. But it was not from Gina nor a member of the girl's family. This message was unexpected and startling.

Chapter 53

Hannah held her phone close to her ear. She replayed the message and listened carefully.

Professor Stein, this is Frank Brubaker. Just heard from my mom, who heard from my Aunt Bonnie. Get this, Professor Stein. My Aunt Bonnie lives in the city, and she told my mom that police have been swarming in and out of a row house near hers all day. And there were bodies. Two bodies were taken out of the house. Aunt Bonnie saw everything from her front porch. She also saw a woman screaming and crying in front of that house. My Aunt Bonnie's neighbors told her that the sobbing woman's daughter was engaged to Ken Graybill, and now he and the girl are dead. They were the ones in the body bags. Can you believe it? Don't know if any of this is related to Matthew Baker, but it sure is strange. Thought you'd like to know. See you in class tomorrow.

Yes, Hannah thought, *it's very strange. Eyewitnesses say that Graybill was the driver who tried to run over my students, and then shortly after that, Graybill dies. So, now the investigation will stop. Literally a dead end. What in the world is going on?*

Hannah quickly flipped open her laptop and scanned the sites that carried local news stories. She read short blurbs under "breaking news" banners: *Two dead in Lancaster City. Police investigating an apparent murder-suicide. Motive for two violent early morning deaths not known.*

Hannah frowned. *Local news stations aren't saying much. Apparent murder-suicide. I wonder what that means. Which one was the victim, and which one was the killer? If Graybill was the killer, why did he murder his girlfriend and try to harm my students? Was he mentally unbalanced? Did he just snap? But if he was sane, then why did he commit these acts? Did he kill the Bakers? Did he kill himself? Darn it all. All I have is questions and more questions and no answers.*

Musical notes interrupted Hannah's thoughts. It was her phone's ringtone. She quickly slid her finger across her phone's screen and accepted the call.

"Hello," Hannah said.

"Professor Stein, it's Will Dotlish here. I have some good news and some bad. Good news is that I went through the recent security footage for Parking Lot B, and, sure enough, I spotted a guy putting a note under your car's windshield wiper. Bad news is he was wearing a baseball cap that shaded his face, and there's a lot of glare. It was a really sunny day. But one thing we have no shortage of on this campus is computer geeks. I'm going to ask the folks in Computer Support for some help. See if they can clean the picture up a bit. Then I'll send it on to the Parkerville police."

"That's great news, Will. I appreciate your help."

"Don't thank me yet. Right now, we don't have much. We can roughly calculate the person's height and weight. But that's about all. I'll get back to you in a day or two and let you know if the computer people can work some magic. I'd like to get enough to ID this guy."

After she ended the call with Will, Hannah's stomach growled. She remembered she had grabbed an early lunch and had not eaten dinner. She went into her kitchen and warmed up some leftovers. Hannah quickly ate her meal and was considering topping off her supper with some dessert when her phone signaled that she had another call. Hannah smiled when she saw the caller was her Aunt Gail.

"Hi, Aunt Gail. You just saved me from temptation. The chocolate chip ice cream in my freezer has been calling to me. Now, instead of devouring a lot of calories, I'll talk to you. How are you?"

"I'm fine, but, honey, your father is not doing well. I visited him this afternoon. He's really gone downhill since I last saw him. The cancer is spreading fast. I don't think he has much time left."

"I had no idea. This is so frustrating. The home is supposed to let me know when there are significant changes. And Michael should've called. My summer class will end in a couple of weeks. But I'll drop everything and fly out to see Dad right now if you think I should. I can make arrangements for someone to cover my class."

"Hannah, why don't you talk to your dad's doctors. Then, you'll know what to do. I'm just relaying my impressions. I think you have time to finish teaching your course before you visit. But don't wait too long."

"Thank you, Aunt Gail. I'll get in touch with the home and dad's doctors tomorrow."

Next, Aunt Gail asked about Sophie and Seth, and Hannah responded appropriately, but her mind kept wandering. She felt like she was in the middle of a surreal paintball game. She was being hit by emotionally charged volleys coming at her from many different directions at the same time, spattering her with dark, gloomy colors. The colors of sorrow, loss, and guilt. She was worried about her father and her students. Hannah had accidentally opened a Pandora's box in her classroom. Malignant forces were swirling around Frank, Brad, and Gina, and it was Hannah's job to protect her charges. Now, in addition, the clock was ticking. Would she have time to resolve her students' issues before she had to leave town and attend to her dying father?

"By the way, Aunt Gail," Hannah said. May I ask you a couple of random, off-the-wall questions?"

"Sure. Go ahead, dear."

"Do you remember calculator watches? And can you think of any reason I might've been afraid of them? I believe I was around five years old when they first came out."

"Afraid? No. Just the opposite. You were intrigued by watches when you were little. You loved them. When your father was home and used to read to you, you'd always beg for one more story. He'd limit you by saying, 'Just five minutes more,' and you'd keep your eyes glued on his wristwatch to make sure you got every minute you were entitled to. Now, those calculator watches were very popular. Yes, I remember them. Your dad just had to have one right away. And he bought one for Michael, too. Gave it to your brother as a birthday gift when Michael turned fifteen.

I think he thought it would help bind them together. Father and son linked because each had one of those super-duper new watches. Why do you ask?"

"No reason, really. I just happened to see one of those old wristwatches today and thought I'd ask you if you remembered them. It's not important," Hannah replied.

But Hannah knew, deep down she just knew, that the watch was important. Very important.

Chapter 54

Tuesday, July 2

The next morning, Brad showed up early for class and happily reported to Hannah that Gina was resting at home and doing well.

"She'll be back in class tomorrow," Brad said.

After sharing this news, Brad blurted out, "I've just got to tell you and Frank what happened to me last night. It's big. I mean really big. I'd tell you now, but there isn't time. It's not something I want others to hear. What do you say? Can you stay and talk after class?"

Hannah nodded, and Brad looked relieved. When Frank walked into the classroom, Brad grabbed his arm and pulled him to the back of the room. The two huddled together for a minute, and then Brad turned and gave Hannah the thumbs-up sign, which she took to mean that Frank had agreed to follow Brad's plan.

After class ended, Hannah could see that Brad desperately wanted the other students to leave as quickly as possible. He stood and impatiently bounced up and down on his toes. He actually pounced upon the last slow-moving girl, helped her slide her things into her backpack, and, gently but firmly, escorted her out. Finally, after only Brad, Frank, and Hannah were left in the room, Brad shut the door to the classroom.

Brad said, "Okay. Good. Now we're alone."

"What's up, Brad?" Frank asked.

"I want to tell you what I heard last night. I think it's important. I was with my Uncle Bob. I told you about him. He's the one who helped me get the transcript pages from Baker's lawyer. Uncle Bob just got back from his vacation in the Poconos, and I wanted to talk to him about what's been happening on campus, with our papers and our research and all."

"Brad," Hannah interjected, "you told us your Uncle Bob is a lawyer. Were you seeking legal advice? I thought you, Frank, and Gina all agreed to alter your final papers to protect the scholarship program. Have you changed your mind?"

Brad looked uncomfortable and squirmed in his chair. "Well, no. I just wanted to run things by Uncle Bob. Ask him if he thought I was a coward for compromising. But I never got the chance to talk to him about my paper. Something else happened."

"What happened?" Hannah asked.

Brad explained that he and his uncle were at the old-fashioned diner across from the mall. They had just finished eating their salads when a small guy who resembled a ferret slid into their booth and sat down next to Uncle Bob.

"It was Marvin Hart. You remember him, Frank?" Brad asked.

"Yup. We talked to him when we were chasing down folks who might've seen the driver of the red car that almost hit us. But he didn't say much."

"Right. But he said a lot last night."

* * *

Brad explained that Hart was nervous. He could not sit still; he kept looking over his shoulder and around the restaurant. When Brad asked him if he thought the FBI or CIA might be listening to them, Marvin gave him a withering look and replied it was more likely to be the DEA. Brad had been teasing, but Hart was serious. Brad was surprised and curious. What did Hart know that would interest someone in the government's Drug Enforcement Agency?

Hart said he needed Brad's uncle's help, and there was no time to waste. The lawyer quickly explained that he was having dinner with his nephew and that the diner was not an appropriate place to conduct legal business. But Hart was insistent.

Marvin said, "It's okay. I tell you it's okay. The kid can eat his dinner and listen while I talk to you. I get it. He's not my lawyer and can repeat what I'm going to say. It doesn't matter. I've got to talk to you right now. I spotted you as I was about to leave the restaurant. It was like it was meant to be. I'll have my say, my conscience will be clean, and then I'm leaving town for a while."

Hart looked at Brad and added, "Your uncle is one of the good guys. He kept me out of jail. Helped me get into rehab and got me community service. He really worked the system for me. I owe him. Owe him big. I probably should go to a police station with what I know, but I'm not walking into one. Too risky."

Marvin turned to Uncle Bob and said, "I'm getting outta here till things get sorted out and cool down. You talk to the police. Tell them everything. Just leave me out of it."

Brad leaned back in his chair and said, "Well, the two of them went back and forth a bit longer. I could tell Uncle Bob did not like the way things were going, but he must have felt sorry for Marvin. The little guy was scared; he was shaking. Then, suddenly, words just tumbled out of Hart's mouth. It was amazing how fast he talked. There was no way Uncle Bob could've stopped him, short of stuffing a napkin in his mouth. And he couldn't do that. After Marvin finished spewing out all he had to say, he tore a corner off my paper placemat, scribbled a phone number on it, pressed the paper into Uncle Bob's hand, and then bolted out the door."

"Okay. So, what did he say before he left?" Frank asked.

Brad replied, "First, you gotta know that when Hart was a teen, he was part of Ken Graybill's crew. Hart used to be close to Graybill, and Marvin said that Graybill was paranoid about going to jail. Graybill always bragged that he was protected; he had insurance. Hart said Graybill had a book where he recorded all his drug transactions: name of his supplier, names of his buyers, dates and places of deals, and more. Marvin said he once took a quick peek at the book but couldn't make much sense of it. The names in it were written in some sort of code."

"That's interesting and all, but why bring it up now?" Frank asked

"You'll see when you hear the rest. Last week, Ken Graybill got a brand-new Corvette, and, according to Hart, Graybill didn't pay for it. Graybill just walked into the dealership and walked out with the key to the car. Marvin saw everything. He's an auto mechanic at that fancy new car place. Hart overheard the man everyone calls Moose arguing with Graybill while they were waiting for the Corvette to be freshly washed. The guy with the moose tattoo kept saying that Graybill had to settle down, accept the car, and stop asking for more, or Graybill would be in big trouble. Big enough to get himself killed. And Graybill just laughed and said he had it all worked out. His special book would make Sorry Face cough up more big bucks. Graybill said he was taken care of for life. Remember, Frank, we heard Graybill mention Sorry Face at Friendly Fred's."

"So, you're thinking Graybill's death may not be part of a murder/suicide, right?" Frank asked. "If Graybill was blackmailing this Sorry Face person, that means Sorry Face had a motive. He might have killed Graybill to put an end to the payoffs."

"Yes. Sorry Face or someone hired by him. I think it's a real possibility. And Marvin Hart thinks so, too, because he wants my uncle to tell the police what he overheard, but he doesn't want to be tied to it. He doesn't want anyone coming after him," Brad said. "And there's something else. Hart saw Moose shove Graybill out of the dealership when Graybill wouldn't pipe down. Graybill, according to Marvin, got real nasty and started cursing his big friend. Hart heard Graybill say, 'Leave me alone, or I'll take you down, too. I wrote about what really happened when the Bakers were murdered. And I have proof.'" Brad paused and then asked, "Now, what do you make of that? What do we do now?"

Hannah answered, "It's not up to us to do anything, Brad. Your uncle will tell the police what Hart overheard, and then it's up to the police. They will determine if there's anything to investigate."

"But we have to do something," Frank said. "Graybill said he knew about the Baker murders and had some proof. That's got to help Matthew Baker. It isn't right for a guy to be imprisoned for years for something he didn't do."

"Slow down, Frank," Hannah said. "You can't jump to conclusions based upon what someone overheard during a heated argument. Perhaps Graybill just wanted to scare his friend, and the written account and proof aren't real, just things Graybill made up. And even if they do exist, we don't know if they will help or hurt Matthew Baker. Let's say others can be linked to the Baker murders, like this Moose character. Nothing changes for Baker if Matthew was the one to wield the knife and kill his family."

Frank looked deflated. "Now I feel like I've fallen back into the same dark hole. Once again, I don't know if Baker is guilty or not."

"It sure is confusing," Brad said. "Never thought I'd be tossed back into the world of Matthew Baker while I was having dinner with my uncle last night. What do you think the police will do with all this?"

Hannah replied, "I don't know, Brad. But it really is up to them. They're the professionals."

The boys reluctantly agreed and left the classroom together. Frank looked glum. He plopped down on a bench right outside the classroom building, and Brad sat down next to him.

Brad said. "I can't believe it. I was so sure I was onto something. I thought we'd have a plan of some sort now. Instead, we have nothing to do. But if the account book and murder evidence are real, where do you think Graybill hid those things? He wouldn't have left them lying around where they could be easily found."

Frank sat up straight and turned toward Brad. "Right. And maybe the police already have them if they were hidden in the house where Graybill died, but maybe they don't. You know there is a way to find out."

"How?" Brad asked.

Frank smiled. "My cousin network. Graybill died in the city, and I have a cousin who's on the Lancaster City police force. Let's get going. I have a plan, and now we have something to do."

Chapter 55

After Brad and Frank left, Hannah remained in the classroom, mulling over what Brad had just said about Marvin Hart, Ken Graybill, the man named Moose, and the mysterious Sorry Face.

Hannah wondered, *Who is Sorry Face? It's Graybill's nickname for somebody who has money or access to money. That person gave Graybill cash and a Corvette to keep his or her secret. The boys used the pronoun 'he' when they spoke about Sorry Face, but maybe the person is a 'she.' And what does the name suggest? Does this person have regrets and is sorry for committing some unlawful or immoral act or acts? Or does the name refer to some facial deformity? Or what? And is it possible Graybill knew something about the Baker murders that the police didn't uncover? If so, what type of proof did he have? And if that proof still exists, could it clear Matthew Baker?*

Hannah's thoughts were interrupted by the sounds of chatter. Students filed into the classroom. Hannah looked at the clock and realized it was time for her to leave. An afternoon economics class would be starting in five minutes. She collected her books and papers, slung her computer bag over her shoulder, and headed back to her office. She gnawed on the questions she had asked herself as she walked, frustrated that she had no idea how to answer them. She was clueless.

* * *

Hannah spent a good portion of the afternoon on mindless tasks. She had trouble concentrating, so she replied to emails and returned phone calls that demanded little of her. Hannah was pleased to see that Will Dotlish had sent her an email. When she opened it, she learned that a Buchanan computer super-nerd had, indeed, performed some magic in record time; she was able to enhance the photo of the person who left the threatening note. Will wrote that he had forwarded the photo and all relevant information to the Parkerville police, and Hannah sent Will a quick thank you note. Yes, it was good that things were moving forward in that regard, but at the end of the day, Hannah regretted that she had not accomplished more. Consequently, she made herself a promise. She would stop being distracted by Ken Graybill and the Baker murders. She would heed the advice she gave Brad and Frank. She would concentrate on her own work. She was, after all, a college professor and not a detective.

On the drive home from Buchanan College, Hannah felt calmer than she had all day. She had veered off the rails, but now she was back on track. However, she still did not know what to do about Ethan Clark. Could he be trusted? As she turned into her driveway, she forgot all about Ethan when she saw red. She literally saw red. Splotches of red were on the walkway leading up to her house. Were they globs of blood? And a red paper was hanging askew on her front door. Hannah gasped. She parked her car and grabbed her cell phone out of her bag. She kept one finger poised over the digit that would automatically dial 911 for her. She cautiously opened her car door, slid out of the vehicle, and looked down at the red blotches. She exhaled. She had not realized that she had been holding her breath; she had been so frightened. Hannah was amazed. She was looking at flower petals. Red rose petals littered the walk. She followed them to the note attached to the front door. On closer inspection, she saw that the paper was cut in the shape of a heart. She yanked it off the door, opened it, and read the words inside.

It took Hannah a minute to process that all was well. She slumped against the door and sighed in relief. And that is how Officer Paul Brown found her after he parked his patrol car and joined her at the front door.

"Everything okay, Mrs. Stein?" Officer Brown asked. "I was driving by to check on your home and spotted you out here."

"Oh, I'm sorry. I was frightened. I saw these red petals from a distance and thought . . . You're going to think I'm silly. But, really, they're fine. Just flowers."

"And the paper in your hand?" Brown asked.

"Just a dinner invitation," Hannah answered.

"Well, I'm glad all is well. I was going to call you later. Might as well tell you now. I did find out that there's a detective on the force named Joe. Joe Miller is his name. He's been out on family leave, so I haven't met him yet. Wanted to let you know. That probably is the Joe you were asking about," Brown said.

Just then, Hannah and Brown saw two men walking toward them. They must have come from the back yard as neither Hannah nor the officer had seen them approach the house. One of the men was wearing a shoulder holster and had a gun. Officer Brown moved his right arm to his right side. His hand hovered over his pistol.

Chapter 56

"Please," Hannah said to her friend Jodi much later that night, "it's late, and I'm tired. I promise to call you back tomorrow."

"How do you expect me to fall asleep without knowing more?" Jodi asked. "Now, let me see if I have this right. While you were talking to this police officer who has been keeping an eye on your house, Ethan and a guy with a gun suddenly appeared. Right?"

"Yes. And the guy with the gun is Ethan's friend, a police detective named Joe Miller. He had stopped by to see Ethan, and Ethan wanted me to meet him. You see, Ethan really did talk to the police for me. He talked to Joe, but Joe didn't follow up. Joe left town a few hours later. His son was hurt in a motorcycle accident in Scranton, and Joe just took off after he was notified. He said his conversation with Ethan just flew out of his head. And I can understand why. His son needed surgery, and it was touch and go for a while. Because Ethan had talked to Joe at Joe's house and not at the station, no one else knew about their conversation. There was no paper trail. So, no one looked into anything while Joe was gone. Joe apologized. He also asked me to forgive him for failing to contact campus security. He had promised Ethan he would take care of that as well. I told Joe that I had spoken to Will Dotlish myself and that he had gone through the parking lot security tapes and now had a picture of the person who left the note on my car. Joe said he would follow up on that."

"Okay," Jodi said, "so, does that change your mind about Ethan? Is he still unreliable, or is he back to being a contender?"

"Oh, Jodi, contender for what?"

"For whatever you'd like. Maybe a lover. Now, tell me about this fantastic dinner you said you had with Ethan tonight."

"You are relentless. I'll cover just the basics. I do need to get some sleep. Well, after Officer Brown and Joe Miller left, Ethan took my hand and guided me to a veritable fairyland. His mom and his sister Lydia had helped him. They had strung little Christmas lights all over the shrubbery and low tree branches in the Clarks' back yard. The whole place was aglow. It was so pretty. And Ethan's mom had helped him set a lovely table for two on their patio with fine china, crystal, flowers, candles, and wine. You get the idea. I felt like I had walked into a very fancy restaurant. Ethan grilled some steaks, and there were side dishes from the Parkerville Diner and a cake from the new French bakery. Everything was delicious. We ate, talked, laughed, and, yes, I had a great time. Ethan is charming. There. Are you satisfied?"

"But, Hannah, how do you feel about him? He seems intent on sweeping you off your feet with all these romantic gestures."

"Jodi, right now, my feet are on the ground. I admit I float a bit when Ethan holds me in his arms, but when I'm not with him, I have my doubts. He's too much. I can't explain it better than that. It's wonderful to be treated so well and flattered and fawned upon, but it's too much too soon. It just doesn't feel real."

"I don't know. It all sounds good and real to me. What more do you want, Hannah?"

"I have to figure that out. But not tonight. Good night, my friend. We'll talk again tomorrow."

Jodi said, "You know we will. I want more details. And please don't tell me you were wearing your baggy old sundress when Ethan wined and dined you in such style."

After Hannah ended the call, she sighed. How could she explain to Jodi what she could not explain to herself? It had been a perfect evening; Ethan had orchestrated an ideal romantic interlude. Thought, time, and work had gone into impressing her, and how could she help but be impressed? Aaron, who had loved her with all his heart, would not have known where to begin; he could not have pulled it off. Hannah was attracted to Ethan because he wasn't like Aaron and, simultaneously, leery of Ethan because he wasn't like Aaron. She knew Ethan desperately wanted her to trust him again, and when she met Joe Miller, it was as if Ethan had gathered together the loose ends that had been bothering her and neatly snipped them off. However, there were still a few stray threads Ethan had missed.

Chapter 57

Wednesday, July 3

The next morning, Hannah was munching on some peanut butter toast for breakfast. When her coffee mug was empty, she refilled it, hoping the caffeine would revive her. Hannah had not slept well. She had been too wound up after such an incredible evening. She could not relax as she kept thinking about Ethan. He had been kind, witty, attentive, and sexy. But she also remembered the Friday night dinner at her home. After their meal on Friday, Ethan had glibly answered all her queries about the note left on her car and the Baker case. But most of what he said had not been true. Now, he begged her to understand that he only wanted to steer her away from danger and protect her, that he was only thinking of her. But was he? Joe Miller had cleared up a lot, but in the middle of the night, Hannah remembered that Ethan had also said that he had contacted another detective, the female detective who had dealt with Sandra Metzler's rape. Last night, she could not remember the detective's name. She was frustrated because she knew it was submerged somewhere in her brain. Finally, this morning, it floated to the surface. Hannah set her mug down on the table and said, "Erin Summers." She wondered if there was a way for her to find out if Ethan had really talked to Summers or made that up as well.

Hannah was startled by the sound of her doorbell. She was not expecting an early-morning caller and was surprised to find Robin Henley standing on her front doorstep. The Henley family lived in the farmhouse up the street, the house where the Bakers were murdered.

"Morning, Hannah. So sorry to bother you so early, but I'm desperate. We're all packed up and ready to go. We have to leave right now to get to the airport on time," Robin Henley rattled this off in record time. "We bought our tickets for this Fourth of July family reunion months ago, and my parents are counting on us being there. I really hate to ask you this favor, but I don't know what else to do."

Hannah could see that her neighbor was upset. "Do you want to come in and tell me how I can help?"

"Can't come in. There's no time. You know Lexi, our German Shepherd. The kids tell me you're one of her favorite people. You spoil her so. I know when you walk around the neighborhood that you always put a dog treat in your pocket for Lexi. And our dog knows it, too. She gets so excited when she sees you. Well, the thing is, our dog-sitter just called. He was supposed to walk and feed Lexi over the long weekend. Instead, he's going to the beach with his girlfriend. And we have to leave, and there's no time to make other arrangements. I know it's a lot to ask, but could you take care of Lexi? I've left instructions on a paper on the kitchen island. There's dog food, a water bowl, treats, and her leash nearby. And our emergency contact info is on the paper, too. Oh, Hannah, we have to leave right now if we're going to make our flight. We'll be back late Sunday night. Can you help us?"

Hannah did not have any plans for the Fourth of July and the long holiday weekend. "All right. But I've never had a dog as a pet. Do you think I can do this? I know Lexi likes me, but will she obey me?"

"Yes. Yes," Robin said. "Lexi loves our family, but unlike many German Shepherds, she's fond of others, too. Just keep her away from cats. She hates cats." Robin grabbed Hannah's right hand and dropped a key on her palm. "Thank you. Thank you so much. You've saved us. This key opens the side door. It's all you need. Although we've thought about it, we've never gotten around to installing a security system. We already walked and fed Lexi this morning. I think that covers everything. I can't tell you how much this means to us. Thank you."

Hannah watched as her neighbor ran down the walk and jumped into the white SUV waiting at the curb. Robin's husband was at the wheel. He waved and tooted the horn, and then they were off. Hannah watched the car disappear and prayed that she, who knew next to nothing about dogs, was up to caring for Lexi, a very large and very energetic German Shepherd.

Chapter 58

Hannah's Wednesday morning class was only half-full. The students who did show up were distracted by thoughts of sun and fun. They fidgeted in their seats. Hannah understood that her students were eager to start celebrating Independence Day. Because the Fourth of July fell on a Thursday, Buchanan College had designated Friday as a vacation day as well; this meant its students would have four consecutive days of freedom. After slugging through the first half of her lesson, Hannah gave up. There seemed little point in fighting a losing battle. Hannah ended class early. Her students cheered, and three rushed out the door. However, Frank, Brad, and Gina remained in the room.

Hannah said, "I'm surprised you three didn't dash out the door along with your classmates." Then Hannah looked at Gina and added, "Gina, I'm glad you were able to return to class today. How are you feeling?"

"Okay," Gina said. "But I still can't get over the fact that Ken Graybill tried to run us down. And now, Graybill and his girlfriend are dead. It's all really weird."

"That's what we want to talk to you about, Professor Stein," Frank said. "Those two peculiar deaths. You see, Brad and I did a little more snooping."

"Oh, no," Hannah said. "I thought we all agreed to leave the snooping to the police."

"Well," Brad said, "our snooping was confined to visiting the police. Nothing more than that. You know Frank has family all over the county, and he has a cousin who's a detective on the Lancaster City police force. And she works on homicide cases."

Frank said, "That's right. We talked to her yesterday, but it wasn't what she said that was interesting. It was what she didn't say."

Brad nodded in agreement and then added, "We asked her a lot of questions about Graybill's and his girlfriend's deaths. But she wouldn't answer us. She said it was an ongoing investigation, and we, along with everyone else, would learn the results when it's completed."

Frank chimed in, "But I got impatient and asked her if she could tell us anything. Anything at all. And she just clammed up. But I've known this cousin all my life. I know how to push her buttons. I told her I thought she didn't know anything because she wasn't important enough to be involved. She snapped back that, of course, she was involved in the case but wasn't going to tell some rude little cousin of hers about the clues they had. So, I pushed a little more. I said that we'd heard that Graybill had recorded his drug deals in a book. Well, her eyes got real big, and she said, 'Really. A book with drug deals. Now, that's interesting.' And then she left us. Never got to ask her anything more."

Brad said, "So, we know the police are still looking into the deaths because the case isn't closed and because Frank's cousin wouldn't answer our questions. And, from the way Frank's cousin reacted when he mentioned the drug book, we think that was the first time she had heard about it. Which means they don't have it. That's why Frank and I wanted to share all this with you, Professor Stein, and with Gina. We thought, if the four of us put our heads together, we might come up with a list of possible places where that book may be hidden."

"Where do you think it is?" Gina asked the group.

"It's not our job to guess," Hannah said. "We have to let the police investigate. Although I should be angry, it's good that the city police now know about the drug book. However, it was bound to come up when Brad's Uncle Bob tells them Marvin Hart's story."

"But," Brad said, "we did speed things up a bit by talking to Frank's cousin. I just wish we'd been able to find out more."

Hannah said, "Please. You have to stop. Poking around in matters like this can be dangerous. Remember that Gina was hurt. You're college students and not professional detectives. Leave the police work to the police."

Gina said, "Before we go, did anyone else see the eleven o'clock news on channel eight last night?" The boys and Hannah shook their heads and answered, "No." Then Gina continued, "Well, I did. They interviewed the mother of the girl who died with Ken Graybill. This woman was sobbing. She said that Graybill and her daughter were deeply in love. She talked about all the wedding plans they had made. She begged anyone who knows anything about their deaths to call a tipline. This woman is convinced that Ken Graybill and her daughter were both murdered by some unknown person or persons. She's raising money now. She wants to offer a reward for information that will lead to an arrest."

Hannah said, "I hope the police will be able to give this mother some answers and closure." Hannah paused and then added, "Now you three should be moving in new directions, away from murder, rape, and drug deals. Just relax and enjoy the holiday. Go have some fun."

Three solemn students left the classroom together. And once out of earshot of their teacher, they made some unusual Fourth of July plans.

Chapter 59

Later that afternoon, Hannah held onto a German Shepherd's leash with one hand while her other hand held her cell phone in the vicinity of her face, so she could talk to her daughter. Hannah walked, lurched, and staggered as the dog named Lexi pulled her down the street.

"Sophie, I honestly think this dog is walking me and not the other way around," Hannah said. Her words were uttered in a staccato rhythm as she struggled to keep up with Lexi.

Sophie giggled. "Honestly, Mom, I just can't picture you walking the Henleys' dog. Now, I feel guilty for changing my plans and not coming home for the Fourth. I could've helped you take care of Lexi."

"Oh, I'll manage somehow. Luckily, the family left me detailed instructions. Don't worry about me. Have a good time with your friend's family. Enjoy the swimming and water skiing on Lake Erie."

"Thanks, Mom. I'm looking forward to it. I don't know what the cell reception will be like in the cabin where I'll be staying, so I'll skip our Sunday call and talk to you sometime next week. Happy Fourth! Love you."

"I love you, too, honey," Hannah said, and then she ended the call.

Hannah was happy Sophie would soon be enjoying a lakeside retreat, but she would miss having her daughter's company. Instead, Hannah would spend the holiday taking care of one very large and frisky pooch. Hannah slid her phone into her pocket and held onto the leash with both hands. After circling the neighborhood three times, Lexi seemed intent on returning home. Hannah was relieved. Lexi had pooped, and Hannah had scooped. They both had taken care of business. Now, it was time to get the dog home and give her a drink of water. As Lexi pranced up the cul-de-sac with Hannah in tow, Hannah spotted a familiar figure at the end of the Clarks' driveway by their mailbox. She heard a familiar chuckle.

"Look at you," Ethan Clark called. "I didn't know you were a dog-walker."

Hannah stopped in front of Ethan and said, "Believe me, this wasn't my idea. The Henleys were in a bind, so I'm filling in as Lexi's dog-sitter." After saying these words, Hannah looked more closely at Ethan's face. She noted that it was bruised and that he was well on his way to having a black eye. "Oh, Ethan, your poor face. What happened?"

Ethan smiled. "Well, you should see the other guy. Believe me; I kicked that chair hard after it beat me up."

"What?"

"Hannah, here's what happened. My mom keeps her gardening tools in a basket. Sometimes she forgets to put it back in the garage, and she leaves it by the back door. Last night, before I turned in, I thought I'd go outside and make sure I brought everything in from our dinner. The moon was bright, so I didn't turn on a light. Bet you can figure out what happened next. I tripped over Mom's basket and fell right into one of the wrought iron chairs on the patio. It did a number on my face. I feel very foolish."

That's funny, Hannah thought. *There wasn't a gardening basket by their back door last night. I saw Ethan walk in and out of the house many times. He brought out trays of food and never had to circle an obstacle. Our dinner ended well after the sun had set. Lily wouldn't go out late at night to garden in the dark. What's up? Ethan's story doesn't make sense.*

Ethan interrupted Hannah's thoughts, "Hannah, last night was very special for me. I hope you thought it was special, too."

"Yes, Ethan, it was great. I can't thank you enough. You went to a lot of trouble for me. I appreciate it. I appreciate it very much."

"No trouble at all for you." Ethan leaned toward Hannah and lightly kissed her on her cheek.

Hannah looked around. "The neighbors. They might see."

"Let them. I don't care about anyone else. I only care about you."

Lexi pulled on her leash. "I better get this dog out of the sun and give her some water," Hannah said.

"Will you be home for the holiday weekend? May I see you?"

"You'll see me walking Lexi. Remember, I'm the emergency dog-sitter."

"I can work around Lexi. I have to meet with someone tonight about a business opportunity, but I'll get in touch with you tomorrow. This is going to be an unforgettable Fourth of July. I promise."

As Hannah and Lexi walked up the street to the Henleys' house, Hannah wondered what exactly Ethan had in mind.

Chapter 60

It was a little past five o'clock when Hannah ended her phone call with Jodi. Jodi had been rushed. At the last minute, the fellow she had met in the grocery store had invited Jodi to join him on a dinner cruise. Jodi did not have time to quiz Hannah about Ethan. So, Hannah had a reprieve. When Jodi asked Hannah if she had plans for the Fourth, Hannah replied that she would be spending the holiday at home, taking care of a neighbor's dog. And Hannah added, almost as an afterthought, that she also would be seeing Ethan. Jodi wished Hannah well and reminded her to discard her old sundress.

"Don't wear that old thing anymore. Not even in front of the dog. It does nothing for you. Find something pretty to wear when you go out with Ethan. Bye for now," Jodi said.

Hannah grinned. *My old sundress is perfect for dog-sitting. It's cool and comfortable. That's exactly what I'm going to change into. And there's no need to tell Jodi.*

Hannah looked at the clock and realized it was time to feed Lexi and check that there was water in the dog's bowl. She ran up to her bedroom, pulled off her clothes, and put on her old reliable sundress.

Just as Hannah was about to leave her home, her cell phone chimed. Her brother's name and number were on the screen.

"Hi, Michael," Hannah said. She pushed the speaker button so she could listen and talk while she put on her sneakers.

"Hi, Hannah," her brother replied. "Just wanted to say hello, wish you a happy July Fourth, and let you know that Susan has, as she puts it, almost definitely scheduled our wedding for the Saturday night of Thanksgiving weekend. I hope you and your kids can come."

"Well, sure. Of course, we'll make every effort to be there. But what's the problem? Why is Susan wobbling a bit with the date?

"You know," Michael said. "A lot depends on Dad. I know Aunt Gail told you he's dying, and they told me at the home that you've been calling and getting updates. There's nothing new to report. The doctors say he's on a downhill slope, but they aren't sure when the end will come. He could linger for a time. Maybe months. Or he could die very soon. Aunt Gail said that you're planning on coming to the Twin Cities in a couple of weeks."

"Yes. Just as soon as my summer class ends."

"Well, good. Best to see Dad while he's still lucid. By the way, Aunt Gail told me you recently asked her about watches. About the calculator watches Dad and I both had. Now, that's strange."

Hannah said, "Yes. I agree. I saw one the other day, and it scared me. But I have no idea why. Those calculator watches were popular when I was little. I was hoping Aunt Gail might know why the watch frightened me. I hoped she'd remember something that I've forgotten. Do you have any ideas?"

There was a long pause, and then Michael said, "Lots of people had calculator watches. They came out around the time Mom died. I do remember you got upset when a neighbor tried to comfort you at Mom's funeral. She told you Mom was in heaven because it was her time to die. You cried and ran out of the room, screaming that we need to stop time. You were very upset. And you know Dad loves to show off and use old-fashioned words. Why, he still calls a watch a timepiece. I bet you mixed all that up in your head when you were small. You probably connected the trendy calculator watch to time and then linked time to death. That must be why a calculator watch scared you. Yes, I'm sure that's it. Let it go, Hannah. Don't worry about that kid stuff from the past. Everyone has to grow up and move on."

Michael spoke a little longer, but Hannah barely listened. The rationalization that Michael had just come up with did not jive with what Aunt Gail had told her. According to Aunt Gail, Hannah had loved looking at her father's watch when he read to her. Hannah was amazed that, within the span of a few hours, she had heard two very odd explanations. One from Ethan and one from Michael. Both explanations were designed to stifle her curiosity and silence her. Why?

Chapter 61

A short time later, Hannah, much to her surprise, was talking to a dog. Hannah was sitting on one of the Henleys' kitchen chairs, and Lexi, the Henleys' German Shepherd, was sitting on the floor beside her. The dog tilted her head when Hannah began speaking. Hannah sensed that Lexi was understanding her words or, at least, was absorbing her feelings.

"Lexi, I have a confession to make. I was concerned. I really don't know much about dogs, so this task is daunting. But just look at us. We're doing okay together. We started out as casual friends, but I think, before this weekend is over, we'll become great pals. I feel we're moving in that direction." Hannah reached down and petted Lexi's head. "What do you think, girl? Do you agree?"

The dog barked. Hannah smiled and said, "I'll take that as a yes. You know, you're one very smart and very beautiful dog. And, in a little while, after you've digested your meal a bit, we're going to take a nice leisurely evening walk. Now, doesn't that sound fine?"

This time the dog did not bark in agreement. Lexi abruptly rose, raced across the room, and started growling by one of the doors in the hallway off the kitchen. Hannah followed and asked, "What's wrong, Lexi? Did you hear something? Is it behind this door?"

Hannah tried to pull the dog away from the door, so she could open it and investigate, but Lexi stubbornly refused to move and continued to growl. Hannah pressed her ear to the door and thought she heard a scratching sound on the other side.

"Lexi, try to stay calm. However, if it's a mouse or a rat, you might hear me scream."

Hannah wedged her body between the dog and the door, grabbed the doorknob, twisted it, and pried the door open as she pushed Lexi back. The hallway was dimly lit, but she was able to see a small black shape with green eyes that meowed once before it vanished into the darkness. Lexi barked and took off after the cat.

"Wait, Lexi. Wait," Hannah yelled.

Hannah quickly ran her fingers along the wall, searching for a light switch. When she found one, she flicked it on. A light suddenly illuminated a steep staircase. Hannah quickly went down the steps, and a dangling chain bounced off her forehead near the last step. She pulled the chain down and turned on a high-wattage bulb that was attached to a supportive beam. Now, there was enough light for her to see the whole basement. Lexi was barking and racing from one end of the room to the other, searching for the cat. Another meow directed Lexi to an alcove where an ancient washer and dryer had been abandoned. They were rusty and covered in grime. Lexi ran back and forth in front of them, trying to locate the cat. Hannah heard another plaintive meow and felt she had to do something to save the small creature.

Hannah spotted a tool bench near the old washer and dryer. A variety of gardening and handyman tools hung on a large square of pegboard above the bench. Miracle of miracles, there was also a length of rope hanging there, too.

"You're not going to like this, Lexi, but I'm not going to let you tear that cat apart. You're a lot bigger, and you have bigger teeth. It wouldn't be a fair fight," Hannah said as she grabbed hold of the dog's collar, slipped some of the rope under it, and tried to remember how she tied a square knot when she was a Girl Scout. Somehow or other, she managed to make a leash out of the rope. She pulled and pushed Lexi in the direction of the heavy tool bench and then tied the rope to the bench. It was hard to ignore Lexi's loud, indignant barking.

"Think of it this way, Lexi. Now you won't get scratched by the cat," Hannah said. However, Hannah did wonder how she was going to save the kitty and keep it from scratching her.

But first, Hannah had to figure out where the cat was hiding. She heard more frightened meows. They seemed to be coming from the dryer. She looked inside. No cat. She found a flashlight in a box on the tool bench and aimed its ray of light in back of the dryer. She spotted a black ball of fur, with a collar around its neck, shaking on the floor.

Hannah spoke to the cat in a soothing tone, "Hey, kitty, I see you have a collar. You must belong to someone. I'm going to help you get back home. Hopefully, you like people and have had all your shots. But just in case that's not true, give me one more minute." Hannah grabbed some thick gardening gloves off the pegboard wall. "Since they're here, I might as well use them. I really don't relish the idea of getting hurt while I rescue you."

Hannah pushed her hands into the gloves and then got down on her knees and looked behind the dryer. There was only a small space between the back of the dryer and the wall. She carefully slid one arm into the space and stretched, but try as she might, she could not reach the cat. She tried calling to the animal, but the cat only meowed plaintively in response and did not move. Hannah walked over to the front of the dryer. She grabbed the sides of the appliance and tried to move it forward, but it was heavy and would not budge. Then she tried joggling it a bit from side to side as she slowly backed up. With each rocking motion, Hannah managed to move the dryer, ever so slowly, away from the wall. Finally, there was a little more room behind the dryer, just enough for Hannah to lie flat on the floor on her side, slither to the cat, and scoop up the animal.

While Hannah was concentrating on her rescue efforts, Lexi had been engaging in a running commentary. Her loud barks reverberated off the cinder block basement walls. The dog was upset. She was intent on protecting the family domain from the intruder and loudly voiced her objections to being thwarted.

"Hush, now, Lexi," Hannah said as she cradled the shaking cat in her arms. "The situation is under control." However, Lexi continued to bark and bark. Exasperated, Hannah said in a stern voice, "Sit. Quiet." And Lexi sat and stopped barking. Hannah was pleasantly surprised that Lexi had responded to her commands.

The room was suddenly silent, and then Hannah heard two things. She heard a thump, the sound of something hitting the floor, and immediately after that, she heard Ethan's voice.

"Hannah," Ethan called, "where are you? Is everything all right?"

"I'm in the basement," Hannah shouted.

In no time at all, Ethan was standing beside Hannah. "I saw you walk up the street a short time ago. I figured you were on your way to take care of Lexi. And then I heard the barking. I think everyone in the whole neighborhood heard Lexi barking. It went on and on and on and on. I got concerned. I knocked on the Henleys' side door, but you didn't answer. The door was unlocked, so I let myself in. What happened? Do you need some help?"

"This is what happened," Hannah said as she placed the cat, that had calmed down, in Ethan's arms. "Hold onto it while I check the ID tag hanging from its collar. I'd like to return this cat to its owner right away. As you heard, Lexi wants this animal outta here pronto."

Hannah slid her hands out of the gardening gloves and then picked up the ID tag. She leaned down and read the information on the tag. She said, "The cat's name is Pepper, and it belongs to the Peterson family. There's also a phone number and an address."

"No need to call," Ethan said. "The Petersons live in the white house with green shutters on the corner. We can return this animal in nothing flat. But how did the cat get in here?"

"I don't know for sure. But I have an idea." Hannah pointed to a broken window.

Ethan nodded. "That's probably why I heard Lexi so clearly."

Before either of them had the chance to say anything further, they heard two high-pitched voices calling, "Pepper. Pepper. Where are you, Pepper?"

"I think," Ethan said, "that we don't have to look for Pepper's owners. I think they are outside looking for their cat."

In a very short time, Pepper was reunited, in front of the Henleys' home, with two red-headed boys under the age of ten.

"Thank you," the taller boy said as he protectively held the cat close to his chest. "We were worried. Pepper's not an outdoor cat. Sorry if she caused you any trouble. Boy, she sure got dirty. Hey, lady, you sure got dirty, too."

Ethan laughed after the boys and the cat departed. "You know, he's right, Hannah. You sure are a sight. You are streaked with dirt from head to toe."

"Oh, no," said Hannah as she looked at her dirt-smudged arms and dress. "I better clean up."

Ethan said, "Tell you what, I don't have to leave for my appointment till nine o'clock. I can take Lexi for a walk right now. That'll give you time to wash up and change. Okay?"

"Are you sure?"

"Definitely. If it'll make you feel better, you can treat me to an ice-cold soft drink when I bring Lexi back. Deal?"

"Deal," Hannah said.

Chapter 62

After Ethan and Lexi left for their walk, Hannah returned to the Henley basement.

Before I get all cleaned up, I should do something about that broken window. I don't want Pepper or any other animal to sneak into the house, Hannah said to herself. *I saw a modern laundry room off the kitchen, so I bet no one has come down here to wash clothes for a very long time. The tool bench is dusty, too. That window may have been broken for some time.*

Hannah circled the basement. In one corner, there was a furnace and water heater. Near them, there was a metal shelving unit where some paint cans and brushes were stored. A clothing rack holding four long, bulky garment bags was against the far wall. None of these things would help her seal off the window. Hannah thought she might have more luck finding repair materials in the barn. There, she had some success. She found a small tarp near a couple of rakes, and on a metal shelf, there were a variety of odds and ends, including a new roll of duct tape. It was an amateur job and a temporary fix, but Hannah was pleased with herself after she sealed the window using the tarp and the tape.

Hannah grinned and thought, *I can now add to my resume that I am Hannah Stein, staunch duct tape advocate, quick window fixer, and emergency dog-sitter. However, I am also Hannah Stein, who is covered in grime. I better hurry and get cleaned up before Ethan and Lexi get back. Time to lock up this place and head home to shower.*

Hannah patted the pocket on the right side of her sundress and frowned. It was empty. She had put her house key and the Henleys' house key on a key ring before she left her house, and she remembered dropping both of them in her pocket. The one on the right side. She looked in her pocket on the other side of her dress, just in case she was mistaken. It held her cell phone but no keys. Now what? Where could the keys have gone? She reasoned that she might have dropped them when she was struggling to get a hold of the cat. And then she remembered the thump. She heard something fall before Ethan came down the stairs and joined her in the basement. Could that thump have been the keys? She walked over to the dryer and examined the floor. No keys. She looked in back of the dryer and spotted something silvery. Once again, Hannah had to retrieve something that was on the floor in back of the dryer, and once again, she was successful. Except this time, she got more than she expected. Her key ring was stuck on a plastic bag. The bag had strips of masking tape around it, and the keys were clinging to one of the strips. After Hannah extricated herself from the back of the dryer, she was able to examine her find more closely. She pulled the keys off the tape and dropped the key ring in her pocket. Then, she looked at the plastic bag and noted that there was a small book inside it.

Hannah thought, *This bag must have been attached to the back of the dryer. I did shake the dryer a lot to move it away from the wall. I bet this book is an instruction manual. People often keep them near their appliances. The sound I heard, the thump, must have been the book hitting the floor when the tape gave out.*

Hannah slid the book out of the bag. It had a cracked plastic cover, and the letters KG were stamped in a gold color on the bottom right corner. She opened the book and discovered it was a financial ledger. It contained page after page of transactions from the years 2004 to 2006.

I was wrong. This is not a user manual. But can I make the leap based on the initials KG? Hannah asked herself. *Could this really be Ken Graybill's account book?*

There was a roughly drawn map on the back of the front cover. A long line was drawn from Canada to Philadelphia, and then there were many shorter lines branching out from Philadelphia to surrounding towns. One red line stretched to the west to Harrisburg, and another blue one angled south to Baltimore. She noted that there were tabs on some pages that divided the book into sections: customers, soldiers, supply, and cops. Money appeared to flow in from the first category and out to the last three. There were dates and dollar amounts in the book but no names. A combination of letters and numbers was by each transaction.

He must have used some sort of code to identify the people he dealt with, Hannah mused. As she flipped through the pages of the ledger, a folded sheet of paper slipped out of the book and fell on the floor. Hannah picked it up and opened it. There was a sketch that resembled a family tree, and there were the same type of letters and numbers by each branch. *I wonder what this means? Could this be a diagram of the whole drug operation, with the kingpin at the top and the lesser lords below?*

Hannah was surprised when she heard Lexi's bark; Ethan and Lexi had returned from their walk. Hannah had lost track of time and realized that she was now dirtier, from her second foray to the back of the dryer, than she was when they left. She looked at the book in her hands and shuddered. It suddenly struck her that she was holding onto something evil. Lives were destroyed when kids got hooked on illegal drugs, and this book was part of that story. Furthermore, someone might have killed Graybill and his fiancée for this ledger. She suddenly wanted nothing more than to hand the book over to the proper authorities and get as far away from it as possible. But Hannah was at a loss. She had no idea which government agency to turn to. Would the ledger be used to support a local, state, or federal case? She would ask Ethan. With his background, he would know. Hannah quickly looked inside the washer, just in case something else might be hidden inside of it. But it was empty.

Hannah heard Ethan and Lexi enter the house, and then she heard the sound of running water in the kitchen. She assumed that Ethan was refilling the dog's water bowl and possibly grabbing a drink of water for himself, too. As Hannah was walking up the stairs from the basement, she heard Ethan's cell phone chime, and when she reached the hallway off the kitchen, Ethan was shouting into his phone.

"Stop threatening me. And don't send those thugs to rough me up again. It's not going to get you your money any faster. I got your message, and I've got everything covered. I'll seal the deal with the doctor's widow this weekend, and I'll get the money from her. No problem. She owns her house free and clear. She can take out a mortgage if there's not enough to pull the full amount from other places. You'll get your money."

Hannah gasped. Her hand flew to her mouth to smother a scream. What a fool she had been. Ethan had been playing her. She was hurt and angry at herself for being swayed by Ethan's romantic moves. But another part of her, a bigger part, was simply furious with Ethan. How dare he take it for granted that she could be manipulated.

Hannah stepped into the kitchen.

Chapter 63

Ethan ended his call. He turned and spotted Hannah.

"Hannah, I thought you were getting cleaned up at your house. Did you hear what I just said?"

"It was hard not to. You were yelling."

"Hannah, let me explain."

"No, Ethan. I don't want to hear any more lies. Just leave."

"But I didn't mean it. I was just buying myself a little time. Hannah, you know you mean the world to me. You know I've fallen in love with you."

"Oh, Ethan, stop. It's over. You don't have to pretend anymore."

"You don't understand. Please, just listen to me."

"No. I've heard enough. Just get out of this house and out of my life."

Hannah strode to the door and opened it. She stood like a stone sentinel by the door, with her arms protectively crossed at her chest, waiting for Ethan to leave. Instead, he quickly crossed the room, closed and locked the door, and stood in front of it, blocking the door with his body.

"Please, Hannah, I need to talk to you. Just give me a few minutes. Then, I'll leave if you still want me to."

"Leave right now, or I'll call 911." Hannah reached into her pocket and drew out her cell phone. Ethan immediately snatched it out of her hand.

"Tell you what, we'll swap. You give me a little of your time, and I'll give you back your phone. And I'll sweeten the deal. I'll truthfully answer your questions. I figure I owe you that. You know you always have questions."

Hannah glared at Ethan but did not respond.

"Come on, Hannah. I can't walk away from you like this. I'm only asking for a few minutes."

Reluctantly, Hannah pulled a kitchen chair away from the table and sat down on it. She chose the one closest to the door. When she sat down, she felt the weight of the ledger against her leg. She had dropped the book into her pocket, the one holding the keys, before she entered the kitchen. Ethan moved a chair close to hers and sat down, too.

"Well?" Hannah asked. "What's so important? You know, holding me against my will is illegal."

Ethan sighed. "This is tough. I hate admitting to you that I'm a phenomenal screw-up. I've wrecked my life and hurt my family. And now I've hurt you, too. What's worse is that I have no excuse. It's the gambling. I've been hooked for years. When I win, I can't stop. I want more. And when I lose, I can't stop because I have to make back what I lost. It's sick. I know it. I'm sick. And now, I've hit rock bottom. I'm in deep, Hannah. Deeper than I've ever been before. I've had an incredible run of bad luck. I owe money to a guy in Philadelphia and to another guy in Harrisburg. Their interest rates are out of sight, but I was desperate to make a big score and get out of this mess. Now they both want to be repaid. But I have nothing to give them. And it's a lot. My folks can't help me. They're tapped out after buying their home and covering my losses for years. I have no one left to turn to but you."

"How much do you owe?" Hannah asked.

"One hundred fifty thousand dollars."

"Ethan, are you serious? Do you really expect me to give you that much money?"

"Hannah, my life is on the line. If I don't hand over a big chunk of my debt, they may kill me. Or, worse yet, hurt my folks and my sister to make me suffer. These people do not make idle threats."

"Ethan, go to the police. Get some protection."

"I can't, Hannah."

"Why?"

"Because I've made mistakes. I didn't leave the Parkerville force because I wanted to work in a bigger city. I was told to get out and move on. People on the force started putting two and two together. They knew too many drug sellers were slipping through our nets; they were too lucky. Yes, I was paid to tip them off. I'm not proud of it, but I kept having gambling debts. I thought things would be different when I became a cop in Philadelphia. But they weren't. I went right back to gambling and right back to needing money. I had contacts, and getting money, lots of money, for passing on a little information to drug dealers was so easy. But, once again, my fellow officers became suspicious. There was no proof to make a case, but I was quietly told to leave while the going was still good. The station didn't want its reputation soiled by the likes of me."

"But, Ethan, if it's a matter of life and death …"

"No. The last thing I need is to have the police poking into my life right now. I've had to make some questionable choices lately. But you can help me, Hannah. I know you can. You don't want my death on your conscience."

"I can't help you, Ethan. I'm not rich. My husband was still paying off his medical school debts when he died. I have two kids in college now, and I don't earn a lot."

"But, if you can't give me the full amount, can you lend me something to hold off the vultures? You must have some savings. You did say you own your home."

"So, all that talk about housing values and mortgages was just a ploy to find out about my finances? It was all a lie, wasn't it? You never wanted to become a real estate agent."

"I said I'd be honest. Yes, I did want to know how you were fixed for money. But I do need a new job, and selling houses is a possibility. Honestly, Hannah, I never dreamed I'd be in such a fix."

"Ethan, I'm sorry you're in a jam, but I can't help you. My husband worked hard to pay off our mortgage. He wanted his family to have a good, secure home. I won't give it away. I have to protect myself and my children."

Hannah quickly rose and started toward the door. Ethan stood up and grabbed her by the arm and spun her around.

"Hannah, you must help me," Ethan angrily shouted. "After all I've done for you, to keep you safe, you owe me."

Lexi growled and moved toward them. The dog still had on her leash from her walk. Ethan held on to Hannah's arm with one hand and tried to reach for the leash trailing behind the dog with his other hand. But Ethan did not move fast enough. In the next instant, Lexi was standing at Hannah's side and barking at Ethan.

"Easy, girl. Quiet," Hannah deliberately and calmly said. "Ethan, let go of me, or I'll tell Lexi to attack. Since you won't leave, Lexi and I will. I can always get another phone."

Ethan relaxed his grip on Hannah, and Hannah immediately backed away from him. She was anxious to get away. She quickly bent down, picked up Lexi's leash, and pulled. The dog was startled and knocked against Hannah's right leg. The movement caused the ledger to fall out of Hannah's shallow pocket and tumble onto the kitchen floor. Ethan bent down to pick up the book, but Lexi growled at him again. The threat implicit in that menacing sound caused Ethan to hesitate and gave Hannah just enough time to grab the ledger off the floor and shove it back into her pocket.

"I saw the letters KG. Is it what I think it is?" Ethan asked.

Hannah didn't answer, but she could feel her face getting hot. She knew her cheeks were flushed.

Ethan noted Hannah's reaction. He emitted a sigh and a low-pitched whistle. "Well, I'll be. People have been going crazy looking for Graybill's account book for a long time. And you found it. Where was it hidden?"

Hannah remained silent.

"Of course," Ethan said. "You must have found it here. You're still covered in dirt. You never went home to shower. Graybill always believed that he had a rightful claim to this place. Makes sense that he would stash his account book here for safekeeping."

"I'm leaving with Lexi now, and I'm giving this book to the police."

"No. It has no value to the police. They can't convict anyone for any of those drug transactions now. That's the beauty of the statute of limitations. But I can use it. It can help me."

"How?" Hannah asked.

Hannah knew her curiosity was getting the better of her. But, as Lexi was by her side, she felt protected. She no longer felt the urgent need to bolt. In addition, Ethan had said he would answer her questions truthfully, and she did have many questions.

"Graybill's ledger is worth a lot to the right person. And I know who that person is. I was on his payroll when I was a Parkerville cop, and he recently hired me to look for the ledger. You won't give me money, but you can give me the book. It'll save me. Believe me, Hannah, you don't want to hold onto it. You don't want to end up like Graybill and his girlfriend."

"What do you know about that? Did you kill them?"

"Me? Of course not. But I won't say who did. There are some things you're better off not knowing. For your own safety."

"From whom? I'm so tired of your lies. Did you ever tell me the truth?"

"You know I did. I was honest about my feelings. I really did fall for you. And you met Joe. He's on the force. He's the real deal."

"And what about my students' questions regarding Sandra Metzler's rape? Is there a Detective Erin Summers?"

"Yes. Only I didn't bother talking to her. There wasn't time to track her down. I was promised money, a lot of money if I got you and your students to stop your investigation. I needed that money right away. I'm sorry, Hannah. I wish I could've handled things differently. I wish you would've just accepted the logical explanations I dreamed up. Every time I thought you were through with the Baker case, you or your students would go right back to it and ask more questions."

"Really, Ethan. Someone paid you to deceive me?"

"Not yet. But I hope to get some money for my efforts tonight. And more if I hand over Graybill's ledger. Maybe a lot more. Hannah, how can I get you to understand? I lied to protect you. I went to great lengths to save you."

Hannah frowned. "What great lengths are you talking about? What did you do? There was that threatening note on my car. Did you leave that?"

"No, that was Graybill. The little creep actually thought you would cave in if he frightened you. Stupid guy. He never could spell 'murdered.'"

"And Graybill was the one who tried to hit my students with his car. Then there was the other note by Audrey's body. Oh, no. Did you kill Audrey?"

Ethan paused. "Of course, I'll never admit this to anyone else. Yes, I had to. I hated that it had to be done. And it really was your fault. You were being so damn difficult and stubborn. I did it for you. You weren't backing off. You needed to believe that you were in danger. I wrote the note as Graybill would have. His misspellings and all."

"No. No. No," Hannah moaned. "How could you? What kind of monster are you?"

"Hannah, don't look at me like that. Why can't you understand?"

Hannah swiped away the tears that were on her face. She gulped for air and then said in a measured tone, "Okay. I've heard more than enough. Stop talking, Ethan. Just shut up. You asked me to listen to you, and I did. Now give me back my phone as you promised, and get out of here."

"I'm sorry, Hannah. I really am. I never wanted it to end like this between us. Just give me the ledger, and I'll leave."

"Go. But I'm not giving you money, and I'm not giving you Graybill's book."

Ethan took a step toward Hannah, but Lexi bared her teeth and growled again.

"All right, Hannah. Have it your way. I'm not going to fight you for the book. Just do me one small favor. Don't give it to the police right away."

"Why?"

"Because I'll bluff and say I have it. Let me try to squeeze more cash out of my deal. Then, I'll have a nice bit of traveling money, and I'll be able to disappear. If I'm gone, there's no reason to hurt my family. If you won't help me, then help them."

"But, Ethan, I don't get it. What makes the book so valuable? You said, after all this time, no one can be prosecuted for anything in it."

"Ah, but there are names in the book. I saw Graybill write in it once. He used some type of code. But after some clever code-breaking geek figures out the names, things will explode, and reputations will shatter. I need to cash in before that happens." Ethan put Hannah's phone on the kitchen table. "I said I'd return it to you, and here it is. See, you can trust me now. Please, Hannah. All I need is a couple of days to make my play and collect some money. Can you give me that?"

Hannah hesitated.

Sensing that Hannah might be swayed by a gentler approach, Ethan pivoted. "You don't have to make up your mind right now. I trust you to be fair. Take some time. Think it over."

"Okay. I promise to think it over, but I won't promise more. Just one last question."

"Naturally. I would expect nothing less from you."

"Graybill, illegal drugs, and the account book. It's easy to see how they're connected. But my students heard about someone called Sorry Face. How does Sorry Face fit into all this? What did Graybill have on Sorry Face? And why the need to shut down an amateur inquiry into the Baker case? Did Matthew Baker really kill his family, or is someone else responsible? And Graybill boasted he had something, some proof, related to the Baker killings. Does it exist or not?"

"You said you had one last question. It's amazing. You just can't help yourself. You can't stop asking questions. But I'll be generous. Honestly, you'd be very surprised if you knew who Sorry Face is. I'm not going to say more than that. As to Matthew Baker's guilt or innocence, I have no idea. What I can tell you is this; a lot of money has been spent to keep Baker in jail. I don't know what Graybill thought he knew about the Baker murders. In all likelihood, Graybill's version of the story and his proof died with him. Let it be, Hannah. Protect yourself and your students. Let it be."

Ethan walked to the door and paused before he opened it. "A couple of days won't change anything for the police, but they could save my life. Think about that, Hannah. And remember, I will always love you."

After Ethan left, Hannah hugged Lexi and gave her a treat. Hannah then guided the dog out of the house, locked the Henleys' door, and walked toward her home with her canine protector.

"Until I get rid of this book, I want you by my side," Hannah said to the dog.

By the time Hannah reached her car in her driveway, she had made her decision. She turned to Lexi and said, "Well, I promised to think it over, and I did. Promise fulfilled. Lexi, we're going for a ride."

Chapter 64

Ten minutes later, Hannah was parking her car in front of the Parkerville police station. Ten minutes after that, the officer at the desk had summoned, upon Hannah's request, Officer Paul Brown. And after an intense hour of filling out paperwork and answering questions, Hannah left the police station with Lexi. Ken Graybill's ledger was now safely in the hands of the Parkerville police. The names in it, the ones Graybill had tried to conceal, would soon be decoded and revealed. Although Hannah felt a twinge of concern for Ethan, she was confident that she had made the right choice.

When Hannah and Lexi returned to Hannah's house, Hannah realized that she had fed Lexi dinner but had not eaten one herself. She slathered one piece of bread with peanut butter and another with jelly, pushed the bread slices together, popped open a can of soda, and set her sandwich and beverage down on a table in her family room. Her simple meal rapidly disappeared in quick, successive bites. Afterward, she pulled her laptop computer out of its bag and typed while she polished off her soft drink. She put names on top of columns: Ken Graybill, Matthew Baker, Sandra Metzler, Sorry Face, and Moose. After a brief pause, she added the name Ethan Clark. Then she filled in what she knew about each of these people and what she wanted to find out. It bothered her that she still had so many questions about the people on her spreadsheet. Looking into the Baker case had not enabled her to find the peace of mind she craved. One unresolved issue had simply led to another with no end in sight. However, she did learn, while she was at the Parkerville police station, that they never had a fire in their building. The story of a fire destroying all of Sandra Metzler's rape evidence was another one of Ethan's fabrications. As there is no statute of limitations in Pennsylvania for the rape of a minor, there was a good chance that whatever had been collected in connection to the Metzler rape was still in an evidence box in the station's basement.

So, if anything new is discovered in conjunction with the rape, Hannah mused, *it might be verified by a piece of evidence that was gathered and collected years ago. But is there anything new to learn about it? So many pieces to this puzzle, and Ethan told me so many lies. Tonight the police showed me the picture Will Dotlish sent them of the man who left the note on my car. It was Ken Graybill. It's not much, but tonight Ethan did tell me the truth about that. I wish I knew why Graybill did it. Was it his idea or someone else's?*

Lexi put her head on Hannah's lap, and Hannah ran her fingers through the dog's thick, silky fur coat.

"You're going to stay here with me," Hannah said to Lexi. "It's been quite a day, and I could use the company. And, I must admit, I like the idea of having a guard dog with me tonight. I'll make up a nice bed for you in the kitchen and set out a water bowl. Just give me a few minutes to send an email. My investigative trio deserves to know that I found Ken Graybill's account book. I want to share the news with them."

Hannah quickly opened a new email and put the email addresses of Frank, Brad, and Gina in the "send to" space. Then she rapidly typed her message.

Chapter 65

That night Hannah had trouble sleeping. She tossed and turned as she replayed the day over and over in her mind. She was tired, but she found it difficult to relax and unwind. She flipped on the light on her bedside table.

Might as well read for a bit, she thought as she reached for a novel. There was always a pile of books on the table by her bed. *I did what I had to do, but, despite everything he's done, I can't help worrying about Ethan. I do hope no one will hurt him or his family.*

Hannah was surprised when she heard the doorbell ring. It was so late, too late for anyone to come for a visit. Was there an emergency? Hannah flew down the stairs and flung open the front door. She was shocked to see Ethan standing in front of her. He was dressed in a Superman costume, and he was holding a bouquet of roses. Hannah was astounded when Ethan flew into her house. He landed in the center of the family room and proclaimed that he would turn her home into a gambling casino. He said, "I will place bets as I fight for truth, justice, and the American Way." Hannah opened her mouth to object, but what came out was a bark, a dog's bark. She barked over and over. The sound shattered her dream and woke her.

Hannah opened her eyes and looked around. She realized that she was in her bed in her bedroom. She must have fallen into a deep sleep while she was reading because she was finding it difficult to wake up. She heard barking, loud barking. And it would not stop. Then a thought trickled into her brain, and she followed it as it seeped into her consciousness. Barking meant dog, and dog meant Lexi, and barking Lexi meant that something was wrong in her house. And now she recognized another sound, the screech of the house security alarm system.

Hannah jumped out of bed, jammed her feet into her slippers, and flung her robe over her shoulders as she raced down the stairs. She followed the sound of Lexi's barks to the back of the house. She flicked on the overhead light in the kitchen. There was broken glass on the floor, and the door to the deck was open. As she walked into the room, Lexi ran out the door, chasing a large black shadow. Seconds later, Hannah heard thumps on the deck and the sound of Lexi whimpering.

"Lexi," Hannah shouted as she sprinted out her kitchen door.

There was no time to say more. Hannah's head exploded in pain. It had been hit by a large, heavy object. Hannah's body swayed from the impact, and she collapsed onto her deck.

Chapter 66

"Hannah, can you hear me?" Lily Clark asked. "Cranston, she's not answering me. Her head is bleeding. What should we do?"

Cranston Clark replied, "I hear sirens. The police and paramedics will be here soon. I heard a few moans. I don't think we should move her."

A short time later, Hannah felt hands gently turn her over and touch her head. Her head felt sticky and hurt. It hurt a lot. Hannah opened her eyes. Lily and Cranston Clark were hovering in the background, looking very concerned. Officer Paul Brown was standing nearby, too. A young woman with a stethoscope around her neck was kneeling beside Hannah and slowly wrapping a bandage around Hannah's head.

"Please, I don't need to be fussed over," Hannah mumbled. "I'm fine."

Lily Clark laughed. "Well, that's got to be a good sign. She's talking now."

"What happened?" Hannah asked. "Why are you all here?"

"What do you remember?" Officer Brown asked.

"I remember that Lexi's barking woke me up. Is Lexi okay?" Hannah asked.

Cranston Clark said, "She's fine, Hannah. But I'm afraid your cloth folding chair is broken. Lexi got her foot caught in it. There's a big hole in the fabric now."

"It looks like someone tried to break into your house. Was the dog chasing someone?" Brown asked.

"Yes," Hannah said. "I remember now. I saw Lexi take off after someone dressed in black. I ran outside to look for Lexi, and then I felt something heavy hit my head."

"Judging from the shards of broken pottery," Brown said, "I think a planter was flung at you."

The paramedic added, "And you were lucky it only grazed your head. But we're going to take you to the hospital, so they can look you over there."

Lily Clark turned to Hannah and said, "I'm so glad we called for help. I told Cranston that something was wrong when we heard all the barking and the house alarm. When I looked out our bedroom window, I saw that your motion detector lights were on. I was surprised to see the Henleys' dog on your deck. And then I saw you, Hannah. Just lying face down and not moving. I was so frightened. Ethan will be so upset when he hears about all this."

Hannah was dazed, but thoughts were beginning to gel. "Where is Ethan?"

Lily answered, "I don't know. He had a business appointment. He hasn't returned, so he must be staying with friends. But don't worry, dear. We'll tell him what happened." She turned to Officer Brown. "Isn't that romantic? They're sweet on each other, and the first person she asked about was our Ethan."

Brown noted that Hannah looked directly at him and gave her head a tiny shake to signify "no," that is not why she asked. The patrolman gave his head a small nod to acknowledge that he understood.

Chapter 67

Thursday, July 4

"Hannah," Jodi gushed over the phone, "I think I'm falling in love. In fact, I may already be there. In love. Doesn't that sound absolutely wonderful?"

Hannah was groggy. Her cell phone's ringtone had awoken her, and she had grabbed for her phone and murmured a sleep-laden "hello" before opening her eyes. She gingerly fingered the bandage on her head. She had a tremendous headache.

"Hannah, you haven't said a word. Don't you believe me? I know I've said that I was in love before, but this may be the real, long-lasting thing."

"Jodi," Hannah replied, "I'm sorry, but I'm not fully awake. Are you talking about the fellow you were with last night, the one you met in the grocery store?"

"Yes, that's the one. Hannah, you wouldn't believe the dinner cruise. It was just great. And, anyway, why are you so sleepy? You're normally up way before I am. I never thought I'd be waking you at ten o'clock in the morning. Are you tired because you had a romantic time with your Superman last night? Is he still with you?"

"Slow down. Slow way down. I have a lot to tell you, but I don't have much time. I need to get up and take care of my neighbors' dog. I'm going to watch the clock and only talk for five minutes, and I promise I will elaborate later. And I do want to hear more about your evening with the man you met at the grocery store, starting with his name, but that will also have to wait until later."

Hannah quickly brought Jodi up to speed. Her friend appropriately gasped in astonishment and uttered supportive words as Hannah related a condensed version of everything that had happened to her since they last spoke. Although her head wound had required five stitches, Hannah assured Jodi that she was fine. She had survived her encounter with the "large black shadow." She had no other words to describe her assailant.

"I know you must regret dating Ethan. But honestly, Hannah, who could have predicted what you were getting into? I'm so sorry I encouraged you to give Ethan a chance. Definitely not the right guy for you. You said Ethan wanted the book. Do you think he broke into your home to get it? Was he the one who threw the planter at you?"

"I really don't know. Maybe Officer Brown will find out for me. He was very helpful and kind when Audrey was killed. Last night, when I went to the Parkerville station, Brown had just started his shift, so I handed Graybill's ledger over to him. Brown was also the patrolman who responded to the 911 call and took Lexi back to the Henleys' house when I went to the hospital. Speaking of the dog, I've got to get moving. The poor animal must be going crazy waiting for me. Jodi, I've gone past the five-minute limit. No time, my friend, to go over anything more now. We'll talk later."

After ending the call, Hannah forced herself to leave her bed and pull a sundress out of her closet. She awkwardly wiggled into her clothes. Every small movement intensified the pain in her head. Hannah was grateful that she could just slide her feet into her sandals and did not need to bend down to put them on. After chugging down a glass of water and some pain relief tablets, Hannah covered her sore head with a sunhat and left her house with her pockets filled with dog treats for Lexi, the wonder dog who had guarded her and her home.

Chapter 68

Hannah carefully walked up the block to the Henleys' home, trying not to jostle her head too much. What she saw from the street surprised her. There were people sitting on the Henleys' front stoop. Three people, to be exact. Three people who just happened to be Brad, Frank, and Gina.

When Hannah got closer, she called out, "Hello. What are you doing here?"

The trio stood up and walked toward Hannah. Brad spoke first. "We all read your email last night. We were blown away by it. You found Graybill's account book."

Gina said in a rush, "Each of us contacted the others after reading what you wrote. You see, we've been trying to figure out where Graybill might have hidden things. We did some investigating after class yesterday and got absolutely nowhere."

"More investigating?" Hannah asked. "I thought I told all of you to relax and enjoy the holiday break."

"Well," Frank said, "in our defense, we were relaxing. We went to Lake Keller. It's a nice place to walk, fish, and have a picnic."

"Yes, I know that," Hannah said. "But why am I thinking that you three had another reason for being there?"

Gina blurted, "Of course, you're right, Professor Stein. But we were all together and safe and just asking a few questions in a very public place in the middle of the day."

Hannah sighed. "So, you went to the mobile home park near the lake, right? Checking out the place where Graybill used to live?"

"Yup," Brad said. "We did. And got nowhere. We talked to some folks, but no one knew much. Just what they'd heard on the news. Ken Graybill's parents had moved away years ago. We heard they live somewhere in California now. So, there was nothing to look at and nowhere to search."

"But, you see, that's why we're here," Frank said. "You found the ledger in this house, so maybe there's more hidden here, too. Stuff that might clear Matthew Baker."

Just then, there was the large pop of a firecracker, followed by the repetitive crackle of smaller fireworks. Inside the house, Lexi barked and barked.

"Oh," Hannah said. "Fireworks. I almost forgot that it's the Fourth of July. I'm sorry. I really can't talk to you now. I have to take care of the dog. And I can't let you enter and rummage around this house. I don't have the Henleys' permission. Just go home. I'll see you all in class on Monday."

There was another round of thunderous, sputtering fireworks, and Lexi barked again. Hannah headed toward the Henleys' side door. Last night, after leaving Lexi in the Henleys' house, Officer Brown had stopped by the hospital to return the house key to Hannah. Now, she had the key in her hand. Hannah unlocked the door and opened it. She was about to walk into the house when a brisk breeze blew her straw hat off her head. When she turned to pick it up, she was surprised. Frank, Brad, and Gina had not left. They were standing right behind her.

"Please," Hannah said, "I thought I made it very clear. You have to leave."

"But," Frank said, "we want to make sure you'll be okay in there. We walked around the house when we got here, just before you came. We were talking over what to do next when you arrived. You see, someone broke off the lock on the basement bulkhead, that large door in the back of the house. Did you see that?"

That surprised Hannah. The old farmhouse had many doors, and she had only used the side door which led into the kitchen. She had never circled the house. Suddenly, there was the sound of more fireworks, a deafening popping and snapping, causing Lexi to bark again and again.

Hannah's head was still throbbing, and the loud celebratory noises and Lexi's continuous barking were causing her to wince in pain.

"Okay," Hannah said, "wait here while I take care of all the dog's needs, and then we'll check out that bulkhead door together."

A short time later, while Lexi was gobbling down her late breakfast in the kitchen, Hannah and her students stood in front of the bulkhead door. The broken lock was lying alongside it.

"There's no way to know when the lock was broken," Brad said. "The lock is rusty, but that doesn't tell us when it was pried off."

"This is the type of door that gives you easy access to a cellar or basement," Gina said. She turned toward Hannah. "You were in the basement. You found Graybill's ledger there. Right?"

"Yes," said Hannah, "But I walked down the stairs off the kitchen to get to the basement. When I was down there, I was in a large room, but I didn't see any doors. No closets and no exits. I'm concerned about this broken lock. If the Henleys had seen it, they wouldn't have left something rusty like this in the yard where their small children could trip over it. I hate to think some damage was done on my watch. And I would like to know what this bulkhead door covers and where it leads. I guess there's only one way to find out."

Hannah's students nodded in agreement. Frank moved toward the bulkhead door and opened it, uncovering a short set of stairs. Frank stepped down the stairs and stood in front of an entry door. When Frank turned the doorknob, he discovered that the door was unlocked, but he could not open it very far. Something was in the way. Frank took a deep breath, put both his hands on the door, and pushed. He heard something on the other side of the door move. Frank had enlarged the opening. Frank pushed hard again. This time he distinctly heard the sound of metallic wheels skittering away. The door swung open. Frank walked through the opening, and the others followed him. There was just enough sunlight seeping through the dirty windows for Hannah to see that she was once again in the Henleys' basement.

"Now, I understand," Hannah said. "The door was hidden. Covered and blocked by this movable clothing rack." She pointed to the metal unit, which had four bulky garment bags hanging from its rack.

"Do you think someone put it in front of the door on purpose?" Gina asked.

"I don't know," Hannah replied. "Everything looks the same as it did when I was last here. Nothing's out of place."

"Well, as long as we're here, Professor Stein, will you show us where you found the ledger?" Brad asked.

Hannah answered, "All right. Since you're already here, I can't see any harm in that."

Hannah led them over to the old clothes washer and dryer and pointed.

"It was taped to the back of this dryer," Hannah explained.

"What about the washer?" Frank asked. "Did you look inside it, too?

"Yes," Hannah said. "I checked inside the washer and dryer. Just dirt and dust."

"And in back of the washer?" Brad asked.

"I must admit that after I found the ledger, I was distracted. Someone entered the house, and then other matters came up that I had to attend to."

"So," Frank said, "something could be back there. Since Graybill liked the dryer as a hiding place, why not the washer? We're here. We've just got to look."

Three anxious faces looked at Hannah, pleading with her to agree.

Hannah sighed. "Okay. One quick look. Then we must put everything back just the way we found it."

Hannah walked over to the stairs, pulled the chain, and turned on the light to illuminate the basement.

She felt lightheaded and sat down on the steps to rest while Brad and Frank worked together to pull the heavy clothes washer away from the wall. Gina grabbed the flashlight from the workbench, switched it on, and aimed its beam at the dark area behind the old washer. It was not an easy task, but the boys managed to slowly move the clothes washer forward.

"Stop, guys," Gina said. "I don't see anything. Nothing's taped to the back of the washer."

"Are you sure?" Frank asked. "I was really hopeful."

"I know," Gina said. "I thought something would be back here, too. But no such luck."

Brad scowled and scratched his head. "Ken Graybill hid his ledger in this basement. He must have thought this was a good place to hide things. So, if I were Graybill, where would I hide other important stuff?" Brad looked around. "It's not a finished room, so all the structural supports are exposed. There's not much down here."

Frank added, "We can look, but I doubt there's anything important attached to the furnace or the water heater. I wouldn't attach something to them because those units break down. Then workers would be down here repairing or replacing them. Same for hiding something among the tools or paint stuff because people do, eventually, use those things. True for the garment bags, too. Folks could empty them at any time or throw them out. There's nowhere else to look. I'm stumped." Frank turned toward Hannah. "We'll put the washer back now, Professor Stein. Thanks for letting us check it out. I would've regretted it if we hadn't tried. Say, are you okay? You don't look so good."

"Don't mind me," Hannah said. "I had a bit of a problem last night. Fell on my deck. But I'll be all right. Just have one big headache. Go ahead. Slide the washer back."

Brad and Frank each grabbed onto a side of the washer and tried to move the heavy appliance back toward the wall, but the washer did not cooperate. It appeared to be stuck.

"That's funny," Brad said. "Why won't it move?"

The boys tried different maneuvers, but the washer seemed intent on remaining in its current position. A frustrated Frank came up with a new idea. Brad and Frank would tip the machine a little to one side while Gina, using the flashlight, would look under it. Frank reasoned that there had to be something impeding their progress and hoped Gina would be able to see what it was.

"Yes, I can see something. Something's hanging from the back right corner. Put the washer down, and then tip it the other way. I'll try to reach it and grab a hold of it," Gina said.

Hannah thought it ironic that she heard the noise of fireworks, accompanied by the yelps of Lexi, just as Gina triumphantly waved a plastic bag in the air. When the noise quieted, Hannah heard Gina scream, "I have it. It has tape around it. It must've slipped off the back."

The boys set the washer down. Gina placed the bag on the washer and opened it. Hannah walked over to the group as Gina slid a paper and a bulky white envelope out of the bag. Gina held up the blood-stained dish towel she found in the envelope. It took just a few seconds for Hannah's students to understand what they were looking at. The boys began to whoop and holler and pump their fists into the air, and Gina did an impromptu dance, moving in circles and wildly waving her arms.

Hannah waited for the pandemonium to subside and then said, "Before we celebrate, we have to read this paper. We don't know what's written here. And we don't know if this old towel is tied to the Baker killings. It looks like this document was signed by Kenneth Graybill, but the signature will have to be verified."

Suddenly, a large figure emerged from the shadows behind the old furnace, walked toward them, and shouted, "Stop. Give those to me. If you don't, you'll die."

Chapter 69

A mammoth man dressed in black was standing in front of Hannah and her students. He pointed his gun straight at Gina. When he shouted, Gina had instinctively grabbed the paper and dish towel off the washer. She protectively held them now, clutched to her chest.

"I mean it," the man growled. "I want those. If I have to kill all of you to get them, I will."

Hannah's head hurt. She was having trouble thinking clearly. "Who are you? How did you get in here? Why do you want these things?" Hannah asked.

The man snorted. "Like I have to explain myself to you, lady. You and this stupid group of college kids. You messed up my life but good."

More fireworks crackled loudly and sputtered, causing Lexi to bark repeatedly in the kitchen.

The big man glared at Hannah and said, "Dumb dog. I should've shot it last night when I had the chance. Couldn't believe it when my guy at the Parkerville station called and told me you turned in Graybill's book. So, I figured you might have more of Graybill's stuff at your house. But that dumb dog came after me when I broke in. Snapping those big teeth and barking like crazy. But I'm smarter than all of you 'cause I decided to look here this morning. And I didn't have to lift a finger. You dumb-asses did all the work for me. So, hand over what you've got. If you don't, no one's gonna hear me shooting all of you and the dumb dog, too. The fireworks will cover up the noise."

Hannah said, "You can have what we found. Whatever it is, it's not worth our lives. You know what? I always keep some cash in my house.

Just let these kids go. If you do, I'll give you the money. I hid it well. There's no way you'll be able to find it quickly without me. Just let the kids go, and I'll help you. What do you say?"

Hannah watched the man carefully. He seemed to be thinking over her offer. Hannah silently prayed that neither the boys nor Gina would do anything rash to provoke the man and cause him to shoot. Above and beyond all else, she had to protect her students and get them safely out of this mess.

"Nah, it's not worth it," the large man said. "You talk too much and ask too many questions. But for a hostage and traveling companion, she'll do just fine."

Without warning, the man grabbed Gina. He pinned her body against his. One meaty arm encircled Gina's throat. His other arm never wavered. His gun was still pointed at Brad, Frank, and Hannah. Gina's eyes widened in fear.

"Please," Hannah said, "I'll be a much better hostage. I'm older and slower. Much more manageable. Trust me."

"No way," the man barked.

"But you can trust me, Maurice," said a new voice. It was Ethan Clark's voice. Ethan was now standing in the basement. He had used the open bulkhead entrance.

Hannah asked herself, *How much did Ethan hear? Does he understand what's happening? Whose side is he on?*

The large man shouted, "Clark! What are you doing here? Nobody uses my real name. It's Moose to you and everybody else."

"Okay, Moose," Ethan said. "Whatever you say. I came to help you out."

"I don't need any help. I have a gun and lots of bullets," Moose said.

"Sure," Ethan said. "You're absolutely right. But you need to know that it's all over. Julian Adams is dead. You're not going to get any more money out of him. Just take Graybill's paper and so-called proof and walk away."

"Huh? Sorry Face is dead? I don't believe it. I just saw him. He settled up with me yesterday afternoon. He's been paying me to control Graybill. Ken had a big mouth when he was drunk," Moose said.

"And I saw Adams very late last night," Ethan said. "He's dead. Booze and pills and a suicide note. He learned that the police had Graybill's ledger, and he couldn't deal with it. Believe me; he's dead. If he wasn't, I would've collected the money he owes me and would be long gone. I'm in a bind over some gambling debts. So, I spent the night in the Henleys' barn. Too much cop activity around my folks' house when I came home. Couldn't believe it when I heard you breaking off that lock this morning and saw you enter this house. I guessed you were looking for something down here."

Moose shook his head back and forth. "Hard to believe Adams killed himself. I thought Adams was smart. But, you know, Graybill was even smarter. Ken always called him Sorry Face and played him for years. Sorry Face never got over the fact that Graybill sold his son tainted drugs. Funny, right? Before his kid overdosed, Adams never knew his own son was buying drugs from us. The very same ones Adams supplied us with and brought in from Canada. Of course, nobody knew that one shipment was bad."

"And now Adams is dead," Ethan said. "It's all over. Let the girl go. There's nothing for you here. Look at these boys. They're wound up like tight little springs just waiting to jump you. End this now before it gets bloody."

"I can handle bloody," Moose said. "Ken and me did bloody in this house. We killed the Bakers and got away with it because I was his alibi, and he was mine. But I was sick and tired of Ken. He kept saying he had something that could link me to the Baker murders. He was always holding that over my head to get me to do whatever he wanted. He was mean. He always wanted more for himself. He never cared about me. Selfish bastard. So, you see, what happened in the city wasn't my fault. I just wanted to find the ledger with Adams' name in it and the Baker evidence, have Adams pay me for the book, and then leave and get away from Ken. But Ken's girl really lost it when she caught me looking through Ken's stuff at her house. Crazy bitch. She grabbed a knife and waved it in my face. So, I shot her, and then Graybill came after me. So, I had to shoot him, too. But I was smart. I made it look like they went after each other."

Ethan frowned. He knew he had to think fast and talk even faster. Ethan said, "But you can still walk away from all this. What you just said doesn't count. Think about it. It was just a wild story to scare us. Right? And it was great. It was a whopper. There's no evidence that you killed two people. The police have that case all wrapped up. Graybill killed his fiancée and then committed suicide. Now, just leave, take whatever it is the girl is holding, and destroy it. Poof! You're home free. Besides, I don't think Graybill really hid anything important. He just liked to play sick jokes on people."

Moose looked uncertain. "I don't know. It sounds too easy."

"I was a cop," Ethan said. "I know the law. Just hand me the gun and prove to everybody that you're completely innocent. You're just a guy who likes to tell wild stories on the Fourth of July. Come on. This is your chance to walk away cleanly, and no one will be after you. Go ahead. Give me the gun."

Ethan stepped toward Moose. "Put the gun in my hand, Moose."

There was another set of thunderous firecrackers. These fireworks were followed by more angry barks from Lexi. Moose was startled by the massive onslaught of noise. When it quieted, he heard someone shout, "Police. Drop your gun."

Moose swung his head around, trying to locate the new threat. He saw a uniformed figure standing on the stairs. Moose fired his gun in the direction of the staircase and yelled, "You can't trick me. I'll kill you all."

Ethan plunged forward. Moose fired at him. The shot narrowly missed Ethan's head. Moose fired again. This time the bullet whizzed by Ethan's ear and pinged off one of the cinder block walls. When Ethan reached Moose, he grabbed onto Moose's right arm, the one holding the deadly weapon. Moose tried to swat him away as Ethan struggled to get the gun. Moose's efforts were hampered by his hold on Gina, but he would not release her. To Hannah, everything seemed to be happening at warp speed. Moose was angry and frustrated. He frantically swung his right arm in random arcs, trying to shake off Ethan. Moose's finger was on the trigger of the gun. He fired wildly, over and over and over. Bullets flew around the room. Some ricocheted off the concrete floor. A bullet hit Ethan in the leg. Ethan screamed in pain. Moose was momentarily distracted as he watched Ethan's body slump onto the floor.

Gina used this opportunity to bite down hard on Moose's left arm, the one that was restraining her, and then she stomped on Moose's left foot with all her might. Moose was in pain. He loosened his grip on Gina, and she immediately slid out of his grasp and spun like a deranged dervish. She now was in back of Moose and repeatedly kicked at his back and legs, which brought him to his knees. With lightning speed, Gina changed position. She faced Moose and delivered a karate chop to his throat. The gun, now empty of ammunition, flew out of Moose's hand. Moose was on his knees, stunned and gasping for breath, when Officer Paul Brown, who had raced down the stairs, reached him. Brown knocked the big man over, handcuffed him, and read him his rights. Minutes later, the basement was flooded with police officers.

Hannah hugged Gina and then rushed over to Ethan. "How bad is it?"

Ethan said, "You know how the heroes in old Western movies always say, 'It's nothing, ma'am. Just a little gunshot wound.' Well, they're wrong. It hurts like hell."

Hannah said, "Thank you. Thank you for trying to help."

Ethan said, "I want you to know, Hannah, that I would've come sooner if I'd known Moose had a gun. I thought four people and a large dog would surely scare him away or cause him to hide until you left. But too much time went by. I just had to come over and check on you. I had to make sure you were safe. You have to believe me. I really do love you."

Hannah did not have time to reply. A paramedic pushed her aside to examine Ethan. Ethan looked very pale, and his eyes fluttered shut as he was hoisted onto a gurney, strapped in, and then loaded into an ambulance. Hannah listened to the wail of the ambulance's siren and wondered how she would tell Lily and Cranston Clark that their son had been shot while trying to save her and her students.

Where did her students go? Hannah had lost sight of her students while she was talking to Ethan. She noted that they were huddled in a corner, reading the paper Gina still held in her hand. Hannah was about to walk over to them when she was stopped by Officer Brown.

"How did you know we were in trouble? How did you get here?" Hannah asked him.

Brown replied, "I put in some holiday overtime. Before I checked out, I decided to swing by your place and make sure everything was okay. No one was there, and I was concerned when I heard the Henleys' dog barking like crazy over here. Then, when I spotted the open bulkhead door and heard what the big guy with the gun was shouting, I called the station for backup and looked for a way to surprise him. The kitchen door was unlocked, so I came in that way and headed down the stairs. I'm sorry so many shots were fired."

"It really was frightening," Hannah replied.

"Can you talk now?" Brown asked. "Your students have agreed to come to the station. We want to interview them while all the events are still fresh in their minds. How about you, Mrs. Stein? You know, you do look a little shaky. I can send a detective over to your home to interview you there if that would help."

"I'm okay. I just have a pounding headache. But I'm worried about leaving Lexi alone. She's been barking a lot. These fireworks are making her very nervous. And I should notify the Clarks. Tell them what happened to Ethan."

"Don't worry. An officer is talking to the Clarks right now. Let's walk over to your house with the dog. I think Lexi will be calmer if she's by your side and in a quieter place."

A quieter place. Hannah savored those words and thought, *That sounds really good right now.*

Chapter 70

Friday, July 5

"Let me get this straight," Jodi said after speaking with Hannah for some time on the phone. "All that happened to you after I talked to you yesterday morning?"

"Yes," Hannah replied. "I know it sounds bizarre, but everything I told you about my Fourth of July is true. The big fellow named Moose had a gun, Ethan was shot, Gina acted like the Karate Kid, my students found Graybill's confession and evidence, and Officer Brown and the Parkerville police swooped in at the end."

"So, the paper in the plastic bag was a confession?"

"Yes," Hannah answered. "The kids managed to read it before Gina handed it over to the police."

"And ...?"

"And last night, the three of them stopped by with a pizza and filled me in. It was a shocker. Remember, Ken Graybill grew up in the Baker house. It's over one hundred years old and has an old-fashioned wide door to its basement. The Bakers never locked the bulkhead door, so Ken Graybill used it to enter the house when the Bakers weren't home. Helen Baker told me she thought things were moved about. I bet Graybill did that to drive the family crazy. Graybill wrote that he often got drunk in the basement. Considered it his private domain. And then there was that fateful night. Graybill was drunk, and the family came home while Graybill and his friend Moose were still in the house. Moose tried to get Graybill to sneak out, but Ken Graybill wanted to confront the Bakers.

Who knows what he thought he would get out of that, but he went into the kitchen and argued with Bruce and Helen Baker. According to his confession, Bruce ordered Graybill to leave, and Ken couldn't stomach that. Graybill still thought the house was his. So, Ken grabbed a knife and stabbed Bruce and then killed Helen because she wouldn't stop screaming. Moose had followed Graybill upstairs and saw it all. When the daughter, Dara, ran into the room, Graybill was spent from repeatedly stabbing Bruce and Helen and dropped the knife. That's why Moose picked up the knife and stabbed Dara, to keep her from running for help. Graybill wrote that when he saw Matthew Baker in the kitchen doorway, he thought about killing him, too, but he forgot about it when he spotted Sandra Metzler running toward the barn. Graybill ran after her. He claims he knocked her down and raped her. He apologizes in his confession. Wrote he didn't mean to and can't explain why he did it. He blames it all on being drunk and angry."

"Interesting," Jodi said.

"What part?"

"Well, all of it, of course. But it's interesting that Graybill felt the need to apologize for the rape and not the murders."

"True. And there's more. Graybill wrote that he was in a daze and staggered around in the barn after he raped Sandra. He heard Sandra moaning and was surprised to see that she was being raped again. But this time by Matthew Baker, and Baker had the bloody knife in his hand."

"So, do we believe Graybill?" Jodi asked. "But why would Matthew Baker rape his cousin right after his parents and sister were murdered? Was it because he was high on drugs?"

"I don't know," Hannah said. "But if we believe what Ken Graybill wrote, then Baker is guilty of rape but not guilty of murder."

"And the blood-stained towel? How does that fit in?"

"Graybill included a postscript to his confession. He wrote that Moose and he were bloody after the murders and used the towel to wipe their hands. It's odd. I understand why Graybill kept and hid the ledger. He was blackmailing Adams. But why did he write a confession and hold onto the towel? Was Graybill planning on using them to help free Baker in the future? Or did he just enjoy taunting his friend Moose and never meant to disclose them? Or was there some other reason? There are still so many unanswered questions. Ethan told me that someone paid out a lot of money to keep people from reexamining the Baker case. Why? And who?"

"Gosh, Hannah, will there ever be an end to this? What now?"

"It's a holiday weekend. It'll take time to sort things out. The bloody dish towel will have to be examined and tested, and handwriting experts will need to look at the confession and the signature," Hannah said and then sighed. "Oh, I almost forgot to mention that the news media have been having a field day with Julian Adams' suicide. Lots of speculation as to why the rich, successful man killed himself. People are saying that he never got over the deaths of his son and his wife. Some claim that there's a moral here, that family and love are more important than position and money."

"What will happen to your students' scholarship program now that Adams is dead?" Jodi asked.

"I got an email from President Daniels about that. Luckily, Adams set up a special endowment fund to cover the program. His death will not change much."

"Well, that's good. So, what's next?"

"Well, for us, it's your turn. Tell me about your Fourth of July and your grocery store man. You mentioned that he may be the one. I want to hear all about him."

And Jodi promptly launched into her love story. Jodi was confident that this romance tale would end with the words "and they lived happily ever after."

Chapter 71

Saturday, July 20

Hannah was loading her suitcase into her car. Soon she would be on her way to the Harrisburg airport and, shortly after that, on a plane flying to Minneapolis to see her dying father. A tearful Aunt Gail had called her early that morning and told Hannah to hurry. The end was near.

Ethan, on the other hand, was steadily improving. After a short stay in the hospital for his gunshot wound, he was transferred to a rehabilitation center. Lydia, Ethan's sister, had called and given Hannah updates on his condition. According to Lydia, Ethan had been lucky. The bullet had landed in muscle tissue. It had not damaged any arteries, veins, nerves, or bones. Hannah, who knew very little about such medical matters, was relieved, but she did not think Ethan was lucky. If he had walked away from his fight with Moose unscathed and had not been shot, then he would have been lucky. Hannah had not visited Ethan. When she called the hospital and rehab center, she had been told that only family members were allowed to visit. This was confusing as this restriction did not jive with Lydia's glowing reports.

Hannah had just finished punching the airport's address into her car's GPS when she heard her name called. Hannah recognized Lily Clark's distinctive voice. Hannah slid out of her car and was surprised to see Lily standing by a large "house for sale" sign in the Clarks' front yard. Lily waved and walked over to Hannah.

"Hannah, dear," Lily said, "I saw you put a suitcase in your car. Are you going somewhere"

"Yes. My father is dying. I'm flying to Minnesota tonight."

"Oh my. That makes what I have to say a bit harder, but it has to be said."

"What is it, Lily?"

"Well, as you can see, we are selling our home."

"But why? I thought you loved the house and your gardens."

"We do, Hannah. We really do. We thought this would be our forever home. We told Ethan that there was no way we would give up the house to settle his debts. But after he was shot, we realized that we love this property, but we love our son more. What good are a house and yard if we don't have Ethan? So, we've made a hard decision. Hard for us and hard for you, too."

"For me?" Hannah asked.

"Yes, dear. I thought you'd be a good influence. Keep Ethan from gambling and keep him grounded. But you failed. Ethan was shot. This isn't working. You understand?"

"I'm not sure I do."

"Then I'm forced to make this very clear. I withdraw my support. I no longer consider you good marriage material for my son. He got shot while he was with you. He has to give you up. It's part of the bargain."

"The bargain?"

"We made a deal with Ethan. We're going to sell this house and pay off his gambling debts. In return, as soon as Ethan can travel, he has agreed to leave Parkerville. We found a good rehab center for him in Florida. Ethan will be able to get physical therapy for his leg and counseling for his gambling addiction. And Cranston and I will be renting an apartment near the center. We'll keep a close eye on our son until he can fight temptation on his own. He needs to leave this place and everyone in it, including you, in order to make a fresh start."

"Oh," Hannah said, "I see."

"Nothing personal, Hannah. I'm sure you'll find someone else, and Ethan must abide by our bargain. His debts endangered our lives. He has to stop gambling, and this is his last chance. You do understand now?"

"Yes. Yes, I do," Hannah said.

After Lily Clark walked away, Hannah looked at her watch.

Hannah thought, *I have time to make one stop on the way to the airport.*

Chapter 72

The young woman at the reception desk of the rehabilitation center was wearing headphones and bobbing her head. Hannah assumed that she must be listening to a song with a fast beat as she was rapidly shaking her head from side to side and appeared to be playing an invisible keyboard.

"Excuse me," Hannah said. There was no reaction, so Hannah waved her hand in front of the girl's face to get her attention.

The receptionist took her headphones off and asked, "Do you need some help?"

Hannah replied, "I'd like to visit Ethan Clark. Do you know where I might find him?"

"Funny you should ask about him," the girl said. "There's a note by his name that says, No Visitors. Only family. But a police detective just came in and said he had to see Mr. Clark on official business. That sounded important, so I let him in. Do you have official business with Mr. Clark, too?"

"Well, I'm a neighbor of his. We have ex officio business. Will that do?"

"Oh, that sounds important. You'll find him in his room down the hall. To your left. Room 132."

"Thank you," Hannah said and smiled. She thought, *Never underestimate the power of a large vocabulary.*

Hannah walked down the hall and found Ethan's room. She knocked on the door, and Ethan called out, "Come in." Hannah entered the room and saw that Ethan was with Joe Miller.

"Hannah," Ethan said from a chair by the window, "good to see you. How did you get past the visitor restriction? No matter. I'm just glad you're here. You remember Joe. He was just about to fill me in on what's been going on regarding Moose and Ken Graybill. You're going to want to hear this, too. Would that be okay, Joe?'

"Hi there, Hannah," Joe said. "I figured since Ethan took a bullet that he was entitled to an update. Besides, the district attorney will hold a press conference sometime tonight or tomorrow. But until all this goes public, just keep what I'm about to say to yourselves. Can you do that?"

Hannah and Ethan nodded. Joe set up a folding chair for Hannah and another for himself near Ethan's recliner.

"Well," Joe said, "this has become complicated. Remember, Ethan, how everyone at the station thought the Baker case was so easy. The kid held the bloody knife, and he had motive and opportunity. Simple to understand. Matthew Baker was guilty. Case closed. But then along comes this confession that Hannah's students found. We had to stop and rethink everything. Our experts determined that the confession was written and signed by Graybill, and they were able to make a fingerprint match to him as well. But we also wanted to learn when he wrote it."

"And why he wrote it," Hannah added. "Sorry for interrupting, Joe. Please continue."

Joe smiled. "It's okay. There's a lot to unpack. The ink was tested. We learned that the confession was written within the last two years. Now, Hannah, that leads to the why. We contacted the city police. They've been investigating Graybill's death. Graybill had been living in Colorado before he returned to Lancaster, so a couple of the Lancaster city detectives talked to folks who knew Graybill in Boulder, including his doctor. They learned that Graybill was sick. He had a rare and aggressive cancer. He told his doctor that he wanted to go back home to die. Didn't want to waste the time he had left on any treatments. He mentioned that there was big money waiting for him in Lancaster County, and he was going to go out in style. He was probably referring to his plan to squeeze money out of Adams."

"Ah," Ethan said. "That explains a lot. If Graybill believed he would soon be dead, then he had nothing to lose by writing the confession."

Joe said, "I agree, and he might have had another reason for writing it, too. After he returned to Lancaster, Graybill reconnected with his high school sweetheart, and she agreed to marry him. She was very religious. Her mother told us that her daughter knew that Graybill was dying, and his fiancée wanted to make sure that they would be reunited in heaven. The girl took Graybill to a revival meeting and begged him to repent his sins. So, Graybill might have written the confession in order to receive some forgiveness from God. However, he did not continue along this religious path. Instead, as Graybill grew sicker, he drank more and lived large. Which explains the Corvette and his reckless behavior."

"But why did he hide the ledger and the confession in the Henleys' basement?" Hannah asked. Then she answered her own question. "Of course, Graybill always felt that the house belonged to him. He probably felt safe there. They were well hidden, so he probably was planning on revealing where they were hidden on his deathbed. But how did he get in? The Henleys had a lock on the cellar entrance, and they locked their doors."

"Remember the broken window, Hannah?" Ethan asked. "You know, the cat got in the basement that way. We have no idea how long that window was broken, and Graybill was a small guy. The window isn't big, but it's big enough. I think he could have slid in."

Joe said, "Now, on to that blood-stained towel. That really sent the station spinning. We always hold something back from the public when there's a murder investigation."

"Right," said Ethan. "The Amish cleaning girl said a decorative tea towel was missing after the Baker murders. I remember because I'd never heard anyone call a dish towel a tea towel."

Hannah jumped in, "Are you saying what I think you are?"

Joe chuckled. "Give me a chance to tell you the whole story. Helen Baker liked to cross-stitch, and the Bakers had two decorative towels hanging in the kitchen. Mrs. Baker was very proud of those towels. One had a house cross-stitched on it that resembled the Bakers' home, and the other had a cross-stitched barn. After the murders, the cleaning girl swore that the only thing missing from the kitchen, which she had just cleaned the day before, was the tea towel with the cross-stitched house. And, sure enough, that was what Graybill hid along with his confession."

"He must have considered it a trophy," Ethan said.

"Not sure what he thought," Joe said. "But he saved it and took good care of it. The lab techs were able to lift DNA off it, and it matched Moose's and Graybill's. So, there you have it. New evidence that suggests that Matthew Baker may not have killed his family. His lawyer filed a motion for a new trial. Now, it's up to the judge."

"What about the knife?" Hannah asked. "Was there anything on it that will prove that Moose and Graybill killed the Bakers?"

Joe replied, "This is embarrassing. We looked high and low in the evidence room for that knife. It's missing. No one knows how, why, or when it disappeared. It could have gone missing days, months, or even years ago. We have the results of the original tests, but that's all. Nothing to link it to Graybill or Moose."

Joe scowled and sighed in disgust. "I hate sloppy work. That missing knife really bugs me. But, on the plus side, I'm confident Moose will still be tried for murder. How can he avoid it? He was smart enough to ask for a lawyer when he got to the station, but six people heard him freely confess to killing Graybill and his fiancée and being involved in the Baker murders. The city has a good forensic team; odds are they'll find some evidence to link Moose to the Lancaster murders. And I just learned that an elderly couple has come forward. They can place Moose at the crime scene at the time Graybill and his girl were killed."

"And the rape? What about the rape?" Hannah asked.

"Thank God for DNA testing. Because she was a minor at the time of the rape, we had Metzler's torn garments safely stowed in an evidence box, and they were tested. The results do point to Ken Graybill and Matthew Baker. Not sure what Sandra Metzler will do now."

Joe Miller's cell phone chirped to signify that he had a text message. He read it and said, "Got to run. My partner's waiting for me outside. Good luck in Florida, Ethan. I hope everything works out for you." And then Joe quickly left the room.

Ethan looked at Hannah, "Uh, did you hear about my folks' plans? They're taking me to Florida. They say they're making the sacrifice for me, but I think they want to leave before it gets out that my name is in Graybill's drug book. My dad's a private person. I don't think he could stand the embarrassment."

"Well, I did speak to your mother," Hannah said. "That's why I stopped by. I'm on my way to the airport. My dad's dying, and you may be gone before I get back. I wanted to see for myself that you're okay and thank you again for putting yourself at risk to help me and my students."

"I didn't do a very good job of protecting you. Just got shot for my efforts. I heard that one of your students, the one named Gina, made all the heroic moves. How do you like that? I messed up from start to finish. However, I do wish you had done what I asked and given me a couple of days before you turned in the ledger. I could have taken Adams for a lot of dough and made a fresh start. But I forgive you, and I really am sorry about the cat."

Hannah did not respond. There was nothing more to say. She stood up and walked toward the door.

"Hannah," Ethan called. "I'm not sorry to leave the Lancaster area, but I am sorry to leave you."

Hannah said. "I hope all the therapy in Florida works for you. Good luck, Ethan, and goodbye."

And then Hannah walked out of the room and out of Ethan's life.

Chapter 73

Hannah had time on the flight to Minneapolis to sit back, relax, and let her thoughts wander. So much had happened after the chaotic Fourth of July. There had been the final push to wrap up her class and correct the last of her students' practice assignments and their research papers. She was so proud of her students. They had come a long way, and each had earned a Conrad Adams Scholarship. However, Julian Adams was not on hand for the photo op this year. It was still hard to process that the great man had ended his own life, and it was startling to learn that a large portion of his fortune had been made by selling illegal drugs. Worse yet was the exposé in last Sunday's paper. A reporter traced the bad drugs that killed Conrad Adams directly to Kenneth Graybill, the drug pusher, and Julian Adams, the supplier. It was horrible. Adams had harmed so many young people, and he inadvertently killed his son and destroyed his wife. Now his terrible secret was in the public domain.

Hannah had learned a great deal from Joe Miller right before her flight. There was much to digest. Graybill was dead and could not be punished for killing Bruce and Helen Baker and raping Sandra. However, Moose would be tried and, no doubt, convicted of murder. And then there was Matthew Baker. With Graybill's confession and the new evidence, Baker's murder sentence would probably be overturned, but he would learn that there was evidence proving that he did rape his cousin. What would he think and feel when he learned all this?

Hannah had not eaten much during the day, and she looked forward to landing in Minneapolis, meeting her friend Adele in the baggage claim area, and then catching up with Adele over dinner. She smiled in anticipation of a sumptuous feast. Adele was a great cook. They would probably linger over one of Adele's multi-course meals and talk into the wee hours of the morning. Hannah would be tired when she visited her father tomorrow, but it would be worth it.

Hannah closed her eyes and envisioned her family reunion. Aunt Gail would be teary-eyed as she warmly hugged Hannah. Michael would be restrained, determined to handle their father's impending death properly. Hannah, however, could not predict how she would react when she saw her dad. She loved her father, but he had traveled and left her alone with Aunt Gail during most of her childhood. As an adult, she understood that he had to earn a living, but as a motherless child, she had felt abandoned. Her father had always been large and hearty; she did not know how she would respond to seeing him in a frail, near-death state.

As her plane approached the Minneapolis airport and began its descent. Hannah thought about that devilish calculator watch. She had pushed the watch into a far, dark corner of her mind. There had been too many other pressing issues, and that wristwatch had not been a priority. But now that she was returning to the place where her mother was killed, thinking about the calculator watch made her feel, once again, uneasy and fearful. Hannah was convinced that the watch was related to her mother's death. Hannah did not know if her father could help her solve this mystery, but there was only one way to find out.

Chapter 74

Sunday, July 21

The next morning, Hannah knocked softly on the door to her father's room in the nursing home. A hospice volunteer opened the door, said a few words, gestured to a chair by her father's bed, and then left. Hannah sat down and stroked one of her father's hands. His eyes fluttered open.

"Who's there?"

"It's Hannah, Dad. How do you feel? Do you need anything?"

"Hannah. You made it. I'm not doing so well, honey. They've got me all drugged up. It helps with the pain, but it makes me mighty sleepy."

"It's okay, Dad. You can go back to sleep if you want."

"No, I want to talk. I have my words now. Sometimes I don't. Sometimes I can't remember things. I want to talk before I lose my words again. I love you. Always have. Okay?"

Hannah swiped at some tears and answered in a choked voice, "I love you, too."

"Good. Remember the good parts. Not the bad. Not your mother's death. Do you still worry about that?"

"Not all the time, Dad. I've had to move on. I've children of my own to worry about."

"I know. After Aaron died, you did well by your kids. I didn't do so well after your mother died."

"I know you tried your best," Hannah said. Hannah plunged ahead before she lost her nerve. "Dad, I'd like to ask you something about Mom's death. Something that's come up recently. I saw a watch. A calculator watch. And something clicked in my brain. An image related to the hands I saw when Mom died. Aunt Gail told me that Michael often fought with Mom, and he had one of those calculator watches. Do you think he might have . . . ? Oh, I know it's a horrible thought, but could he have pushed Mom down the stairs?" Hannah started to tremble. She had said it. The words were out there and could not be stuffed back inside her.

"Oh, no. No, Hannah. I never thought you'd remember."

"What are you saying, Dad?"

Her father sighed. He shut his eyes. Hannah thought he might have succumbed to the drugs and fallen asleep, but his eyes fluttered open again.

"Hannah, it was an accident."

"Then Michael should have explained what happened to the police. Why didn't he?"

"Not Michael. They were my hands. My watch. Your mother said she was going to leave me. Michael was too much for her. She needed help. Wanted me to stay home. But I needed the big Canadian contract."

Hannah's father paused. He took a big gulp of air and then continued. "We argued. She was trying to get away. I wanted her back in the bedroom. So, I tried to grab her. But she swung at me. And then she fell down the stairs. I didn't mean to hurt her. I didn't."

Hannah was stunned. How could her father be responsible?

"But you weren't at home."

"Yes. I was. I drove a long way. Stopped at a motel. Slept for a couple of hours, but the place was too noisy. I left. I got home that night."

Hannah's father paused. He looked worn out. He quietly said, "Your mother was broken and bloody after she fell. I panicked. Used the back staircase and ran out of the house. I took your mom's purse and some jewelry. Dropped them in a restaurant dumpster. I drove around and around. After I calmed down, I waited in an empty parking lot. Drove home in the morning. The police were there. They told me that your mom was killed by a robber. I was relieved. I was safe. But it's not right. Don't blame Michael now."

More tears flowed down Hannah's face. This time not for her dying father but for herself. Not her grown-up self. No, she cried for the scared little girl who had witnessed her mother's murder and had been crippled by that life-altering event.

"Dad, how could you? If it was an accident, why not just admit it? I was so confused and hurt. I didn't speak for months.

"I know. I felt guilty about that. But, Hannah, if I'd told the truth, there would've been an investigation. Maybe a trial. I would've lost the Canadian job. I needed the work and the money. I did the right thing. I had to protect my family. Say you understand."

Her father held onto Hannah's hand. He looked at her and silently pleaded with Hannah to agree with him. Hannah was numb. She opened her mouth, but nothing came out. No sounds and no words. Hannah's father closed his eyes again. He squeezed Hannah's hand right before he died.

Chapter 75

Friday, August 9

"Now what?" Jodi asked. "You got through your dad's funeral, and you've been home for a week. Are you going to tell or not tell?"

Hannah and Jodi were sitting on Hannah's deck. Jodi had driven to Parkerville from Pittsburgh in record time in order to spend the weekend with Hannah and offer her some much-needed solace. Actually, Jodi needed comforting, too. Two days ago, Jodi had stopped at her local supermarket to pick up some groceries. She was happy and surprised when she spotted the love of her life in the produce aisle. She waved and walked over to him. He turned a bright red and stammered a greeting. The woman standing beside him introduced herself. She was his wife. To make matters worse, the jerk had actually called Jodi later that evening. He apologized for not telling her he was married but thought it was good that everything was now out in the open. He saw no reason for anything to change between them. Jodi told him off, cussed, cried, and then decided it was time for her to visit her best friend. Jodi knew she would survive, but she knew she would get to that point much faster with Hannah's help. Now, they both were relaxing on reclining chairs on Hannah's deck, sipping white wine and nibbling on appetizers. Jodi was on her third glass of wine, and Hannah was slowly nursing her usual half-glass allotment.

"You know," Hannah said, "I wish I could just freeze this moment. Good friend, good food, good wine, and good weather. It's perfect. And, to answer your question, no. I haven't decided what to do about my dad's confession."

"But, Hannah . . ."

"I know I should make up my mind. But I worry about the ripple effects if I tell anyone. In addition, I don't know if I should believe him. My dad had symptoms of dementia. And even if what he said is true, I really don't want to tell my children that their grandfather killed their grandmother. What good would that do? Now, Michael is a different story. If I know, then I feel he should know. But my dad and Michael didn't get along. I don't know if Michael can handle this right now. Or ever. He's really struggling. He doesn't know how to grieve for Dad."

"And then there is that other possibility," Jodi said.

Hannah winced. "Yes. I know. What if Dad decided to take the blame to protect Michael, and Michael is guilty."

Jodi nodded. "So, now what?"

Hannah said, "I wait and remain in limbo. I've lost both my parents and Aaron. If Michael is innocent, I don't want to accuse him of something he didn't do and risk losing him, too. Maybe Michael will reveal something in the future. Maybe not."

Hannah sipped her wine and then said, "It has been such an odd summer. I finally learned more about the tragedy that occurred right up the street. Got some closure there. But I still have unanswered questions about my mother's murder. My father always blamed my mom's death on a reckless thief. He could've clung to that tale. Was he thinking clearly when he confessed? Or did the drugs and his dementia mess up his memories? Why did he change our family's story? And where does that leave me now?"

Chapter 76

Sunday, August 18

This Sunday was a "double party" day. One of those rare and hectic days when Hannah had to bounce from one social event to another. First, there was the picnic at Lake Keller at noon. When she arrived, she saw that Frank's large family had gathered in one of the pavilions. They were proudly celebrating Frank's scholarship and the fact that he was now a Buchanan College freshman. His father had pumped Hannah's hand when he was introduced to her, and Frank's mother had embraced her in a big hug. It was obvious that they were very proud of their son and grateful to the teacher who had helped him. Frank handed her a plate overflowing with food and found Hannah a seat at one of the crowded picnic tables. In answer to his relatives' inquiring looks, Frank repeatedly said, "Here's my teacher. I owe it all to her."

Gina waved to Hannah from another table, and Brad arrived a short time later, accompanied by a very tall middle-aged man. After most of the guests had eaten their first round of food, people broke off into smaller groups. Some took a walk around the lake. Parents with small children headed toward the playground area, and the teens set up a corn hole game. Several of the older men took turns cranking an old ice cream maker. Gina, Brad, and Frank walked over to the picnic table where Hannah was sitting and grabbed three spaces that had just been vacated on the bench across from their teacher.

The tall man who had walked in with Brad squeezed in next to Hannah, extended his hand, and said, "Hi. I'm Bob Lowry. Brad's Uncle Bob.

I'm mighty pleased to meet the famous Professor Stein. I've heard a lot about you."

Hannah laughed. "I'm far from famous. What exactly have you heard about me?"

"Well," Bob answered, "I heard you performed a miracle. You got my smart but lazy nephew to actually do some schoolwork. What's more, he had a grand time in your class. If that doesn't make you famous, I don't know what will."

Hannah smiled. "Thank you, but Brad, as well as Frank and Gina, did the work. I just steered them in the right direction. I'm very proud of all of them."

Bob said, "I am, too. But I must admit I didn't like it when Brad told me that bullets were flying near you and your students. I sincerely hope that is not part of the course curriculum." Bob's last comment was uttered in a stern tone.

"Of course not," Hannah answered. She was flustered. "Believe me; I was shocked and surprised. I never wanted to put my students in danger."

"Gathered as much," Bob said and grinned.

"Sorry about that," Brad interjected. "I should've warned you about my Uncle Bob's wry sense of humor. He likes to tease."

Hannah smiled and relaxed.

Bob said, "I still can't get over this whole thing. Who would've thought that three curious teenage kids and one English teacher would find a way to free Matthew Baker?"

"I've been out of town. I had to deal with a family matter," Hannah said. "I haven't heard the latest about the Baker case."

"Let's remedy that. Why don't we circle the lake and talk? I'll fill you in on the breaking news," Bob said. "I figure I can safely leave the boys in Gina's care."

"I don't get it," Gina said. "Why is everyone surprised by the way I handled Moose? I have three older brothers. They learned karate, so I learned karate. Nothing unusual about that."

Brad, Frank, and Gina joined the other young people playing corn hole while Hannah and Bob slowly walked around the lake. Uncle Bob, as Brad had mentioned, was well-connected with law enforcement people and lawyers in Lancaster County. In addition, Matthew Baker's lawyer was a friend of Bob's. During their walk, Hannah learned that a judge had ruled that there was enough evidence for a new trial for Matthew Baker, but the prosecutor, considering the weight of the evidence, Baker's time served, and public sentiment, decided there was no point in prolonging the inevitable. Baker would soon be cleared of the murder charges and released. And Baker would not be charged with rape. For fourteen years, Matthew Baker had languished in prison and been called a murderer. Sandra Metzler felt her cousin had suffered enough. Meanwhile, sufficient evidence had been accumulated to try Moose for murder in the fall.

On the way home from the picnic to change for the next party, Hannah thought about Bob Lowry. He had been very easy to talk to. He was not a handsome man, but when he smiled, which he did with some regularity, he changed. Suddenly, he was no longer an average-looking guy. He became a man with an inner fire, an interesting and intelligent fellow who drew people to him. All of that probably explained why Hannah agreed to have lunch with him next week. Hannah was amazed that it had been so easy for her to accept this date. It must have been because she felt comfortable with Bob. He reminded her of someone. Then she laughed at herself. Of course, Bob reminded her of Aaron.

Chapter 77

The second part of Hannah's "double party" day was not as much fun as the first. She was dressed more formally and uncomfortably. She had not worn heels in some time, and they were pinching her toes. But she felt she had to get dressed up for Will Dotlish's retirement party as it was being held in a fancy place, and campus bigwigs would be there. Will was beaming when he greeted Hannah at the door of the posh restaurant near Buchanan College. His face was flushed with excitement.

"I got a good crowd," Will said. "I know most came for the free food, but it's great that many did come because they appreciate me. After all, campus security is important. All the highfalutin learning in the world won't sell the place if you don't have students, and students will only come if the college is safe."

Hannah agreed and hugged Will. She found her place card and then sat down at a table with other members of the English department. Dr. Eileen Balinkowski, the department head, was sitting to Hannah's right.

"Hannah, I want to extend my sympathies. I heard your father died," Dr. B said. "I've also been meaning to tell you that I'm happy you and your students were not harmed on the Fourth of July. But seriously, Hannah, you must be more careful. These escapades could have ended in a disaster for you and the college. We'll talk soon. Your next round of Conrad Adams' Scholarship students will be more restricted in regard to their areas of research. Understood?"

Hannah nodded. She ate her meal without tasting much of it. She clapped and smiled as speakers both roasted and toasted Will. She murmured appropriate words when asked a question, but all the time, she was unsettled. Dr. B did say she would have more Conrad Adams students, so that was good. However, their research topics would be limited. Now, that seemed unfair. She wondered how restricted they would be.

When the retirement party ended, Hannah left and walked to her car. She had parked it in a nearby campus parking lot as the restaurant's small lot was full. Hannah was agitated, but there was nothing to do right now. She would have to wait and see what would happen next.

* * *

Meanwhile, a figure, moving in and out of the shadows, headed in the opposite direction. This solitary soul had a purposeful stride and was heading home to a large Victorian mansion near the college.

The walker smiled and thought, "It's all worked out so well. Graybill and Moose only dealt with Adams. Never with me. Now Graybill is dead, and Moose will go to prison. Adams is dead, too. There are no links to me and my offshore accounts. All is well. Shame about spending so much money on those sleazy police officers to keep a lid on the Baker case. Such a waste. But Graybill had a history with the Bakers. I didn't want the police to reexamine the case and pressure Graybill to talk. He might have accidentally let something slip about Adams, and I couldn't depend on Adams after his wife and son died. He weakened. Still, he was strong enough to do what I asked. Once arrangements were made, Adams regularly deposited money into the accounts of the police officers who were working for us. Once again, no money trail to lead anyone to me. And Ethan Clark, the last pawn in my chess game. He failed. He was supposed to find and destroy Graybill's ledger. But that's not a problem now. Now that Adams is dead. Thank goodness my name is not in that silly book, and Clark has no reason to tie me to Adams. Too bad Clark was only injured and not killed. But Clark will be in Florida soon and out of the way. All my minions are accounted for. Yes, it's all worked out very well. Men are so easy to manipulate. I think I'll set up my drug ring again now. Why not? I've waited long enough. But no business on Buchanan's campus. Got to protect my college."

The contemplative figure paused and gazed lovingly at the magnificent white three-story home in the distance and thought, "The renovations

I've completed cost more than I dreamed, but they were worth it. My house is beautiful. And soon, I'll have the money to bring the place back to its original glory on the inside, too. The walls need to be decorated with more masterpieces. And I will splurge again on trips and cruises. First-class all the way. Too bad my salary isn't enough to cover my needs. But I've learned to compensate and then some. However, I will have to keep an eye on Hannah Stein. Clark was supposed to rein her in, but that didn't work. Instead, she got close to the truth. Closer than I would've expected. But still, no one suspects me, and no one ever will."

Dr. Eileen Balinkowsky's smile widened. She knew she had upset Hannah Stein at dinner, and that thought pleased her very much. Dr. B began to hum the Buchanan College fight song and walked a little faster toward her home, marching in time to the beat.

Author's Note

The Class Assignment Is Murder is a work of fiction. It was, however, inspired by a real event. A teenage boy who lived near my home really did murder his family and then rape his cousin. For years, I was haunted by this tragedy as I knew one of the victims. Although I searched, I never found a satisfactory explanation for these horrific crimes. Writing this fictional work has enabled me to control the narrative, give my characters reasons for their acts, and attain some closure. Sadly, there are many cases of triple murders and rape. My book does not recount any of these crimes; it is the work of my imagination.

There are two acts of anti-Semitism in the book. It may interest the reader to know that these were based upon real events. In 1987, a short time after my family moved into our home in Lancaster County, Pennsylvania, we found cruel anti-Semitic chalk drawings on our driveway. The message was clear—Jew, You Must Be Murdered. We were shocked. We had moved from Minnesota and didn't know anyone in the area. I was worried about my children. My son was three years old, and my daughter was a sixteen-month-old toddler. For a long time, I was afraid to let my children play in our yard. I had never experienced anything like this before. The local police reported the incident as a hate crime. I included this incident in the novel to demonstrate that all acts of hate, even those others claim can be easily washed away, are damaging.

The other anti-Semitic incident, the swastikas painted on the front doors of a synagogue, occurred in Lancaster City a few years later. This time there was an outpouring of support. Members of the whole community gathered to wash the hateful symbols off the temple's doors, but the fact that this had to be done was simply wrong and jarring. The vandals used the Nazi swastika to instill fright.

In the novel, these two incidents are both moved to 2005 when Hannah and her family come to Lancaster.

Acknowledgments

Writing a book is similar to a mythical quest for me. I enjoy girding myself for the battle, doing research to insure that what I write is logical and based upon facts. I take long walks to prepare for the challenge, plotting my story along the way. Next, my characters begin to talk to me, and when they persistently chatter in my head, the magic moment arrives. With an outline to guide me, I begin to write. However, I still have to fight the demons of uncertainty and despair that occasionally try to grab me. I need help to achieve the coveted prize, a published book. Thank goodness, I have people. I have people who act as my wise wizards and supportive soldiers. I have people to thank on this acknowledgment page.

From the bottom of my heart, I am grateful to all the readers who critiqued my work: Gail and Richard Blumenthal, Lisa Brooks, Peggy Brown, Sharon Gates, Julie Goldemberg, Barbara Goss, Marybeth Toole, and Gail Sanderson. A special thank you to Susan Barnes and Adele Ruszak who were my primary readers and with me through the whole process. They were incredibly generous and kindly coped with the many times I switched things around in my mystery. Their help was invaluable! I also am indebted to Lisa Barr who suggested ways for me to make my opening chapter more captivating and compelling. I am very grateful this busy author took the time to help me.

I could not have written my mystery without the tech support of my husband Steve. He really is the wind beneath my wings. He also acted as a reader and graciously helped me block out the fight scene, too. He is wonderful and the love of my life.

I also thank my family for all they have done to encourage me. I send hugs to my daughter Julie Goldemberg and her husband Daniel Goldemberg, my son David Kleinman and his wife Erin Nightingale, and my grandchildren: Max Goldemberg, Lucas Kleinman, Nina Goldemberg, and Sophie Kleinman.

I am grateful to the folks at Sunbury Press. Thank you for choosing to publish my mystery!

And, last but not least, thank you to my readers. I am thrilled that you read my book! I hope you will read my historical novel, *Love, Faith, and the Dented Bullet*, published by Sunbury Press, too.

Discussion Questions for The Class Assignment Is Murder

1. Hannah is haunted by the murders and rape that occurred in her neighborhood. Are people more strongly affected by violence that happens close to home than by the news reports of violence in other places in the world? Why?

2. Hannah struggles to remember a traumatic event that occurred when she was five years old. What is your earliest childhood memory? Can people accurately remember events that happened when they were very young? Do our early memories shape and define us?

3. Jodi and Hannah are good friends, but in many ways, they are very different. Do we normally seek out or avoid friendships with people who are different than we are? Is that old expression "opposites attract" true? What is gained from having a friendship with someone who is not a lot like you?

4. Why was Hannah wary of dating? Why was she ready to date at this point in her life? In your opinion, what complicates a woman's search for love "the second time around"? Are the challenges widows and divorced women face when they begin to date again the same or different?

5. Brad explains that in Pennsylvania children and teenagers who commit murders are charged as adults. Does this make sense to you? Are there factors that should be taken into consideration when a young person commits a murder? If so, what are they?

6. Consider Sandra Metzler's reaction and her family's reaction to the rape. Is being raped by a family member more or less traumatic than being raped by a stranger.? Do you think women ever fully recover from being raped? Do you agree with Sandra's decisions?

7. What can be done in families and in the community to help young people avoid turning to drugs and violent behavior? Do troubled teens exhibit reliable warning signs to indicate that they are in trouble and need help? If so, what are they?

8. Was Hannah right or wrong to go along with the dictates of President Daniels? Are there times when it is appropriate to take a stand for intellectual freedom, even if there are severe consequences?

9. Do you think Michael is innocent or guilty? How will Hannah interact with him in the future?

10. Hannah's father said he was trying to protect his family, but did he? Do you think his actions were justified? Is his confession true? Is he innocent or guilty?

11. What is your opinion of Ethan? Is he a hero or a villain at the end of the novel?

12. What do you think will happen to Hannah in the future?

About the Author

CAROLYN KLEINMAN is a retired English and English as a Second Language teacher. She has BS and MA degrees from the University of Minnesota. Carolyn has always been a reader and a storyteller and enjoys writing books that explore how people respond to life-changing events. Her first novel, *Love, Faith, and the Dented Bullet,* is a historical fiction book that describes what happens when a WWII Holocaust survivor meets a Mennonite farm girl in 1947. She enjoyed crafting the twists and turns in her mystery, *The Class Assignment Is Murder*. Both novels are published by Sunbury Press. Carolyn lives in Lancaster, Pennsylvania, with her husband Steven and is very proud of her two children and their spouses and her four grandchildren.

www.ingramcontent.com/pod-product-compliance
Lightning Source LLC
Chambersburg PA
CBHW011342010726
47493CB00009B/2914